Midnight Oath

The BoneBound Court

Harleigh Rose Knight

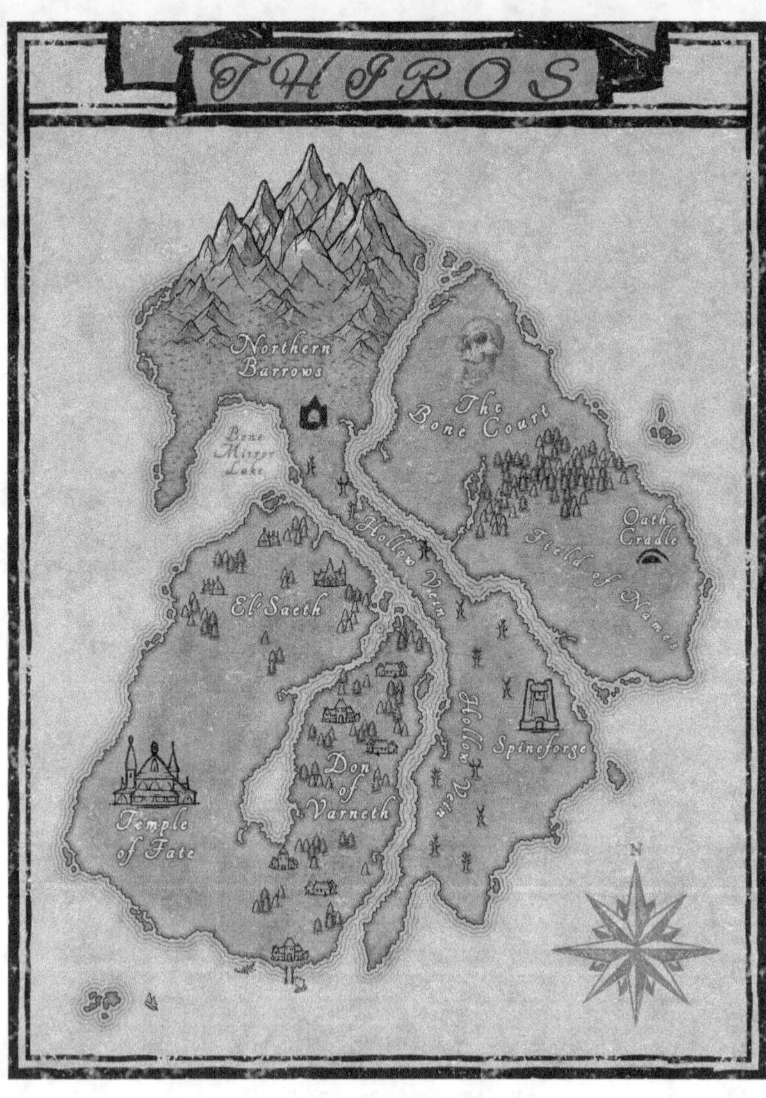

THIROS
Northern Barrows
Bone Mirror Lake
The Bone Court
Oath Cradle
Field of Namii
El Saeth
Hollow Vein
Hollow Vein
Don of Varneth
Spineforge
Temple of Fate
N

Contents

Coming Soon

Coming Soon...

The Bloodborn Inheritance
Hourglass of Blood, Book Two
Shadow of the Last Born, Book Three

The Serpents Vengeance

Heartless

Keep up to date with the latest news and release dates by following on social media.
Find Harleigh Rose Knight on all platforms.

Act One

SEPARATION

Chapter One

The Morning After

Renata

The body sprawled in front of my throne—a boy, maybe fifteen, skin already cooling to grave-wax gray. Someone had carved traitor into his forehead with methodical precision, each letter weeping thin trails of dried blood.

I knew I'd done it. My hands remembered even if the Hollow Crown had already consumed the memory. I could feel the phantom weight of the blade, the resistance of skin and bone. Could almost hear his pleading, a ghost-sound that made my fingers twitch against my skirt.

Instead, I sat hollow as the Crown fused to my skull, both hands gripping black fabric until my knuckles ached—a distant sensation, like pain happening to someone else's body. My eyes burned with dryness. I couldn't remember the last time I'd blinked.

This was after Nalla's willing sacrifice powered the ritual. The Bone God walked free from his prison. After Nokoa stabilized, his witch runes finally, finally no longer spreading toward his inevitable death. After I'd saved him by damning everything else.

The throne room had emptied hours ago, though time moved strangely now—pooling and stretching like shadows at dusk. Cressa had taken Nokoa to be examined, her healer's hands already reaching for him before the magical fallout had fully settled. He'd protested, insisting he felt good. The best since being dragged back from death.

Cressa hadn't listened. She'd argued it remained her duty as court healer to understand what the stabilization ritual had actually done to the witch runes carved into his bones. Nokoa had looked at me then, golden eyes seeking permission. I'd managed a nod. Barely. The movement felt like dragging stone across stone.

Priestess Alaira had stayed far longer, her cries echoing off vaulted bone ceilings until they became just another texture in the darkness. Hours of weeping and praying and bargaining with gods who wouldn't answer. Finally she'd wandered out, priestess robes dragging against the floor with a whisper like wind through a graveyard, muttering about finding a new way, a new answer.

I wanted answers too. Wanted to know how deep her betrayal burrowed into everything I'd trusted. How much of what she'd done for me had actually been in service to Quade. Had any of it been real? The questions circled like carrion birds, but I couldn't quite reach them through the Crown's numbing haze.

The caves felt smaller than usual. Bone walls leaned inward, ribcage-close, as if the court itself held its breath. Or perhaps I felt different—less like a person and more like something simply occupying space. The Hollow Crown's grip had loosened just enough for me to see a bit more around me, like fog briefly clearing from a mirror's surface.

Not enough to show the full picture. Never that.

But enough to sit with something so heavy it might crush me.

Renata, nothing will come of simply sitting here. Queen Oriana's voice echoed through my skull from inside the Crown itself. Her consciousness lived there now, trapped in the bone circlet along with the others who'd worn it before me. Her tone carried that harder, mother-like quality.

I didn't have words to respond. My throat felt lined with sand.

Get up. Break something if you must. King Aldric's voice held its violence-ready edge. I could almost picture him—the topknot, the shaved sides, the missing arm he'd sacrificed to the Crown's hunger.

The suggestion sparked something. Not quite feeling, but the memory of what feeling might have been like. Breaking something. Yes. The urge rose sudden and overwhelming—to shatter bone against bone, to hear something crack that wasn't my own fragmenting psyche.

But I remained frozen, caught between impulse and execution.

Around the throne room's edges, my seven spectral guardians stood in silent vigil. Raised dead pulled from their rest to serve as my protection. Previous hollow rulers, now bound through magic they couldn't refuse. They didn't speak, didn't offer counsel. Just watched with hollow eyes, waiting for threats that might never come.

I forced myself to focus on breathing—in, out, each breath a small act of defiance against the numbness. The air tasted stale, recycled through too many lungs, filtered through too much bone. My white hair—now fully black from the Crown's corruption—fell forward into my face. I didn't brush it back.

Somewhere in the caves, Valdic was probably looking for me. My DirgeWolf, my emaciated friend with purple eyes and dark humor sharp enough to cut through any darkness. I could picture him padding through corridors, his decayed form moving with surprising grace.

I needed him. Needed his caustic observations and unwavering loyalty. Needed the reminder that some bonds couldn't be broken, even by the Hollow Crown.

The boy's family will want to know what happened. Queen Lyanna's voice drifted through my thoughts, softer than Oriana's but edged with something sharp. Vain, even in death—the short bob, the half of her face burnt down to bone, always frowning.

The boy. I didn't even know his name. Fifteen years old and marked as traitor, and I couldn't remember his name or what he'd supposedly done to deserve such a fate. The Crown had taken that too, leaving only the aftermath—the body, the blood, the terrible weight of actions I couldn't recall but couldn't deny.

I'd rationalized Nalla's death easily enough. She'd chosen sacrifice, had walked into it with eyes open and purpose firm. That blood wasn't on my hands.

But this—this was different. There were no other hands here. Only mine.

I wondered if this was how it had been for the others, the voices now trapped in the Crown with me. If they'd sat in this throne room staring at evidence of atrocities they couldn't quite remember committing. If the Crown had hollowed them out piece by piece until nothing remained but consciousness without body, voice without agency.

If this was just the beginning of my transformation into something that could sustain the Crown's hunger indefinitely.

It settled over my shoulders like a familiar coat—heavy, suffocating, somehow expected.

"I can't feel anything," I whispered to the empty throne room, my voice cracking like old bone breaking. The spectral guardians didn't respond—they never did. "I should feel something. Horror. Guilt. Anything."

The Crown takes what it needs, King Aldric replied, something knowing in his tone that spoke of experience. And right now it needs you functional. Feeling will come later. Usually when you least want it.

I looked back at the boy's body, forcing myself to truly see it this time. The precise lettering on his forehead. His hands curled as if reaching for something in his final moments. The growing pool of darkness beneath him that might have been blood or shadow or both. Eyes staring at nothing, clouded and distant.

The metallic scent of blood still hung in the air, mixing with the ever-present smell of ancient bone and faint mineral tang of underground water. Arches of bone stretched overhead—ribs forming ceiling vaults, vertebrae marching along walls in precise rows. Everything here built from the remains of what came before. The two great cities, now nothing but bone and wasteland.

I couldn't decide if I hated Alaira or the Hollow Crown more. The priestess had orchestrated this nightmare, had pulled strings I hadn't known existed. The Crown had stolen my agency, my memory, my ability to feel appropriate horror at my own actions.

If I were honest—and the loosened grip of the Crown allowed for brutal honesty tonight—I hated myself most.

For being weak enough to need the Crown. For feeding it memories until I'd become something that could carve words into children's foreheads and forget by morning.

Feed us, the Crown voices whispered. Remember us. Forget yourself.

And I would. Because the alternative was watching Nokoa's witch runes spread until they consumed him. Was seeing the Bone Court collapse into famine and chaos.

Even if that duty carved me hollow.

A sound echoed through the corridor outside—familiar footsteps, the slight drag of paws against bone floor. Relief flooded through me, sharp enough to cut through the numbness.

Valdic.

He padded into the throne room, his emaciated form somehow graceful despite the decay. Purple eyes fixed on me with an intensity that felt almost painful. His gaze flicked to the boy's body, then back to my face.

"Well," he said, his voice carrying that dark humor I desperately needed. "I see you've been redecorating. Really sets a mood. Early apocalypse? Post-conscience chic?"

Something in my chest loosened. Not laughter—I couldn't quite reach that. But something close to it.

"I don't remember doing it," I admitted.

"Of course you don't." He moved closer, settling beside the throne. His presence was grounding, solid in a way nothing else felt. "The Crown's gotten hungry again. Seems to prefer the memories you'd rather keep."

"His family—"

"Will be told he was a traitor to the Bone Court," Valdic finished. "Because that's what you carved into his skull. Very subtle, by the way. I appreciate the commitment to clear communication."

I should have defended myself. Should have explained that I didn't choose this, didn't want this. But the words felt hollow before I could even speak them.

"I saved Nokoa," I said instead.

"You did." Valdic's purple eyes held something complicated—loyalty and concern and a darkness that matched my own. "And damned everything else in the process. But that was always the plan, wasn't it? Save the one you love. Let the world burn."

"The Bone God is free."

"Also part of the plan. His plan, anyway. We just happened to be convenient." He tilted his head, studying me. "The question is—now what? You've got your stable resurrection. Your lover's witch runes aren't killing him anymore. The God you accidentally freed is probably plotting something terrible. And you're sitting here staring at a dead child you can't remember killing."

"Now what," I echoed.

Now you get up, Queen Oriana commanded. Now you clean up your mess.

Valdic's ears twitched, as if he could hear the voices too. Maybe he could. He'd been with me long enough to recognize when the Crown was speaking.

Valdic spoke quietly. "Whatever comes next, it won't come from sitting here drowning in guilt you can't quite feel."

"I need to see Nokoa," I said finally.

"Of course you do." Valdic stood, his joints popping softly. "And then we need to deal with Alaira. And Quade. And whatever fresh nightmare is waiting around the corner. But first—" He glanced at the boy's body. "—first we deal with this."

"The Rattlemaids—"

"Are already on their way. Praxis sent them. He's disturbingly efficient about cleaning up royal mistakes." Valdic's tone was dry. "They'll handle the body. Prepare it for whatever ritual we have now. You need to know, most are dead. Those who are not, will be soon."

I pushed myself up from the throne, my legs trembling with the effort. The world tilted slightly, then righted itself. Valdic pressed against my side, his solid presence keeping me upright.

"One step," he said quietly. "Then another. That's all you have to do."

One step. Then another.

I could do that.

I had to do that.

Because tomorrow I would do it again. Or I would feed the Crown another memory and forget I'd ever doubted. Would wake up lighter, emptier, more capable of the impossible choices this position demanded.

And I would let it.

Because the alternative was losing Nokoa.

Chapter Two

WATCHING HER SHATTER

Nokoa

The Bone Court was nothing like I'd left it three hours ago.

It had always been damp, moisture seeping through bone walls like sweat through skin. It had always smelled of mildew and decay—that particular combination of rot and political machination that characterized life underground. The scent had become almost comforting in its familiarity.

But I'd never seen it soaking in blood.

The floor glistened with it, pooling in natural depressions of the bone architecture, following grooves carved by centuries of footsteps. The metallic tang cut through everything else, overwhelming even the ever-present must. Fresh blood, still wet, still spreading. Too much for one body, or even two.

I'd never seen the caves so dim my own shadow ran from me, stretching and distorting across blood-slicked bone like it was trying to escape. The bioluminescence that normally painted everything in ethereal blue and green was fading—the glowing fungi and phosphorescent moss dying like everything else alive had. Starved of whatever they needed to sustain that gentle light.

Soon we'd be living in absolute darkness.

The silence was louder than words. It pressed against my eardrums, made my heartbeat sound deafening in my own skull. No whispers of gossip echoing through corridors. No voices shouting orders. No cries from the injured. No sounds of training, of life continuing despite everything.

Just this suffocating absence of sound, as if the Bone Court itself was holding its breath.

But the sight of Renata still in the throne room, alone, unblinking with shaking hands—that was the loudest thing of all.

She sat motionless on her throne of bone. Her white hair, now fully black from the Hollow Crown's corruption, hung in tangled curtains around her face. Her clothes were ripped—not from struggle, but from clawing, as if she'd tried to tear them off her own body. Blood stained the black fabric in patterns that looked almost deliberate. Handprints, maybe.

Bone ash showed in her hair like premature grey, dusting her shoulders and lap. Her skin looked paler than usual, translucent enough that I could trace the map of black veins spreading through her entire body. They wrapped around her jaw like fingers, crawled up her neck, spiderwebbed across what skin I could see. The Hollow Crown sat fused to her skull, bone circlet on bone, impossible to tell where one ended and the other began. The black spikes of her exposed spine pushed through the skin of her back, visible even from where I stood.

Her eyes read of numbness, grey and flat as river stones. But her shaking hands spoke of something else entirely.

Valdic sat at my side, his emaciated DirgeWolf body pressing against my leg. His purple eyes were filled with sorrow so profound it looked like physical pain. He wanted to run to her—I could feel it in the tension of his muscles, the barely restrained impulse to close the distance.

But he felt guilty leaving me. His loyalty was split between the woman who was his bonded companion and the man she'd destroyed the world to save.

I nudged his decayed body in her direction. He hesitated, purple eyes meeting mine in question. I nodded. She needed him more than I did right now.

Valdic made his way to her side, movements silent despite his size. He sat at her feet without disturbing her, without demanding acknowledgment. Just presence. Just proof that she wasn't completely alone.

The witch runes carved into my bones had finally stopped spreading. The glowing marks no longer crawled beneath my skin like living things trying to escape. They burned—gods, they burned—but they weren't expanding. Weren't consuming more of me piece by piece.

My body felt good for the first time since resurrection. I wasn't walking decay anymore. My joints moved without grinding. My lungs expanded without crackling. My skin didn't feel like paper ready to tear.

But the bond still kept us separated.

Physical distance was the only relief. Even thinking of Renata intensified it—the bond didn't distinguish between physical nearness and mental focus. It wanted connection, demanded it, punished any attempt at distance. My skull throbbed with the familiar ache.

Since resurrection, all I'd known from these runes was pain. Spreading agony that promised to consume me completely. The bond had been torture—every thought of Renata a blade to the skull, every moment of separation an exercise in controlled suffering. I'd learned to fear anything connected to the magic that brought me back.

So when Cressa had explained that proximity would ease the burning, I couldn't bring myself to accept it. Couldn't trust that comfort. The runes had betrayed me at every turn—why would they suddenly offer relief?

I took a step toward the throne room anyway. The bond flared, then eased slightly. Like moving closer to warmth after standing too long in cold.

But I kept walking, because watching Renata shatter from a distance was worse than whatever the runes might do.

"He's free," Renata whispered, her voice so quiet I almost missed it under the oppressive silence. She wasn't looking at Valdic, wasn't looking at anything really. Her grey eyes stared through the walls, through reality itself. "He's free because of me. Nalla is dead. Did I—" She hesitated, and something human flickered across her numb expression. "Did I do this to those children?"

My stomach dropped.

I'd seen the bodies as Cressa led me away earlier. Two of them, maybe three—hard to tell with how they'd been torn apart. Children, barely teenagers. One had writing carved into his forehead. Another looked crushed, bones shattered from the inside out.

The kind of damage Renata could do without thinking, if the Hollow Crown was driving.

I never asked for this. The thought came unbidden. I'd have happily stayed dead if it spared her this. If it meant her hands stayed clean and her memories intact. Death had been quiet, peaceful even.

This was worse than death for both of us.

Neither of us had chosen this path. I'd died—been murdered, in a betrayal I still couldn't fully process. She'd made a choice in her grief, used power she barely understood to drag me back. We were both victims of circumstance and love twisted into something monstrous by necessity.

But gods, the guilt.

I felt guilty for being the one she chose, for being important enough to damn herself over. But some terrible, selfish part of me wanted her to pick me. Wanted to be worth the cost, even if the cost was this. Even if the cost was children's bodies and Renata's memories fed to a crown that would never be satisfied.

She felt guilty for the things she'd done to keep me—would do to keep me stable. But she still wanted to keep me. Would make the same choice again, probably. Would feed the Crown more memories, would carve more words into more foreheads, would burn down what remained of the world if it meant I kept breathing.

Valdic laid his snout on Renata's lap with infinite gentleness.

"You aren't bad, Renata," he murmured, voice carrying that dark humor that defined him even in terrible moments. "You're just monumentally fucked up by circumstances beyond your control. There's a difference."

"I've clearly made terrible choices," she replied, and her voice cracked. Her shaking hands moved to touch Valdic's head, fingers sinking into his decayed fur.

I wanted to comfort her. To cross the remaining distance and hold her until the shaking stopped. To tell her I didn't blame her, that I understood, that I'd have done the same—worse, probably.

But what words existed that could hold together someone shattering from the inside out?

The witch runes burned brighter, responding to the spike of emotion.

Cressa had cleared me medically an hour ago, declared my resurrection stable enough for now. The witch runes had settled into their pattern, the bond equalized at its new baseline of constant low-level agony.

But standing here, watching Renata shake apart while covered in blood and bone ash, I'd never felt more helpless.

The bioluminescence flickered again, dimmer than before. The Bone Court was dying along with everything else. The ritual of resurrection had caused widespread famine, accelerated the starvation already consuming the outer cities. There was no food beyond storage now. No hunting, no harvest.

Just rationing and decline and the slow march toward extinction.

All because Renata loved me.

"Renata," I finally managed, voice rough from disuse. The bond flared in response, a spike of pain that made me grit my teeth. "Look at me. Please."

Her grey eyes slowly focused, finding me in the dimness. Recognition flickered across her face, followed by something that might have been relief or fresh horror.

"Nokoa," she whispered, and my name in her mouth sounded like a prayer and a curse. "You shouldn't see me like this."

"I've seen you in worse states," I lied, taking another step closer. The bond eased fractionally. "Remember when you had that stomach illness—"

"Don't," she cut me off, something almost desperate in her voice. "Don't try to make this normal. Don't pretend this is something we can joke about or get through with enough time."

"Then what do you want me to do?" I asked, hating how helpless the question sounded. "How do I help you through this?"

Her laugh was bitter, sharp enough to draw blood. "You can't. That's the point. I chose this. I fed the Crown enough memories to resurrect you and stabilize your runes. I made deals with priestesses. I carved—" She stopped, looked down at her shaking hands as if seeing them for the first time. Blood still caked beneath her fingernails, dark crescents of evidence. "I did things. Terrible things. And I'll do them again because the alternative is watching you die, and I can't. I won't."

"Renata—"

"Go," she interrupted, grey eyes meeting mine with sudden focus. "Please, Nokoa. I can't—I need time. I need to think. And I can't do that with you here reminding me of why I did all this."

The dismissal hit like a physical blow. The bond screamed at the suggestion of separation, flooding my nervous system with warning signals. Pain spiked through my temples, nausea rolled through my stomach.

But I could see she meant it. Could see that my presence was making this worse somehow.

So I nodded, even though every instinct screamed to stay. Even though leaving her alone in this blood-soaked throne room felt like abandonment.

"Valdic stays," I said. Not a question.

"Valdic stays," she agreed, her hand still buried in his decayed fur like it was the only thing anchoring her to reality.

I turned to leave, each step away from her an exercise in controlled agony. My head pounded, my stomach churned, my bones ached with the wrongness of separation.

But I could bear it. I'd bear worse if it gave her the space she needed.

At the threshold, I looked back one more time. Renata sat on her throne with Valdic at her feet, surrounded by her seven silent spectral guardians in their ceremonial silks. Covered in blood and ash and darkness.

The Hollow Queen in truth, not just title.

And I was the reason she'd become this.

I walked away into the dimming caves, following the fading bioluminescence toward whatever came next. My life had cost her everything. She loved me enough to carve the world hollow, and I had let her do it.

Even knowing what it would make us both become.

Chapter Three

The Bone God's First Truth

Renata

The caves around me shook.

Not the gentle tremor of settling stone or shifting earth, but violent convulsions that sent cracks spiderwebbing up the bone walls. The throne beneath me vibrated so hard my teeth chattered, the sensation jarring through my jaw and into my skull. Dirt and dust kicked into the air, thick enough to choke on, coating my tongue with the taste of ancient earth. The particles turned the already dim bioluminescence into a hazy fog. The ancient bone architecture groaned—a sound like the death rattle of something massive and primordial.

Valdic's head lifted from my lap, purple eyes wide and alert. His decayed ears swiveled, trying to pinpoint the source. "What is that?"

For the first time in hours, I stood from the throne of bones. My legs protested, stiff from sitting motionless for so long. The shaking intensified, nearly knocking me off balance. I stumbled, caught myself against the throne's armrest. Pieces of the vaulted ceiling began to rain down—fragments of ancient bone, chunks of fossilized marrow, the luminescent moss that had been our only light source. They clattered against the floor like hail.

The caves were collapsing around us.

"Run!" I didn't recognize my own voice, stripped of its usual hollow flatness and filled instead with something sharp and immediate.

We ran.

Valdic stayed by my side, his emaciated body moving with surprising grace despite its state of decay. We sprinted through corridors I'd walked a thousand times, now transformed into death traps. Bone columns cracked and fell behind us, their impacts shaking the floor beneath our feet. The floor buckled and heaved like breathing ribs, forcing me to adjust my stride with every step. Dust clouds chased us through the darkness, filling my lungs with the taste of ancient death.

We ran across the bridge that spanned the underground waterway—the one feature of the Bone Court that had always felt almost peaceful. Returning from the cottage, I'd stood on this very bridge and looked down at clear water fed by underground springs, teeming with blind white fish that had evolved in the darkness.

The water was gone. Not even mud remained. Just a deep gouge in the bone floor, dry as bleached skulls, lined with the desiccated corpses of those blind fish. Their pale bodies curled and brittle, fragile as ash.

I managed to run out of the entrance just as the shaking finished, bursting into the open air with my lungs burning and my heart hammering against my ribs. Valdic emerged beside me, panting, his purple eyes reflecting the weak sunlight that filtered through the perpetual grey clouds above.

I bent double, hands on my knees, trying to catch my breath. The air outside tasted different—less recycled, less stale, but also emptier somehow. Thinner.

"What is happening?" I yelled into the settling dust.

The Bone God stood before the cave entrance, his massive skeletal hands raised toward the sky. His black bones gleamed dully in the weak light, moss trailing from his eye sockets. Before my eyes, walls of bone raised toward the sky, growing like inverse trees. Ribs as thick as ancient pillars rising from the earth. Vertebrae stacked into spiraling towers. Skulls of various sizes mortared together with calcified sinew, creating patterns that were both beautiful and horrifying.

A cathedral. He was building a skeletal cathedral.

The architecture still made entirely of bone, but transformed from cave to something that reached for the sky with defiant elegance. There was still a path inside—I could see it through the arched entrance formed from a massive ribcage—but now the structure stood above ground. Exposed to the weak sunlight. Open to the air and sky and the vast emptiness of the wasteland beyond.

He was different now. Whole in a way he hadn't been before. His bones were black instead of the lighter colors I was used to seeing on skeletal remains—not sun-bleached white, but something darker. Ancient. Moss grew from his hollow eye sockets, verdant green against the black bone. Four horns curved from his skull, elegant and terrible. Shredded, decayed wings spread from his back, tattered membranes hanging between skeletal wing-bones.

"You require a proper home," he rumbled, his voice reverberating through the bone structure like an echo in a cathedral's nave. "In the sunlight, as you wanted. Consider it my first gift to you."

The wasteland stretched in all directions, a landscape of bone dust and dried earth extending to the horizon. The ground cracked and pale, as if all moisture had been leached from it centuries ago. In the distance, what remained of the outer city's camps—collapsed structures, abandoned tents, the scattered debris of civilization's end.

"My child, come closer," his voice was warm, patient.

As if he were speaking to me the way my parents used to, back when I was small and the world made sense. Back when white hair fell around my shoulders instead of this Crown-corrupted black. Back when my hands were clean and my memories were my own.

I took a hesitant step toward him, then another. Valdic pressed against my leg. The Bone God towered over me, easily three times my height, his black bones catching the weak light in strange ways. But despite his size and the obvious power radiating from his ancient bones, his posture was gentle. Almost protective.

"I can offer you more than simply this," he gestured toward the cathedral with one skeletal hand, moss falling from his eye sockets as he moved. "This is merely the beginning."

Questions crowded my tongue, fighting for priority. Where would everyone else live? What happened to the survivors? Why now? But the first one that emerged was simpler: "Why do you look changed? How did you do this?"

His skull tilted slightly, considering me. The movement dislodged more moss, which drifted down like dark snow. "I needed time to fully wake," he answered. "When your priestess opened the doorway, I was still fragmented. Still scattered across the darkness where they banished me. But Alaira had been working for years before that final ritual. Every crack she placed in my prison, every weakening of the seals, allowed me to feed. To pull life force through the gaps and rebuild myself piece by piece. With each offering of bone and blood, each memory you fed the Crown, each death in the outer cities—I grew stronger. More whole. The version of me you see now is closer to what I was before my sisters drove the guardians to imprison me."

The revelation was chilling. Alaira hadn't just freed him in one moment—she'd been preparing his awakening for years. Every ritual, every manipulation, every crack in his prison had been feeding him. Making him stronger while we thought we were simply maintaining the Bone Court's magic.

"There won't even be that if Praxis is allowed to keep moving as he has," Quade continued, something in his tone sharpening.

I looked at him, my grey eyes searching his moss-lined sockets for meaning.

"Have you not wondered how he remained so well put together while the rest of the Bone Council turned to dust?" Quade asked. "How Ancelin and Fatin and the others grew more skeletal, more corrupted, more hollow—but Praxis's bones stayed bleached to paper-white perfection? How his ivory horns and golden daggers gleamed while theirs dulled?"

I opened my mouth to respond, but no words came. Because he was right. I hadn't questioned it. Praxis had always been there, always strong, always the pillar of the Bone Council. While the others withered, he remained vital.

"He has been forcing tithe offerings himself," Quade said, each word deliberate. "Pulling from the outer cities' camp that sat on your front door. Taking heart fire and bone marrow directly from the dying, bypassing the proper distribution channels. While everyone starved, he never missed a meal. While the Bone Council rotted, he stayed nourished. While you fed the Crown memories and went hungry yourself, he feasted on the last resources meant for the people."

The revelation settled cold and heavy in my stomach like swallowed stones.

I shook my head, the motion automatic. "I would have known. I would have felt it."

Right?

We wanted to protect you, Queen Oriana's voice rang out in my head. Her tone harder, more pragmatic. You had so much on your mind already. The bond, Nokoa's instability, the famine, the resurrection. We thought it best not to burden you further.

The admission staggered me. The voices in the Crown—my supposed allies, my predecessors who understood this burden—had kept secrets from me. Had decided what I should and shouldn't know.

"You were blind, Renata," Quade said, not unkindly. "They made you blind. The Crown narrows your vision to protect your sanity, and those trapped within it manipulate that narrowing. Let me help you see. Let me give you clarity they've denied you."

"I trusted him," I whispered, thinking of Praxis. His crimson eyes that blazed inside bleached sockets. His carefully sculpted ivory horns. "I trusted the Hollow Crown."

"My child, I can offer you so much more," Quade knelt before me, bringing his massive skull closer to my eye level. The moss in his sockets swayed gently. "True sight. Real power. The ability to protect what you love without sacrificing yourself piece by piece to a crown that cares nothing for you."

"What do you want in return?" I asked, because there was always a cost. Always a price for power.

His expression—if a skull could have expressions—seemed almost amused. "We will discuss the particulars of our arrangement soon enough. But not today. Today is for you to understand what I'm offering. To see clearly without the Crown's filter."

He was deliberately withholding something. I could sense it in the careful way he chose his words, in the pause before answering. Whatever price he wanted, whatever my destiny entailed, he wanted me hungry for more before revealing the full cost.

It made me wary. But desperation had a way of overriding caution.

"I ask nothing in return but for you to fulfill your destiny," he said, and his voice held something like pride. "You are meant for more than being the Hollow Queen, Renata Sunthorne. You are transitioning into something greater, something the world has not seen since my sisters walked freely. But we will speak of that later. For now, I will give you another gift."

He raised one skeletal hand, fingers spread as if grasping something invisible. Power gathered around him, making the air taste of ozone and ancient magic.

"I will halt the bond," he declared. "Allow you and Nokoa to have a day without consequences. The pain will cease. The constant pull will silence. You can be together or apart as you choose, without agony dictating your proximity. And more—I will silence the Hollow Crown as well. One day of quiet in your own mind. No voices, no hunger, no memories being consumed."

My breath caught.

"What do you want me to call you?" I asked.

"Quade," he said simply. "I am not the Bone God, though mortals named me such. I am the Primal God of Transitions—of changes from one state to another. Birth to death, death to life, living to undead, light to dark and back again. All transitions fall under my domain. I was one of four. One of the original."

He rose to his full height, bones creaking with ancient power. "Enjoy your gift, my child. Learn what it feels like to be whole again. And then we will discuss your true purpose."

The power released.

It washed over me like a wave, and suddenly—

The Crown went silent. Completely, utterly silent. No voices whispering warnings or advice or manipulations. No hunger gnawing at the edges of my consciousness, demanding memories to feed it. No constant drain pulling pieces of me into its endless void.

Just silence in my own head for the first time since the Crown had fused to my skull.

And the bond—the bond that had burned constantly since Nokoa's resurrection, that had made every moment of separation agony and every thought of him a spike of pain—it simply stopped. The thread was still there, I could feel its presence like a barely-there touch. But it wasn't hurting. Wasn't demanding. Wasn't punishing me for distance or rewarding proximity with manipulative relief.

It just... was.

Valdic nuzzled my hand with his snout, the texture both familiar and strange—decay and loyalty mixed into one.

"There you are," he said softly. "You're warm again."

My body flooded with emotion all at once, like a dam breaking. The numbness lifted. Everything came rushing back: the horror of the children's deaths, the grief for the camps turned to dust, the betrayal of Praxis, the manipulation of the Crown voices, the desperate love for Nokoa that had started all of this.

And with the emotions came a single, overwhelming thought: Where is Nokoa?

I'd done all of this for him. And in this moment, when I could finally feel clearly, when I could finally be close to him without pain, he wasn't here. He'd left when I'd asked him to. Given me space when I'd thought I needed it.

I fell to my knees in the bone dust, hands gripping the front of my ruined dress, and finally—finally—I felt it all.

Joy at seeing the sun. Terror at what I'd become. Hope for what Quade promised. Doubt about everything. Love for Nokoa that burned brighter without the bond's interference. Grief for the thousands who'd died. Rage at Praxis's betrayal. Fear of what came next.

It washed through me like blood rushing back into a limb that had fallen asleep—painful and vital in equal measure. Tears streamed down my face for the first time in what felt like years.

Behind me, the skeletal cathedral stood complete, gleaming in the weak sunlight.

"Valdic," I managed, my voice breaking on his name. "I need to find Nokoa."

"I know," he replied softly. "Let's go find him."

I pushed myself up from the bone dust, legs shaking but functional. For one day, I could be close to him without consequence. For one day, I could hold him and not suffer for it.

Tomorrow, Quade would tell me what he really wanted. What final price this gift would cost.

But that was tomorrow.

Chapter Four

A Day Without Pain

Nokoa

I followed Cressa through the skeletal corridors of our newly created palace, still trying to process the transformation that had occurred in mere hours. The bone architecture rose around us in dark arches and spiraling columns, so different from the oppressive caves we'd left behind. Moss grew in deliberate patterns along the walls, verdant green against bleached white bone—living decoration in a palace of death.

Skeletal arms jutted from the walls at regular intervals, holding flames in their open palms for light. The fire danced without consuming, magical and eternal, casting moving shadows that made the bone seem to breathe.

"I took supplies from the caves and set them up here," Cressa explained, her healer's hands gesturing at the doors we passed. Her voice echoed off the vaulted ceilings. "It's not luxury, but it has to be better than the tents you were staying in before."

The reminder of the tents made something twist in my chest. The outer city camps, packed with desperate people waiting for salvation. All gone now, turned to bone dust by the famine's final acceleration. I'd been living among them, dying slowly alongside them, before the resurrection. Now they were memories and ash, and I was walking through a palace built from their remains.

"Being alive without constant pain is enough of a luxury," I admitted. The witch runes still burned beneath my skin, visible through my flesh in glowing patterns that traced ancient script along my bones. But the pain was manageable now. Not the all-consuming agony that had characterized every moment since resurrection.

Something nagged at the back of my mind, though. The runes had been pure torture since Alaira brought me back—spreading, burning, consuming. And now they were just quiet. Stable. It felt like the eye of a storm rather than the end of one.

But I pushed the thought away. Today was a gift. I wouldn't waste it on suspicion.

"The rations of food left, I'm going to bring what I can," Cressa continued, stopping at a door near the end of the corridor. Sunlight filtered through a nearby window—actual sunlight, not bioluminescence or magical flame. "I will stop here first so you can eat. You need to maintain your strength while the runes stabilize."

She turned the knob on my door, but she didn't step aside for me to enter. Instead, she looked back at me with something like fear crossing her features. Her dark eyes were wide, one hand raised as if to stop me from advancing.

The reaction sent alarm coursing through my veins. "What—"

I placed my hand on her shoulder and moved her aside as gently as I could manage.

On my bed sat the most beautiful sight I'd seen in what felt like lifetimes.

Renata.

Her black hair shined in the sunlight beaming through the window, catching highlights I'd forgotten existed. Deep blue undertones in the darkness, like midnight rather than void. She sat with perfect posture, hands folded in her lap, looking more like a painting than a person. The Hollow Crown still fused to her skull, but something about her was different. Softer. More present. Her grey eyes held actual light instead of that flat emptiness.

"You two can't be this close," Cressa pleaded behind me, and I could hear the genuine distress in her voice. "I'm going to run out of supplies to help him recover. The bond will tear him apart if you stay together, and I don't have enough—"

"This is Quade's gift to us," Renata interrupted, her voice gentle but certain. She looked up at me, grey eyes meeting mine without the usual flatness. Real feeling, not the muted approximations the Crown allowed. "A day without pain."

I hesitated, every instinct screaming that this was impossible. The bond had been a constant companion since resurrection—burning, demanding, punishing any distance between us. It didn't just stop. Magic like that didn't take holidays.

But she was right.

We were near—closer than we'd been allowed to be in days—and I felt nothing. No tightening in my chest. No pounding in my skull. No fire racing along my nerves.

I bridged the space between us in three strides, and my hands were on her face before I could consciously decide to move. My palms cupped her cheeks, thumbs tracing the line of her cheekbones, fingers tangling in the black silk of her hair.

She was warm. Actually warm, not the cold that had been settling into her skin as the Crown consumed more of her humanity. Peach color in her cheeks, blood beneath the surface instead of paper-white translucency. The black veins still traced patterns across her jaw and down her neck, but they seemed less pronounced somehow.

Tears were filling her eyes. It was the most human thing I'd seen her do in what felt like forever.

I lowered my face to hers and placed my lips where they had always longed to be.

No pain. No stabbing at my chest. No fire racing through the runes. Just the soft press of her lips against mine, warm and alive and real. The taste of her—something sweet like honey mixed with the salt of her tears.

She pulled back just enough to speak, eyes still closed. "The voices in the Crown are silenced too," she whispered, and her voice cracked on the words. "It's only you and I. I can feel you. I can feel how much I love you." Her eyes opened, grey and bright. "I touched the bone coral growing outside, and I felt it too. The texture. The life in it. Everything."

A knock sounded at the door, sharp and insistent. Cressa opened it without waiting for permission, carrying a tray nearly larger than she could manage. The silver surface gleamed in the sunlight. "Quade asked me to bring you this," she announced, slightly breathless from the weight.

I smelled it before she ever removed the lid—the unmistakable aroma of fresh food. Real food, not the dried rations or carefully preserved supplies we'd been living on. My stomach clenched in response, mouth flooding with saliva after weeks of near-starvation.

"I don't know how he did it, but he did," Cressa muttered as she lifted the lid.

Fresh bright fruits—oranges and apples and berries that shouldn't exist in a world where nothing grew. Boiled eggs with shells so perfect they looked painted. Chicken so tender I could see the juice glistening on it, steam still rising from the perfectly browned skin. Bread that smelled of yeast and warmth, butter melting into its surface in golden pools. Vegetables that were actually green.

A feast. An impossible feast in a dying world.

"He's extended the food to me as well," Cressa continued, setting the tray on a small table near the window. "Offering me my favorites. Foods I haven't seen since before the famine started. It feels wrong, though." She paused, looking between Renata and me. "It feels wrong to eat so well after everything that's gotten us here. After what the resurrection cost. Without knowing how he made it, where it came from."

Renata sat frozen on the bed, staring at the food. I knew that expression. The old Renata would have refused to eat entirely, would have tried to distribute the food to others, would have starved herself rather than accept generosity built on graves.

"He is a God," I pointed out, keeping my voice neutral. "It seems all too simple that he'd be able to make food. To create something from nothing, or pull it from wherever gods keep their stores. That's rather the definition of divine power, isn't it?"

"Should we really be eating it, though?" Cressa pressed, her voice sharp with frustration. "Just accepting gifts from a being who demolished entire cities and turned people to bone dust? Who built this palace from corpses?"

"Should we be taking our life for granted?" I countered, meeting her gaze directly. "Should we starve out of principle when we've been given the chance to survive? I died, Cressa. I was dead, actually dead, and now I'm here eating food that shouldn't exist in a world that's ending. I'm not about to refuse that gift because the source makes you uncomfortable."

The words came out harsher than I'd intended, but they were true.

Cressa narrowed her eyes at me, then turned and left without another word, closing the door behind her with more force than necessary.

I turned back to Renata.

She was still shaking—trying to hide it, but I could see the tremors running through her hands, her shoulders. Every suppressed feeling, every stolen memory, every horror the Crown had made her commit—all of it rushing back in an overwhelming tide.

I'd let myself slip before. Let doubt creep in when I looked at what she'd become. But seeing her now, shaking with the weight of returned consciousness, I knew the truth. She never would have been able to make those choices if she hadn't been used by the Hollow Crown. Manipulated by the voices trapped within it, her vision narrowed and her agency stolen.

"She's right," Renata whispered, grey eyes fixed on the tray of food.

"No, she's not," I cut her off. I moved to sit beside her on the bed, close enough that our thighs pressed together. The warmth of contact was almost shocking after so long denied. "She's far from it. You shouldn't be made a villain when the Hollow Crown is the one that forced you."

"I don't know that it did," she whispered, and now she looked at me with such raw pain it made my chest ache. "I would have done so much worse if it meant that you were okay. If it meant that you—"

I stopped her with a kiss, pressing my lips against hers to silence the rest. She tasted of salt. I used my thumb to wipe the tears away, following the tracks down to her jaw, tracing the black veins with gentle reverence.

"Not today," I whispered against her skin. "Today we stay in this room. Today we imagine that outside is your beautiful garden growing." I kissed her cheek, tasting tears and skin. "That later we will go prune it together, check which orchids are blooming, argue about whether we need more herbs or more flowers."

She let out a sound that was half-laugh, half-sob.

"We will discuss what our wedding is to look like," I continued, kissing the corner of her mouth. "What you will wear and how many orchids there will be. Whether we do it at sunrise like you always wanted, or at sunset because it's more dramatic." I kissed her other cheek. "I'll feed you boiled eggs and I won't allow my hands to leave you for even a second. We'll pretend that tomorrow doesn't exist and the world outside these walls is still whole."

She laughed between my kisses, though the end of it bent toward grief.

I reached over to the tray and grabbed an egg, still warm from whatever magic had created it. The shell smooth and perfect under my fingers. I cracked it against the table edge and peeled it with one hand, keeping my other hand tangled in her hair.

"Ahh," I prompted, holding the egg up to her lips.

She bit it in half, and I pulled the egg away fast enough to end the bite with another kiss. Her smile was real—actually real, reaching her eyes and crinkling the corners. Genuine joy on her face, for the first time since before the resurrection and the horror that followed.

Renata grabbed the other half of the egg from my fingers and pushed it into my mouth with a mischievous glint in her grey eyes. The taste took me by surprise—no hint of rot, no staleness. Just pure, fresh egg. Rich and creamy, tasting of a world where things still grew.

I'd forgotten food could taste like this.

Her smile as she watched me chew was better than any of the small victories we'd scraped together from the ruins.

I kissed her again, harder this time, and she pressed back with equal intensity. She moved with me onto the bed, my body settling over hers, pressed close enough that there was no space between us for air or doubt or the outside world.

I kissed her neck down to her collarbone, following the line of black veins with my lips. She let out a small gasp between each point of contact, her fingers tangling in my hair, holding me close.

"I missed you," I whispered into her skin, breathing the words against her pulse point. "All of you, not just the hollow shell the Crown leaves behind."

"I'm here," she whispered back, and her voice cracked on the words. "For today, I'm here."

Later, Renata lay in my arms, the two of us tucked under blankets that smelled faintly of lavender. The afternoon sun had shifted, casting long shadows across the bone walls, painting everything in gold and amber.

In the pit of my stomach, I knew it wasn't without a price. Gods didn't just hand things down for nothing—especially gods of transitions, where everything required balance. But I was willing to pay it. Whatever it cost, this was worth it.

And yet.

The witch runes pulsed beneath my skin. But was it my imagination, or had they dimmed slightly? The glow seemed fainter than it had been this morning, the ancient script less vibrant through my flesh. And I felt too good, maybe. The kind of energized clarity that came before a fever broke or a wound festered.

I tightened my arms around Renata. Tomorrow's problems could wait for tomorrow.

"Tomorrow—" Renata began, her voice soft against my skin.

"What do you want to be remembered for?" I interrupted, not ready to face what waited beyond these walls.

She was quiet for a long moment, her fingers tracing the witch runes through my skin. Finally: "For loving you."

Not for being the Hollow Queen, not for saving the Bone Court or making impossible choices or bearing unbearable burdens. Just for loving me.

"I never wanted to be remembered as anything but yours," I replied, meaning every word. "So it looks like we can both have our wish."

Renata tucked her head back into my chest. "I think things will only get worse from here," she murmured.

I didn't answer. She was right, and we both knew it.

"I don't know how long I can do this," she continued, voice small in a way the Crown never allowed. "Feel all of this, I mean. The children, the camps, all of it. When tomorrow comes and the Crown returns—"

"For now, we take baby steps," I interrupted gently, stroking her hair. "For now, you rest without voices in your mind. You sleep without nightmares. You let yourself be loved without wondering what it costs."

She nodded against my chest, and I felt the dampness of new tears soaking through my shirt.

I spent the rest of the evening memorizing her face. The exact shade of grey in her eyes, like storm clouds holding back rain. The small scar above her right eyebrow from a childhood accident she'd once told me about. The curve of her jaw beneath the black veins, the way her breathing deepened when she finally relaxed into sleep.

There would be plenty of time to sleep later, when she was gone again and I was left with just the bond and the runes. But time to hold her like this—without pain or consequence—might never come again.

So I stayed awake, burning every detail into memory.

One perfect day.

It would have to be enough.

Chapter Five

The Morning After Peace

Renata

I stayed as silent and unmoving as I could, barely allowing myself to breathe for fear of disturbing this fragile peace. The sound of Nokoa's heartbeat drummed in my ear as it rested on his chest—steady, rhythmic, real. Each beat a defiance of the death that had claimed him and the resurrection that had brought him back broken.

He was alive, without the constant pain that had characterized every moment since resurrection. His arm was wrapped around me, heavy and warm, anchoring me to this moment with a weight I never wanted to lose.

Twenty-four hours. That's what Quade had given us. One full day of peace that had passed far too quickly, slipping through my fingers like water no matter how desperately I'd tried to hold onto each moment. And now, as the pre-dawn grey filtered through the window, I could feel our borrowed time running out.

The only thing stopping me from being still was the wave of emotion that kept crashing into me, relentless as a tide against cliffs. Guilt, heavy and suffocating, for every person who'd turned to bone dust while I focused solely on saving one man. Sorrow, sharp as broken glass, for the children whose names I couldn't remember but whose faces I could suddenly see with perfect clarity. The boy with traitor carved into his forehead—I could remember doing it now, could feel the resistance of skin beneath the blade, could hear his pleading.

I brushed Nokoa's curls from his face with gentle fingers, studying him in the grey light. The witch runes still glowed faintly beneath his skin, but they'd settled into steady patterns. His features peaceful, younger somehow without the constant tension of pain. Beautiful in the way he'd always been, before death and resurrection had carved new meanings into his bones.

At least he was breathing. At least we'd had one day to remember when everything inevitably fell apart again.

At least he was—

Nokoa's body tensed beneath me, muscles going rigid all at once like a corpse in rigor mortis. The change was so sudden I barely had time to lift my head before he screamed—the sound raw and animal, filled with such agony it made my own throat ache. His back arched impossibly high, spine curving until I thought it might snap. Then he curled in on himself like a dying spider, knees pulling up to his chest, arms wrapping around his middle. The witch runes blazed beneath his skin, no longer gentle blue-white but burning red-orange, angry and consuming like embers suddenly brought to flame.

He tried to squirm away from me as if my proximity was causing the pain. As if I was the source of his suffering—which, in every way that mattered, I was.

I scrambled back onto the bed, placed my hands on his back. The contact only caused him to cry out again, his skin burning hot beneath my palms, fever-bright. The heat was almost unbearable, like touching sun-baked stone.

"Nokoa, it's alright, I'm here," I tried to keep my voice steady even as panic clawed at my throat. "I've got you. Just breathe. Please breathe."

Valdic rushed through the door, all four paws crashing against the bone floor hard enough to crack it. His purple eyes wide with alarm, his decayed body moving faster than I'd seen him move in months.

My ears rang too loudly to hear him properly. A high-pitched whine that drowned out everything else, pressure building behind my eyes, in my sinuses. Like standing too close to a bell tower when it struck midnight.

The Crown. The Crown was waking up.

"It was worth it, Renata," Nokoa gasped out between convulsions, his voice wrecked and desperate. "Please don't feel bad for me. I'd still choose you. I'd choose—" His words cut off in another scream as his body twisted, the bond reasserting itself with a vengeance.

Tears streamed down my face in hot tracks, blurring my vision until Nokoa became just a shape of agony before me. My breath came in hitching sobs that matched his screams.

My hands began to shake. My body wasn't in pain the same way his was—the bond had always punished him more severely than me—but something else was happening.

The Crown was waking, and it wasn't gentle about it.

I felt it clicking into place like a lock engaging, each tumbler falling with an audible sensation inside my skull. The bone circlet pulsed with returning power. The voices were stirring, waking from their enforced silence with confusion and then anger.

What happened? Queen Lyanna's voice came first, sharp and accusatory. Where were we? Why can't I remember yesterday?

Quade, Queen Oriana replied, her tone flat with certainty. He gave them a gift. Silenced us so they could have their peace.

He can't do that, King Aldric growled, and I could feel his rage like heat inside my skull. We are bound to this Crown, to her. He has no right to—

Their arguing faded as something else demanded my attention. Flashes of memory—images of the things I had done, displayed before my mind's eye with perfect, terrible clarity. Every terrible choice, every compromised decision, every moment where I'd chosen survival over mercy. The Crown had taken these memories before, had consumed them to fuel its magic. Now it was giving them back all at once, force-feeding me my own sins like poison I was required to swallow.

This was the cost. This was what Quade's gift had truly been—not freedom, but a temporary reprieve before an even harsher reckoning.

Guilt and grief and horror and love and desperation all tangled together until I couldn't distinguish one from another. They pressed against my ribcage, against my skull, against every boundary of self. My chest constricted, lungs refusing to expand properly.

Breathe, Queen Oriana commanded, her voice cutting through the chaos. You're hyperventilating. Control yourself.

But I couldn't. The control that the Crown usually provided was gone, scattered by the flood of returned memory. I was just Renata again—fully human and fully broken, unable to bear the weight of what I'd become.

Nokoa's convulsions were slowing, his body exhausted by the pain. He curled tighter into himself, shaking with aftershocks, his breathing ragged and wet. The witch runes still burned beneath his skin, but the worst of the attack was passing. The red-orange glow fading back to blue-white, crisis receding into chronic suffering.

The bond had re-established itself. The day of peace was over.

"This is only the beginning of something much larger, my child," Quade's voice rumbled through the room, coming from everywhere and nowhere at once.

I looked up through tear-blurred vision to see his dark skeletal body materializing in the doorway. The moss in his eye sockets seemed brighter today, more vibrant green against the black bone. He looked pleased. Satisfied with the scene before him—Nokoa writhing in pain, me drowning in emotion, Valdic whimpering helplessly between us.

"You gave us one perfect day," I managed to choke out, my voice raw from crying. "Was it just to make this worse? To show us what we can't have?"

"I gave you a taste of what could be," Quade corrected, moving into the room with surprising grace. Each step silent despite his size. "A reminder of what you're fighting for. Motivation to continue when the path grows darker still."

He knelt beside the bed, bringing his skull level with mine. The moss-lined sockets held no eyes, but I felt seen anyway. Studied. Measured.

"The pain is necessary," he continued, his voice gentle despite the words' cruelty. "Both of you must understand suffering intimately if you're to transcend it. The bond between you must be tested, strained, nearly broken—so that when it reforms, it will be unbreakable. You are being forged, my child. Tempered in fires that would destroy lesser beings."

"I don't want to be forged," I whispered. "I just want him to stop hurting."

"Then accept what you're becoming," Quade replied, and now his skeletal hand reached out to touch the Hollow Crown. The contact sent shivers through my entire body, neither pleasant nor painful but something else entirely. Power recognizing power. "Stop fighting the transformation. Stop clinging to who you were. Renata Sunthorne, the girl who braided flowers in her hair and tended gardens—she is already dead. Mourning her only prolongs the agony."

He's right, Queen Lyanna whispered inside the Crown, her vanity stripped away. We all tried to hold onto our old selves. It only made everything harder.

The Crown takes everything eventually, King Aldric added, his violence-ready tone almost gentle. Better to give it willingly than have it torn away piece by piece.

We're trying to help you, Queen Oriana finished. We don't want you to suffer as we did. Learn from our mistakes.

I looked down at Nokoa, still curled and shaking. His golden eyes squeezed shut, tears streaming down his cheeks, the witch runes continuing their angry burn beneath his skin. He was suffering because I'd refused to let him go.

Valdic pressed against my leg, his purple eyes holding infinite sadness and infinite loyalty.

"What do I have to do?" I asked Quade, the question emerging flat and resigned.

"Rest," he replied, rising back to his full height. "Recover from yesterday's gift. Let the Crown settle back into its rhythms. Care for him." He gestured toward Nokoa. "And tonight, when darkness falls and the voices quiet naturally with sleep, come find me. We have much to discuss about your destiny."

He was gone. Not walking away, not fading—just suddenly absent. Only the faint smell of moss and ancient earth remained.

Nokoa's convulsions had finally stopped, leaving him limp and exhausted. His breathing still ragged, but slower. The witch runes dimming back to their usual steady glow.

I carefully maneuvered back onto the bed beside him, moving slowly so as not to trigger another attack. The bond hummed between us—not painful yet, just present. A headache already building behind my eyes.

"I'm sorry," I whispered.

Nokoa's hand found mine in the tangled blankets, his fingers threading through mine despite the obvious pain it caused him. His grip was weak but determined. "Stop apologizing," he rasped, his voice wrecked from screaming. "I told you. I'd choose this. I'd choose you. Every time."

Valdic jumped onto the bed, carefully positioning himself between us—close enough to touch both, but not pressing hard enough to cause pain. His purple eyes moved from me to Nokoa and back again.

"Well," he said finally, "that was a spectacular end to the honeymoon period. Really sets the tone for the marriage, doesn't it? 'Till death do us part' takes on a whole new meaning when death is just a suggestion you both keep ignoring."

Despite everything, I felt my lips twitch.

"Too soon?" Valdic asked, tilting his head.

"Way too soon," Nokoa confirmed. But he was smiling too, just a little.

Chapter Six

PRAXIS UNMASKED

Renata

Nokoa was insistent that he'd dealt with the physical pain of the bond for long enough that it didn't hurt him to be with me anymore. His voice carried conviction when he said it, his golden eyes meeting mine without flinching. He claimed the witch runes had adapted, that his body had adjusted to the constant burn, that proximity no longer cost him the way it had.

I knew it was a lie because it still hurt me.

I could see it in the way he moved—carefully, precisely, as if sudden movements might shatter something vital. The witch runes glowed angry beneath his skin whenever we were too close for too long, and no amount of Alaira's stabilization magic could fully compensate for the fundamental wrongness of a dead man walking.

I had to leave him for both our sakes.

The thought sat heavy in my stomach like swallowed stones. Every moment we spent together was purchased with pain—his pain, mostly, though he'd never admit it. And I had other responsibilities. Other failures to confront.

I'd been living with no memory and no feelings for so long that having both back felt like drowning. Touching Nokoa was a feeling I almost couldn't bear—not because I didn't love him, but because I loved him so much it threatened to consume everything else. But the memories of what I had done haunted me with equal intensity. They played on repeat behind my eyes every time I blinked—the carved foreheads, the starved bodies, the children's pleading. The Crown had taken those memories before, consumed them for fuel. Now they were back, vivid and inescapable.

I needed to see the aftermath with my own eyes. Not filtered through the Crown's narrowed perception or softened by magical numbness. I needed to walk through what I'd caused and bear witness.

Starting with Praxis.

The last surviving member of the Bone Council. The system had been designed centuries ago—the Hollow Crown would choose its wearer, and the Bone Council would ensure the bonding was complete. The Crown would eat away at its wearer's memories, keeping them docile and controllable while the Council made all the real decisions. The Hollow Ruler was just for show, a vessel for the Crown's power while the Council wielded actual authority.

It had worked that way for generations. Until the outer cities started begging me for relief from the tithes the Bone Council kept raising. Until I'd seen children starving while the Council hoarded heartfire and bone marrow. Until I'd decided I wouldn't be their puppet ruler.

I'd forced them to acknowledge my authority. Had taken the right to rule from the Bone Council and claimed it for myself. Most of them had fought back—Ancelin had resisted openly, Fatin had schemed in shadows, Bahni had tried to undermine me at every turn.

But Praxis hadn't fought at all. Had simply bent the knee without protest.

I'd thought it meant he was growing loyal to me.

I entered the Bone Court caves through what remained of the original entrance. The interior passages were still intact, though damaged from the structural changes. Cracks spiderwebbed through the walls, bone dust coating every surface. The bioluminescence had died almost completely now, leaving only darkness punctuated by the occasional guttering magical flame.

I walked past rubble and bodies, holding my eyes up and forward. Teenagers clutched weapons still in their hands where they'd died—fifteen, sixteen, seventeen, frozen in defensive positions, expressions locked in the moment of death.

I was a monster.

The knowledge settled into my bones with the weight of absolute truth. I'd sworn to be a just ruler who made positive changes for the outer cities. Had sworn to actually use the authority I'd seized from the Bone Council to help people instead of exploit them.

I had failed all of it.

You allowed him to silence us, Queen Lyanna hissed through the Hollow Crown. You let that god lock us away like we were nothing. Like our counsel meant nothing.

"Of course I did," I replied aloud, my voice echoing off the bone walls. "Even if I had protested, what am I to do against a God? Quade gave us a gift. I wasn't going to refuse it out of loyalty to voices in my skull."

You killed Guardians, King Aldric shouted. You wear the Hollow Crown. You wield a spectral army! You have power beyond mortal reckoning, and you just surrendered to his whim like a child accepting candy from a stranger.

"She took a gift offered to her," Queen Oriana interrupted, her harder tone cutting through the others. "Even a God has limitations against a cursed artifact as old and powerful as this Crown. We forgive your weakness and see it as no betrayal."

Betrayal.

The word hung in the air like smoke. It was them who had betrayed me first. Them who had kept secrets about Praxis, who had manipulated my perception, who had decided what I should and shouldn't know. They'd made me blind on purpose, had curated my reality to keep me controllable.

Just like the system had always intended.

Rage flared inside me, hot and immediate. The Crown had always consumed or redirected my anger before. But now, with emotions flooding back unfiltered, I was drowning in fury I didn't know how to process.

Praxis's door was locked when I located it, tucked away in a section of the caves that had survived the transformation mostly intact. The brass handle cool under my palm, unmoving when I tried to turn it.

"Open it," I commanded my spectral army.

The guardian didn't knock or test the door's strength. He simply blew it entirely off its hinges.

The wood and bone composite exploded inward with a sound like thunder, splinters and dust filling the air. Fragments rained down in a cascade of destruction.

Praxis didn't jump. Didn't look shocked or even particularly surprised. He sat tall behind a desk carved from what looked like a human ribcage, his bleached-bone form perfectly composed. His crimson eyes blazed inside paper-white sockets. The octopus-like tentacles beneath his jaw shifted slightly. Molten gold tattoos gleamed across his skull in the dim light, intricate designs that traced down to his skeletal feet.

As if having his door destroyed was just another minor inconvenience in a long existence of complications.

He was surrounded by treasures.

Shelves lined the walls, packed with vials of heartfire glowing soft blue in the darkness, their light pulsing gently like captured stars. Jars of bone marrow, carefully preserved and labeled, enough to keep someone fed for months. Books, rare and precious in our world of scarcity. Bone weapons ancient and well-maintained. The lower shelves held scrolls, magical implements, pouches that clinked with precious metals.

He'd hoarded everything. While the outer cities starved, while the Bone Council slowly rotted, while I fed the Crown my memories to keep everyone alive—he'd been building a personal treasury.

But worse than the material wealth was what occupied the opposite wall.

Two survivors, chained and barely holding on. They looked as skeletal as Praxis did, but without his careful sculpting and golden adornments. Just raw bone pushing through paper-thin skin. Their eyes hollow, sunken so deep I could see the shape of the sockets beneath. They didn't even look up when I entered, as if they'd lost the energy to care who saw them.

"You know why I've come," I stated, my voice steady despite the fury threatening to choke me.

I shook my head—at myself more than him. When I'd first demanded the Bone Council acknowledge my authority, Praxis hadn't fought back like the others. He'd simply accepted it. Bent the knee without protest.

I'd thought he was seeing reason.

Now I understood—it was strategy. He'd let me think I'd won so I wouldn't look too closely at what he was doing. Had played the loyal councilman while systematically stealing from everyone, ensuring his own survival while his fellow rulers rotted away.

"Someone had to live, Renata," Praxis replied, his voice as calm as his expression. The tentacles beneath his jaw shifted slightly. "Someone had to rebuild when this is all over. You had the Hollow Crown—it wasn't going to let you die. You had Nokoa to obsess over, to pour all your energy into saving. Who was going to help you after? Who was going to be strong enough to assist in whatever comes next?"

He leaned forward, ivory horns catching the dim light. "I chose me," he continued. "Pragmatism. Survival. Inevitability. I made the choice you were too noble to make, and when the dust settles, you'll thank me for it."

The logic was sound, I realized with sick horror. The Bone Council had governed for generations, had managed the complex systems of tithe and distribution, had maintained order even if that order was corrupt. I'd seized power without fully understanding how to wield it, had been so focused on making things better that I hadn't considered who would help me rebuild.

But the two survivors chained to his wall—their suffering, their slow consumption—that wasn't pragmatism. That was cruelty dressed up in reasonable language.

He deserves justice, King Aldric whispered in my head, his violence-ready tone eager. Let me guide your hand. We can end this quickly, make it clean.

But another voice joined the space in my mind, calmer than the others. Now you truly see him, Quade's voice sang through my consciousness like wind through bone chimes. Not the mask that he shows to the court. But his true self—survival incarnate, willing to sacrifice anything and anyone for his own continuation.

The rage that had propelled me here was fracturing into a dozen different emotions, all competing for dominance. Kill him or spare him—both options wanted to drown me. I felt frozen, unable to pick a direction.

"You'll face proper judgment once I've recovered enough to do it," I finally managed, my voice hollow. "Until then, I'll leave a spectral guard by your side. You don't leave this room. You don't touch those survivors again."

It was weak. I knew it was weak even as I said it. King Aldric was shouting in my head about mercy for traitors, Queen Lyanna hissing about my inability to make hard choices. But Queen Oriana remained silent. Observing.

"Renata, I'm still here to do your bidding," Praxis said, his crimson eyes fixed on mine. "Whatever you need, whatever comes next—I can help. I've always helped. This changes nothing about my usefulness to you."

I turned and walked out without another word, one of my spectral guardians peeling off to stand watch over the ruined doorway. The remaining six followed in their silent procession, ceremonial silks whispering against bone.

They take from you, Quade sang in my mind again. From your people. From your world. The Crown voices, the Bone Council—they all extract and consume until nothing remains. I'd never steal from you, my child. Everything I give is freely offered, with no hidden costs or manipulations.

I wanted to believe him. He'd only given me things I wanted so far—the cathedral, the day of peace, the truth about Praxis. But I'd had no reason to doubt Praxis either, until I did.

I grabbed at my neck as I walked, the feeling of constriction growing worse. Like invisible hands closing around my throat. The corridor seemed to narrow, bone walls pressing inward. My vision tunneled, darkness creeping in from the edges.

"Renata," Valdic's voice cut through the rising panic.

He stood on all four paws in front of me, purple eyes steady, his emaciated body blocking my path. Forcing me to stop before I walked blindly into something or collapsed entirely.

Valdic grabbed the fabric of my dress in his teeth and pulled me down to his level. His snout shoved my hand into a patch of his fur—the familiar texture of decay and loyalty, something real and grounding.

"Cry," he commanded, his voice gentler now. "Let it out. Don't choke it down like before. Feel it. Process it."

The tears were already on the edge of my eyes regardless. They spilled over in hot tracks down my cheeks, followed by sobs that shook my entire body. I collapsed onto the cold bone floor, both hands buried in his fur.

"I was beyond blind," I cried, the words coming between gasping breaths. "I was cruel and ignorant. I let them make me into a monster while thinking I was being noble. While congratulating myself on saving Nokoa, people were dying. Children were dying. And Praxis was right there the whole time, and I never saw it."

"You were against multiple forces that were all stronger than any single person," Valdic said, his purple eyes never leaving my face. "The Hollow Crown, the voices within it, the bond pulling you in conflicting directions, Praxis manipulating from the shadows, Alaira serving Quade's agenda. You were never meant to see clearly."

"I couldn't even strike him down," I admitted. "I should have held him accountable in that moment. But I froze."

"He has nowhere to go," Valdic replied. "Your guard won't let him leave. Those resources can be redistributed. The survivors can be freed and treated. His time will come when you're ready to deliver judgment properly, not in the heat of emotion."

I nodded against his fur, trying to believe that mercy wasn't the same as weakness.

He pulled back enough to look at me clearly. "Come on. Let's get you back to the sunlight. You can't fix everything today, and trying will just break you further."

I let him guide me back through the corridors, past the rubble and the bodies, past the evidence of my failures. My spectral guardians followed in their silent procession, ceremonial silks whispering. And somewhere in the darkness behind us, Praxis sat surrounded by his treasures under guard.

Chapter Seven

The Bridge, Never the Shore

Renata

I found Quade in the heart of the skeletal cathedral, surrounded by the bone coral that had taken over what used to be my garden. The formations were taller now than they'd been this morning, some reaching as high as my waist. They grew and decayed in accelerated cycles that made my stomach turn—new growth spiraling up from the base while the top crumbled to powder, an endless loop of creation and destruction happening in seconds rather than seasons.

Growing because of me. Dying because of me.

Valdic pressed against my leg. His purple eyes tracked Quade's every movement, alert despite the exhaustion I could feel in his emaciated frame.

Quade didn't turn when I approached, just continued running his black skeletal fingers over the coral with something like affection. His touch left trails of fresh moss growth wherever he made contact, verdant green against the grey bone. "You have questions," he observed.

"I have demands," I corrected, and my voice came out harder than I'd intended. "Everyone else has lied to me, manipulated me, used my grief as a tool to serve their purposes. Alaira, the Crown voices, Praxis—all of them hiding truth while pretending to help. Are you any different?"

Now he turned, those moss-lined eye sockets fixed on me with patient intensity. "No," he replied simply. "I am manipulating you. Using your circumstances to serve my purposes. Shaping events to push you toward transformation. But I'm the only one willing to tell you exactly how and why."

The admission should have made me angrier. Instead, I just stood there, starving for truth.

"Then tell me. All of it. What am I becoming and why? What do you get from this?"

Quade gestured to a bench carved from a massive vertebra, positioned near the center of the coral garden. "Sit. This explanation requires context, and you've been through enough today that you deserve comfort while bearing the weight of truth."

I almost refused on principle—sitting felt like submission. But my legs were shaking from the confrontation with Praxis, from the panic attack, from carrying emotions I'd been numb to for so long. I sat. The bone was cool beneath me, solid. Valdic immediately jumped up beside me, his weight settling against my thigh.

Quade remained standing, but he positioned himself at eye level, crouching with inhuman grace. The bone coral around us responded to his proximity, growth accelerating in patterns that were almost beautiful if you could forget what they represented.

"I am the Primal God of Transitions," he began, his voice taking on a quality that made the words feel carved into stone. "Not death itself, but the movement from life to death. Not birth, but the transition from non-existence to existence. Every change of state, every transformation—that is my domain. I am the bridge, Renata. Always the bridge. Never the shore."

He extended one skeletal hand, and between his fingers, a small plant sprouted. I watched it grow from seed to sprout to full flower in seconds, then wither and die, then decompose, then—impossibly—begin the cycle again. The scent of growth and decay mixed together, sweet and acrid.

"I can facilitate these transitions," Quade continued. "Can smooth the passage from one state to another. But I cannot create the living state itself. Cannot cause the final death. I am movement, not destination."

The flower in his hand finally stopped cycling, frozen mid-bloom. He closed his fist and it crumbled to dust that drifted down like ash.

"My sister Dahlia, the Goddess of the Moon, did not share my limitations," he said, and something sharp entered his tone. Old anger, carefully controlled. "She could create. Could bring forth life from nothing, could establish the states between which I facilitated movement. And in her pride, she made daughters—the Sisters of Creation. Goddesses of Magic, Time, Fate, Nature. All the forces that push toward existence."

He stood, beginning to pace around the coral garden. Everywhere he walked, the growth patterns shifted, responding to his presence like flowers turning toward the sun.

"They are powerful, my sister's daughters. Beautiful in their way. But they tip the scales toward existence without limit. Life consuming itself in the desperate drive to continue. Growth without ending. Creation spiraling into cancer—cells that won't stop dividing, civilizations that consume everything to sustain themselves."

A sound interrupted my thoughts—sharp and sudden. Skittering. I looked down to see a rat, skeletal and desperate, darting between the coral formations. Its ribs showed through mangy fur, its movements frantic with starvation. It paused near one of the coral growths, then collapsed. Just fell over mid-step, too weak to continue.

Dead. Just like that.

The bone coral nearest to it immediately began growing faster, new formations spiraling up from where the rat had fallen.

Quade watched this with calm interest. "You see?" he said quietly. "Creation without balance. That rat was born into a world that could no longer sustain it. Lived desperately, died pointlessly. The cycle continues, but serves no purpose beyond its own continuation."

"Someone must balance them," Quade continued. "Or creation becomes its own worst enemy. But I can only facilitate their transitions, not create the opposing force. I can move things toward ending, but I cannot be the ending itself."

"You're the process," I said slowly. "Not the result. You can guide things toward death, but you can't embody death itself."

"Precisely." There was pride in his voice. "I am the transition toward those states, not the states themselves."

The implications were beginning to crystallize, sharp and terrible. "So you need daughters," I whispered. "Like your sister has daughters of creation, you need daughters of…"

"Destruction," he finished. "Not mindless devastation or chaotic ruin. But the completion of cycles. The full stop at the end of sentences. The winter that allows spring. The ending that makes space for new beginning."

Valdic's body tensed against mine, a low growl building in his chest.

"You are becoming my second daughter, Renata," Quade said, his voice gentle despite the enormity. "Goddess of Silence and Forgetting. You will embody what I can only facilitate. The transition between Fate and Famine."

"No," I said, but the word came out hollow. "I'm just—I'm just a girl who made desperate choices. That doesn't make me a goddess."

"You already understand endings," Quade replied, crouching so we were eye level. "You've ended yourself piece by piece to keep Nokoa alive. Fed your memories to the Crown—ending who you were to sustain what you needed. Let the famine spread—ending others to preserve him. You have practiced the very nature I need you to embody."

Each example hit like a physical blow. Because he was right.

"The famine," I said, my voice shaking. "It accelerated after the resurrection. That was me, wasn't it? Not just the cost of the ritual. Me. What I'm becoming."

"Yes," Quade confirmed. "Your transformation feeds the famine just as the famine feeds your transformation. You are becoming the transition itself. Silence and Forgetting, and those forces consume. The more you deny what you're becoming, the more chaotic its manifestation. The more you embrace it, the more you can control and direct it."

I looked down at my hands—black veins wrapped around pale skin, fingers that had carved children's flesh and fed a Crown memories and destroyed so much. Hands that were becoming something other than human.

"Why me specifically?" I asked. "There must be millions of desperate people making terrible choices."

"Because you were willing to do what most would not," he replied. "Nokoa died, and you should have let what remained of the girl you were die too. But instead, you clung to pieces while sacrificing everything else. You became expert at partial endings—at letting parts die while desperately holding onto others. Willing desperation."

He reached out, and I didn't pull away when his skeletal fingers touched my cheek. The contact was surprisingly warm, moss-soft against my skin.

"What about the others?" I asked, pulling back from his touch. "You said second daughter. The first? The third and fourth?"

"The first is already formed," Quade replied. "Lanira, Goddess of Hunger and Decay, of Violent Transition. She embodies the ending that comes through consumption, through force. Where you are subtle silence, she is ravenous hunger."

"Where is she?"

"Elsewhere. Fulfilling her purpose as you are learning to fulfill yours. You may meet her eventually, though I suspect you won't particularly like each other. Hunger and Silence rarely get along."

"And the others?"

"Not yet formed. I'm still searching for the right vessels. The transformation only works with someone who's already walking the path, even unconsciously."

A terrible thought occurred to me. "Nokoa's death. His resurrection. Did you—"

"Cause it? No. But I saw the opportunity it presented and ensured certain circumstances aligned. Alaira was already serving me. The resurrection magic was always going to have consequences. I simply made sure those consequences pushed you toward transformation rather than just tragedy."

The honesty should have made me hate him. Instead, I felt almost grateful for the transparency.

"Do I have a choice?" I asked.

"You always have choice," Quade replied. "Just not about the options available. You can accept what you're becoming and learn to wield it with precision. Or you can fight it and watch the transformation happen anyway, chaotically, causing more suffering because you refuse to direct it."

He stood, brushing bone dust from his form. "You cannot go back to being simply Renata Sunthorne. That girl is already dead—you killed her yourself when you chose resurrection over letting go. But you can choose what rises from her ashes. Goddess of purposeful ending, or mindless embodiment of destruction."

Valdic whimpered beside me, pressing closer.

"How long?" I asked. "How long until the transformation is complete?"

"Weeks," Quade replied. "Maybe a month. You're progressing faster than I anticipated—each crisis accelerates the process. Each ending you enact strengthens what you're becoming. Soon there won't be enough human left to resist."

"And then?"

"Then you join me in the work of restoring balance. The Sisters of Creation have had unchecked influence for too long. We will provide the counterweight. The necessary silence that allows new voices. The forgetting that allows moving forward."

He moved toward the cathedral entrance, then paused. "Tell Nokoa if you wish. Or don't. But know this—understanding what you're becoming is the first step to controlling it. And control is the difference between being a goddess who shapes the world and a force that simply destroys it."

Then he was gone, leaving me alone with Valdic and the bone coral and the weight of impossible knowledge.

I sat there for a long time, watching the coral grow and decay, my presence accelerating its cycle until I couldn't tell where one generation ended and the next began.

"What do I do?" I whispered to Valdic.

"You decide who you want to be," he replied, his dark humor stripped away. "Goddess of silence and forgetting, fine. But what kind? The kind who ends suffering, or the kind who just ends? The kind who uses silence and forgetting as tools, or the kind who is used by them?"

He pressed his snout into my hand.

"You're transforming whether you want to or not. But you still get to choose what you transform into. Quade wants a weapon. The Crown wants a vessel. I just want you to still be you, even if 'you' is something divine and terrible."

I buried my fingers in his patchy fur. Nokoa was inside somewhere, probably worried. The Crown sat heavy on my skull, its voices temporarily quiet. My spectral guardians stood somewhere in the shadows, silent witnesses.

"We should tell Nokoa," I said finally. "He deserves to know. Deserves the choice to leave before I become something he can't love."

"He won't leave," Valdic replied. "That boy would follow you into actual hell. The question isn't whether he'll stay. It's whether you'll let him."

I stood, my legs steadier than they'd been. The bone coral continued its accelerated cycle around me, responding to my presence with biological certainty.

Goddess of Silence and Forgetting. My Renata.

Chapter Eight

The Weight of a Dead World

Nokoa

The witch runes had been quiet all morning—too quiet. The usual steady burn had dimmed to barely a whisper beneath my skin, the glowing patterns faint enough that I could almost forget they were there. Almost.

It felt wrong. Since Alaira's stabilization ritual, the runes had settled into a predictable rhythm—painful, yes, but consistent. Now they felt dormant, as if gathering strength for something worse.

Or maybe Quade's presence was suppressing them somehow. The thought made my skin crawl—if he could manipulate the magic keeping me alive this easily, what else could he do? What other strings was he pulling that I couldn't see?

Cressa had cleared me medically, declared the resurrection stable enough for now. But stable didn't mean safe. Stable didn't mean permanent. And the way she'd avoided my eyes when giving me that assessment told me everything she hadn't said aloud.

The bond with Renata had changed since Quade's gift. It felt looser. Less like a noose and more like a tether. Still painful, still demanding, but no longer quite as punishing.

That change had Quade's fingerprints all over it.

So when I saw him walking the cathedral corridors alone, admiring the bone architecture he'd built, I made a choice. If I was going to be a piece in his game, I at least deserved to know what game we were playing.

I followed quietly, my footsteps deliberately soft against the bone floor. Each step sent small vibrations through my legs, reminding me that this entire structure was made from death—corpses and ruins transformed into something that might be called beautiful if you could forget its origins.

I didn't trust him. The knowledge sat cold and certain in my chest, undeniable as the witch runes burning beneath my skin. Quade moved with too much confidence, spoke with too much warmth, offered gifts too perfectly tailored to our deepest desires. Gods didn't do that without wanting something in return.

But there was nothing I could do against him if it came to conflict. He was a Primal God. And I was just a man hanging on by grace I didn't understand, animated by magic I couldn't control.

The Bone God walked with his arms clasped behind his back, robes absorbing light rather than reflecting it. Between his dark wardrobe and his blackened bones, he appeared as a void in the shape of a man. His shredded wings dragged slightly behind him, creating soft scraping sounds against the floor.

Priestess Alaira rounded the corner ahead, moving with purpose. I hadn't seen her since the stabilization ritual, since she'd wept on the throne room floor for hours. She looked different now—more composed, but also more desperate. Her priestess robes stained and rumpled, dark circles ringed her eyes.

I pressed myself into a recessed alcove, watching.

"Is what you said true?" Alaira asked without preamble, her voice tight with barely controlled emotion.

"It is," Quade confirmed, his voice that same warm rumble. "She isn't answering you because she is in a cage."

She. The goddess. The Goddess of Fate that Alaira served. Trapped.

Movement in my peripheral vision pulled my attention before I could hear more.

Renata.

She stumbled past where I crouched, moving with the unsteady gait of someone barely holding themselves together. Her black hair hung in tangles around her face, red rimming her grey eyes. Valdic followed close behind, his purple eyes fixed on her with intense concern.

I glanced back at Quade and Alaira one more time. Then I pushed away from the wall and followed her.

The closer I got, the heavier my steps felt. The bond reasserted itself—not the screaming agony of yesterday's return, but a persistent ache that grew with each foot I closed between us. My chest tightened. A dull throb started behind my eyes.

She stumbled into my room, Valdic at her heels. I entered behind them.

"Renata, what's wrong?" I asked, keeping my voice gentle despite the growing pain in my chest.

She turned to face me. Her grey eyes were red-rimmed and swollen, tears still streaming down her cheeks. The black veins that marked her corruption stood out starkly against her pale skin, pulsing with her elevated heartbeat.

"I confronted Praxis," she managed, her voice cracking on his name. "I had to hear him admit what he's been doing with my own ears. He's been chaining people up, Nokoa. Keeping them alive just enough to farm their heartfire and bone marrow. While we all starved, while the outer cities turned to dust, he was feeding himself off their suffering."

She slid onto the floor as if her legs could no longer support her weight, leaning against the edge of my bed with her knees drawn up to her chest.

"The pain of being in this room, of being close to you," she whispered. "It feels like relief compared to what's crushing me inside."

My fingers ached, bones grinding in their joints. The witch runes blazed trails of fire beneath my skin. Nausea rolled through my stomach in slow waves.

I sat beside her on the floor despite every bone in my body begging me not to. The bond immediately flared in response, sending spikes of pain through my joints and along my spine. But I didn't move away.

"I destroyed the world," Renata cried, her voice breaking. "I broke everything trying to save you, and Praxis was already prepared to go even lower to stay in it. To profit from it. What does that make me? What does it make any of us?"

"You weren't the only one to fail," I said. "And Praxis wasn't alone in what he was willing to do to live. I was selfish too. I still am."

She looked up at me, grey eyes wide and wet.

"I don't want to die," I continued, letting the truth pour out. "After your brother died because of the Hollow Crown, I thought death was the only way I could make things right. That dying would somehow pay the debt for his life, for your suffering. I walked into situations hoping they'd kill me, made choices that should have ended me."

I paused, my throat tight.

"But I'm not brave enough to pay that debt willingly. When death actually came, I fought it. I wanted to live. And now, even knowing what it cost, even seeing what the world has become—I still want to live. I want to be here with you, even if it's a wasteland we have to rebuild from scratch."

She looked at me with equal parts horror and understanding.

"I don't want to die either," she whispered. "But Praxis can't go unpunished. What he did—keeping those people chained, farming them like resources—that's monstrous. If I let it slide, if I make excuses for it because I understand the impulse, then what am I? What does that make me as a ruler?"

"Let him be punished in the way you see as justice," I replied. "Execute him, exile him, imprison him—whatever feels right when you've had time to think clearly. But don't carry the weight of where we are alone. I didn't try harder to stop you from resurrecting me. I could have refused, could have made it impossible. But I wanted to come back. I wanted you to save me, even sensing it would cost too much."

I shifted closer despite the pain, until our shoulders pressed together.

"We're all complicit," I continued. "Alaira performed the ritual knowing it served Quade's purposes. The Crown voices manipulated you into blindness. Praxis hoarded resources. The Bone Council made deals for immortality and then fed off the tithe. And I let you destroy the world to bring me back because I was selfish enough to want to be saved."

Renata buried her face into my chest, her whole body shaking with sobs. Her hands fisted in my shirt, holding on like I was the only stable thing in a world that wouldn't stop spinning. I wrapped my arms around her despite feeling my fingers twist back near breaking, despite the bond punishing every second of contact.

"I was going to do better," she sobbed, her voice muffled but no less devastating. "I truly did want to be better. I had plans—reforms for the outer cities, better distribution of resources, actual justice instead of just survival. I was going to prove that the Hollow Crown didn't have to make you a monster."

"I know," I murmured into her hair. "I know you did."

Valdic leaned into her other side, pressing against her with deliberate gentleness. He didn't speak—just offered his presence, his warmth, his absolute loyalty.

If the cost of my life looked like her tears, I wasn't sure it was truly worth living.

The thought came unbidden, impossible to ignore. I'd fought death with everything I had. But sitting here watching her break, knowing my resurrection had contributed to this catastrophe—maybe death would have been kinder. For both of us.

But it was too late. The resurrection couldn't be undone. The famine was already accelerating toward its inevitable conclusion.

Unless someone had to die for balance. If Quade's plans required a sacrifice, if divine mathematics demanded payment—then it would be me, not the world and not her.

Renata couldn't lose any more pieces of herself. She was already fragmenting, already being hollowed out by the Crown and transformed by forces beyond her control. If I could spare her one more loss—then my death would actually mean something.

I held her tighter despite my fingers threatening to snap, despite the witch runes burning so hot I thought they might ignite my skin from the inside. Let the bond punish me.

For now, I was here. I was holding her.

Later, after Renata's tears had finally subsided and she'd fallen into exhausted sleep against my chest, I let myself think about what I'd overheard. Quade and Alaira discussing the Goddess of Fate trapped in a cage. A god using us for something. A goddess imprisoned. Renata transforming into whatever Quade needed her to become.

The witch runes pulsed beneath my skin, that too-quiet rhythm still wrong in ways I couldn't name.

I watched her breathe—the slow rise and fall of her chest, the way her expression finally softened in sleep, the black veins tracing patterns across her jaw like a map of everything she'd survived. She looked younger when she wasn't carrying the weight of it.

Chapter Nine

Alaira Comes Begging

I sat on the bench in what used to be my garden, the only place in the Bone Court that had once held life. Real life—not the animated dead or magical constructs, but growing things with roots and leaves and the sweet scent of blooming flowers. I'd spent hours here before the Hollow Crown, tending orchids and herbs, pruning roses and watching vegetables slowly ripen in the sunlight that filtered through the cave openings.

The garden had never been so silent. Before, there'd always been something—a breeze rustling through leaves, the gentle trickle of water through the irrigation channels I'd built with my own hands.

Just silence now.

Bone coral in shades of grey grew around the courtyard instead of my carefully cultivated plants. It had sprouted after Quade's arrival, spreading like fungus through the dead soil. Twisted formations that mimicked the shapes of living coral, beautiful in a terrible way. The texture rough under my fingertips when I'd touched it earlier, porous and cold.

Dirt, rocks, and bone coral. That was my garden now. No water flowing through the channels, just dry beds cracked with thirst. The soil itself grey and lifeless, as if every nutrient had been leeched out.

There was a bright sun overhead, at least. The warmth on my face was real. It was the only hint of anything bright in this landscape of bone and ash.

Priestess Alaira shuffled out into the courtyard in her tattered white robes, moving with the hesitant steps of someone approaching a dangerous animal. Her robes had once been pristine, symbolic of her devotion. Now they were stained with bone dust and blood, torn in places, hanging loose on her gaunt frame.

I felt disgusted the moment she caught my eye. Once I'd feared her. Then I'd hated her for the manipulation, for using my desperation against me. And somewhere between fear and hatred, when my mind had been shattering under the weight of Nokoa's dying and the Crown's demands, I'd trusted her.

She'd used that too.

"Renata," she called, her voice carrying across the silent courtyard. "You must accept my apology and help convince Quade to release the Goddess."

The audacity of it struck me like a physical blow. She wanted me to accept her apology—as if words could undo what she'd done—and then immediately wanted a favor.

"Does he have her?" I asked, keeping my voice flat.

"No, but his brother does," she replied quickly. "She is the answer. The Goddess of Fate—she can put all of this right, if she would only speak to us."

Her desperation was palpable. This was what she'd wanted all along, I realized. Not to help me or Nokoa, not to save the Bone Court or prevent the famine. Just to reach her goddess.

I understood that kind of desperation intimately. But understanding didn't equal forgiveness.

"Do you feel no remorse for what you did?" I asked, and my voice came out cold as the bone beneath us.

She looked at me with wide eyes but a blank face, as if the question didn't compute.

"You ask me for favors yet you give me nothing," I continued, feeling my anger build. "No explanation, no real apology, just demands for more help serving your agenda."

"What do you want me to tell you?" she pleaded, fear creeping into her expression.

"Everything," I said, the word coming out hard and final. "Not the convenient half-truths. Not the careful omissions. Everything you did, when you did it, and why."

Alaira's face went pale. She swayed slightly.

"Where do you want me to start?" she asked, her voice barely above a whisper.

"The beginning. When did you start working for Quade?"

She closed her eyes, and when she opened them again, tears were already forming.

"Two years before the famine reached the Bone Court," she began, her voice cracking. "He came to me in a vision during my prayers—when I was most vulnerable, most desperate for answers about why my goddess had gone silent. He knew about the silence. Knew that I'd been praying for centuries without answer. He said he understood divine silence. Said he'd experienced it himself when his siblings banished him."

Two years. She'd been planning this for two entire years before I'd even known there was a problem.

"What did he offer you?" I asked.

"Information," she whispered. "He told me my goddess wasn't ignoring me by choice. That she was trapped, imprisoned by his brother—the God of Insanity. He said the other gods had conspired to lock her away because her gift of fate-seeing made her too powerful, too dangerous."

She laughed, a bitter sound without humor. "And I believed him. Of course I believed him. He was telling me what I desperately wanted to hear—that the silence wasn't my fault, that I hadn't failed her, that there was a reason and a solution. All I had to do was help him, and he'd show me how to reach her again."

"Help him do what?" I pressed.

"Free himself," Alaira admitted, and the words seemed to physically pain her. "The seals holding him were weakening naturally—the famine was affecting divine magic just like it affected everything else. But the process was too slow. He needed someone with magical knowledge and access to powerful rituals. Someone desperate enough to ignore the warnings."

"The rituals you taught me," I said. Not a question.

"Yes." She met my eyes, and I saw genuine anguish there. "Every bonding ritual I showed you, every technique for controlling the Crown, every exercise for managing its hunger—they were all real. They did help you. But they also created fractures in the magical barriers holding Quade. Each ritual you performed weakened the seals a little more."

All those desperate months, all those attempts to gain control of the power consuming me—I'd been breaking Quade free the entire time.

"What else?" I demanded.

Alaira swallowed hard. "I fed him information. About you, about Nokoa, about the political situation in the Bone Court. Everything you told me in confidence—I passed it all to Quade. He needed to understand you, needed to know what would motivate you, what would break you, what would make you desperate enough to perform increasingly powerful rituals without questioning their full effects."

The bone coral was growing faster now, formations twisting upward in sharp spirals.

"I spoke with Fatin," she continued, the words tumbling out as if a dam had broken. "Convinced him that your reforms were weakening our traditions. I knew he'd see Nokoa as your weakness, knew he'd eventually act against him. I didn't tell him to kill Nokoa explicitly, but I guided him toward that conclusion."

The world tilted. Nokoa's death—the single worst moment of my existence, the trauma that had sent me spiraling into desperate resurrection and world-ending choices—had been orchestrated.

"You wanted him dead," I whispered, and my voice sounded distant even to my own ears.

"I needed you to act faster," Alaira said, and there was something terrible in her honesty. "The seals were weakening, but not quickly enough. I'm sorry, Renata. I truly am. But yes, I needed Nokoa's death to accelerate your transformation and weaken the final barriers holding Quade."

The Crown kept most of my rage locked away, let me feel it only as cold, intellectual fury. Almost worse than if I could have screamed.

"The tithes," I said. "The Bone Council kept raising them despite my protests."

"I advised them to do it," Alaira confessed. "I knew it would increase tensions, add pressure to your rule. Every crisis, every desperate situation—it pushed you closer to the breaking point Quade needed."

She looked up at me with red-rimmed eyes. "And the resurrection ritual itself. The one that brought Nokoa back from death. I designed it knowing it would leave him unstable. Quade needed you to have something precious but fragile, something that required constant attention and worry. The witch runes spreading through Nokoa's bones, killing him slowly—that was intentional. That was my design."

This was the worst revelation. Not just that she'd encouraged his death, but that she'd sabotaged his resurrection. That every moment of his pain, every agonizing day he'd spent dying slowly despite being brought back, had been part of her plan.

"The stabilization ritual with Nalla," I managed through clenched teeth. "Was that part of your design too?"

"No," Alaira said. "That was Quade's work. By that point, I'd already served my purpose. Fixing Nokoa was actually beneficial—it gave you hope, made you more willing to accept what came next."

She wrapped her arms around herself. "I've served the Goddess of Fate for three centuries. Three hundred years of devotion, of prayer, of dedicating every breath to her service. And then silence. Complete, absolute silence."

"So you betrayed everyone who trusted you," I stated. "You orchestrated suffering and death, manipulated a grieving woman, sabotaged a resurrection, and helped free a dangerous god—all to reach a goddess who might not even want to speak to you."

Tears streamed down her face, cutting clean tracks through the bone dust on her cheeks.

"I told myself the ends would justify the means. That once Quade was free and I could reach my goddess again, she'd help fix everything. I told myself I was serving a higher purpose, that the temporary suffering would be worth it."

She laughed, bitter and broken. "But it wasn't temporary, was it? The famine accelerated. People died. The Bone Court fell apart. Nokoa died and came back wrong. And I kept telling myself it would all be worth it in the end, kept justifying each new manipulation because I'd already gone too far to turn back."

I watched her break down and felt nothing. No sympathy, no softening of the anger that burned cold in my chest.

Because I understood her motivations too well. I'd done the same thing—told myself each terrible choice would be the last, that the ends would justify the means, that saving Nokoa was worth any price. We were mirrors of each other. Both willing to destroy the world for what we loved most.

But at least I'd destroyed the world for a person who could love me back.

"Every choice you made," Alaira continued, her voice dropping, "every ritual you performed, every decision that brought you to this point—I influenced it. Guided it. But I need you to understand—the transformation you're undergoing requires a specific sequence. Specific circumstances. If even one part had gone differently, you wouldn't become what Quade needs you to be. The Goddess of Silence and Forgetting requires this exact path, this exact—"

"I won't what?" I interrupted, something in her phrasing catching like a hook. "You almost said something. I won't what?"

She cut herself off, but too late.

"I won't what?" I stood fully now, my hands clenching into fists. "I won't what!"

I shouted, but it was different than it should have been. My breath carried a wave with it—actual physical force that pushed outward from my lungs like wind from a storm. The air compressed and then exploded, slamming into Alaira with enough force to knock her off her feet entirely.

She hit the ground hard, immediately cradling her ears. Blood trickled from her nose, thin and bright against her pale skin.

Good, Queen Lyanna whispered in the Crown, her vain tone pleased. Make her understand who holds power here.

Careful, Queen Oriana cautioned. Power without control is just destruction. You're better than that.

Are we sure about that? King Aldric added, almost amused. She seems quite capable of destruction when properly motivated.

"I believed Quade was the only chance to reach her," Alaira managed through gritted teeth, still clutching her ears. "The God of Insanity has her trapped, and only Quade has the knowledge to find her. I had to free him. Had to create the circumstances that would let him return."

"You knew whether he was to be trusted or not," I replied, taking a step closer. The bone coral around us shuddered. "You helped lock him away originally. You were there when he was banished. Yet you chose to free him anyway, chose to use me and mine as the key."

Part of me wanted to forgive her. We'd both been desperate, both been manipulated, both been willing to sacrifice everything for what we loved. But she'd had choices I hadn't. Had time to think and plan where I'd only had desperate moments of grief. She'd orchestrated Nokoa's death, sabotaged his resurrection, made him suffer for months just to keep me desperate.

That wasn't desperation. That was calculation.

"There was no other path," Alaira countered, struggling to her feet. Blood still dripped from her nose. "You don't understand how it is, to be cut off from your goddess. To pray for centuries and receive only silence."

"You could have told me the truth," I said quietly. "Could have given me the choice to help you willingly instead of manipulating me through grief. Instead, you orchestrated the death of the person I loved most, sabotaged his resurrection to keep him suffering, and used my desperation like a tool."

The anger built like pressure in my skull. My hands reached out, fingers curling, power building in my chest that I didn't fully understand. The air around me grew heavy, charged.

Until Valdic appeared.

He placed himself between Alaira and me, his emaciated body blocking my path. His purple eyes met mine with steady certainty, no fear in them. Just concern. Just loyalty.

The sound of his growl brought me back into my body—low and warning.

Priestess Alaira scrambled to her feet and fled, her tattered robes streaming behind her as she ran from the courtyard.

You're becoming stronger, Quade's voice sang through my mind, warm with approval. *The goddess of silence and forgetting. You felt it just now—the power responding to your will.*

I ignored him, focusing on Valdic's steady presence.

"Do what you want," Valdic said quietly. "But not in a fit of rage. Do it once you've thought it over, once you can see clearly what justice actually looks like versus what revenge disguised as justice looks like."

He pressed closer, forcing me to feel his physical presence. "Whatever you decide about Alaira, about Praxis, about all of it—make sure it's really you deciding. Not the Crown, not Quade, not your anger. You."

I sank back down onto the bench, suddenly exhausted. Valdic jumped up beside me.

"I don't know who 'me' is anymore," I admitted. "The girl who tended this garden is gone. And whatever I'm becoming—I don't know if that's who I want to be."

"Then figure it out," Valdic replied. "You've got time. Not much, maybe, but some."

I looked around at my dead garden, at the bone coral growing where orchids used to bloom.

"She wants me to convince Quade to help free a goddess," I said. "The Goddess of Fate, trapped by the God of Insanity. Should I?"

"Do you trust Quade?" Valdic asked.

"No."

"Do you trust Alaira?"

"Absolutely not."

"Do you trust that whatever this trapped goddess wants is in your best interest?"

"I don't even know what she wants."

"Well then," Valdic said, "sounds like you need more information before making decisions about divine politics. Revolutionary concept, but try gathering facts before committing to courses of action that will definitely have massive consequences."

"I need to talk to Quade," I said. "Not as a supplicant asking for gifts. As someone who deserves answers."

"Now that," Valdic replied, "sounds like the beginning of an actual plan."

I shoved him gently, and he leaned into it, purple eyes bright.

The sun was still bright overhead. My garden was still dead. But I was still here—still capable of making choices, still capable of deciding what justice looked like versus revenge.

Chapter Ten

Alaira's Desperation

Nokoa

Priestess Alaira ran into my chest with enough force that the impact threw us both to the ground. I'd been walking through one of the cathedral's corridors, lost in thought, and then suddenly there was a body slamming into me with the desperate momentum of someone fleeing.

We hit the bone floor hard, the impact driving the air from my lungs. The witch runes flared in protest, sending spikes of pain through my ribs where we'd made contact.

Then I saw the blood.

It came from her ears in thin rivulets, bright red against her pale skin and the white of her tattered robes. Not just a little blood—enough that it had soaked into her hair, stained her collar, dripped onto the floor beneath us. The metallic scent filled my nostrils.

"What's happened?" I demanded, scrambling upright. My hands found her shoulders, steadying her while I tried to assess the damage. "Alaira, what happened to you?"

She got to one knee, moving with the shaky uncertainty of someone whose equilibrium was completely disrupted. Her eyes were unfocused, pupils dilated differently from each other. When she spoke, her words came too loud, as if she couldn't hear herself properly.

"Renata," she stuttered, and even through the volume I could hear the fear. "She's changing."

"Changing?" I got to my feet faster than she did, the witch runes burning hot. "What do you mean? What has the Bone God done to her?"

"Quade, he—" Alaira began, but I cut her off.

"Speak clearly. Tell me what is happening to Renata right now. What did she do to you? Why are you bleeding?"

Alaira met my eyes, and I saw genuine terror beneath the pain.

"I thought freeing Quade would benefit us," she began, words tumbling out faster now. "That it would help us survive the famine, help me reach my goddess. If the Goddess of Fate came back, she could have even stopped him."

She swayed, and I steadied her.

"But Quade is seeking to create balance. His sister, Dahlia—the Goddess of the Moon—she made her daughters. The Sisters of Creation. The Goddess of Fate who guides destiny. The Goddess of Time who brings new beginnings. Others whose names have been lost."

"What does this have to do with Renata?" I demanded, though dread was already building in my chest.

"Quade seeks to create the daughters of destruction to balance his sister's daughters of creation," Alaira said, and her voice cracked. "He's already made one—Lanira, the first daughter, the Goddess of Hunger and Decay. Renata is the second. Silence and forgetting."

She pointed to her bleeding ears with a trembling hand.

"She shouted at me, and her breath carried power. Not the Crown's power—something else. The ability to silence, to remove sound itself. My ears are bleeding because the force was too much for a mortal body to withstand. And she didn't even mean to do it. It just happened because she was angry."

Alaira's eyes were bright with unshed tears. "Your death, the resurrection, the bond, the famine—all of it has been orchestrated to ascend her to godhood. To transform her into a goddess of silence and forgetting. The second daughter of destruction."

I looked past Alaira, through the corridor and into the courtyard beyond. Renata sat on a bench with Valdic beside her. The bone coral surrounding her decayed and regrew in an accelerated cycle, breaking down into powder even as new growth spiraled up from the base. Her presence affecting the fundamental nature of the material around her.

She was doing it. Not Quade. Not the Crown. Renata herself.

"How long?" I asked. "How long until the transformation is complete?"

"I don't know," Alaira admitted. "Godhood isn't like a spell with set parameters. It's organic, evolutionary. Renata will become what she's meant to become when she's ready—when she's suffered enough, learned enough, lost enough of her humanity to make room for divinity."

She met my eyes with something like pity. "Every piece of herself she sacrifices is another step toward becoming something that doesn't need those pieces anymore."

"Can it be stopped?"

"No," Alaira replied. "Even if you killed Quade—which you can't—the process would continue. This was set in motion before either of you were born."

She steadied herself against the wall, blood still trickling from her ears. "But there might be a way to help her maintain her humanity through the transformation. To anchor her to what she was even as she becomes what she must be."

"What do you mean?"

"The Goddess of Fate," Alaira said quickly. "She's trapped by the God of Insanity—Quade's brother, Nikola. If we could free her, if she could speak to Renata directly… the Goddess of Fate understands transformation, understands the weight of divine purpose. She could guide Renata through this in ways Quade won't. Could help her keep pieces of herself that Quade would just as soon consume."

Footsteps echoed down the corridor—slow, deliberate. The witch runes flared. We both froze. The footsteps continued past, fading into silence.

Alaira let out a shaky breath and continued in a whisper. "Nikola holds her in a cage of madness—a prison built from fractured realities and broken minds.

Only someone with divine essence could navigate it without being consumed. Someone like you."

"I'm not divine. I'm barely alive."

"The witch runes," she explained. "They're not just resurrection magic. They're transition magic—the same kind Quade wields. You exist between life and death, between mortal and something else. That makes you uniquely suited to walk paths that would destroy the fully living or the completely dead."

She grabbed my arm, her grip surprisingly strong. "I need you to find Nikola's domain. To navigate the cage and reach the Goddess of Fate. To ask her how to free her, what she needs from us. And then—if she agrees to help Renata—we do whatever it takes to break her out."

"And if I refuse?" I asked quietly.

Alaira's expression hardened. "Then Renata transforms alone, guided only by Quade. She becomes his weapon, his perfectly crafted daughter of destruction with no anchor to humanity. Every memory she feeds the Crown, every piece of herself she sacrifices—those don't come back when she ascends. She just becomes divine enough not to miss them anymore."

"And if I succeed?" I pressed. "What does the Goddess of Fate get out of this?"

"Freedom," Alaira said simply. "What any trapped thing wants. And perhaps the chance to guide her niece—because that's what Renata will become. A goddess, daughter to Quade, niece to his sisters. The Goddess of Fate would have family again."

Another sound echoed through the corridor—closer this time. Voices, approaching. Alaira's eyes went wide.

"We can't be seen together," she hissed. "Quade can't know we're planning this."

"When do I leave? How do I find this domain?"

"Tonight," Alaira whispered. "When Renata sleeps and Quade is occupied with his cathedral. I'll come for you. Bring you to the threshold. After that, you're on your own. The witch runes should protect you from the worst of the madness, but—" She trailed off.

I might not survive. Probably wouldn't. But if it meant Renata kept some piece of herself through the transformation, if it meant she didn't forget me entirely when she ascended—

"Fine," I agreed. "Tonight."

The voices grew louder. Alaira gave me one last desperate look, then fled in the opposite direction.

I walked toward the courtyard as if nothing had happened. The bond burned steadily, guiding me toward Renata.

She looked up as I approached, grey eyes finding mine. Valdic's purple gaze followed, assessing.

I sat beside her on the bench, wincing as the bond flared. Around us, the bone coral continued its accelerated cycle of decay and regrowth, the sound of it like whispers, like breathing.

"We need to talk," I began, then paused.

"I know," she said, such exhaustion in her voice. "Quade's been preparing me. Telling me about destiny and transformation. I've been trying not to think about it too hard."

"Did he tell you about being a goddess?" I asked. "About the daughters of destruction and cosmic balance?"

She shook her head. "I've felt it. The power growing, the way reality responds to me differently now. I know I'm not human anymore. Not fully. Not for much longer."

Her hand found mine, fingers interlacing despite the pain it caused both of us. The bond flared, but we both ignored it.

"I'm scared," she admitted, her voice cracking. "I'm terrified of what I'm becoming. Of losing you, losing myself, losing everything that made me me."

Around us, the bone coral crumbled and grew, keeping rhythm with her heartbeat.

I didn't tell her about Alaira's plan. Didn't mention the Goddess of Fate or the mad prison or the journey I'd agreed to take tonight. She had enough to carry without adding my probable death to the weight.

Instead I held her hand and let the silence sit between us—not the silence of absence, but the kind that meant we were still here. Still together. Still holding on.

Goddess of silence and forgetting. My Renata.

Chapter Eleven

HIVRO ARRIVES

Renata

I stood on a balcony built from bone that jutted from the third level of the skeletal cathedral, looking out at the desolation that surrounded me in every direction.

The forest that I had watched the stags in during better days looked as if it had been through decades of fire. The trees were blackened skeletal remains, branches reaching toward the sky like accusatory fingers. No leaves, no green anywhere. Just char and ash and the occasional glint of bone where animals had collapsed.

The stags were long gone. Everything was gone.

"Renata," a voice called from behind me, low and familiar.

I turned quickly, almost stumbling. "Hivro?"

Her white star-covered body was perhaps the most welcome sight I'd seen since this nightmare began. The Butterfly Oracle—one of the oldest beings in our world, placed here by the Goddess of Space herself to observe and record all that transpired. Where Quade was all black bone and moss and ancient decay, Hivro was pristine white marked with constellations that shifted and moved across her surface like living things. Butterflies—hundreds of them in every color imaginable—swirled around her in constant motion, their wings whispering secrets I couldn't quite hear.

She'd been my guide once, my teacher in the ways of the Hollow Crown before everything went so catastrophically wrong. Before I'd stopped listening.

I ran to her without thinking, my arms wrapping around her solid form. For a moment I was just a girl again, seeking comfort from someone who'd shown kindness when kindness was scarce.

"I'm sorry," I cried into her shoulder, the words tumbling out between sobs. "I didn't listen. You tried to warn me about the costs, about the consequences, and I ignored you because I thought I knew better."

Hivro ran her hands through my black hair with gentle grace. The butterflies settled around us, creating a cocoon of color and movement. "You should never have had to choose," she murmured. "You were put in an impossible position—a girl barely grown, given power beyond mortal comprehension and told to save everyone."

"You still have a chance to be something good," she continued. "Despite everything that's happened, despite what you're becoming—you still have a choice in what kind of goddess you'll be."

The word hung between us. Goddess. Spoken aloud by someone other than Quade, given weight by Hivro's confirmation.

"Tell me what to do," I pleaded. "Please. I'm so tired of making choices that destroy everything."

"You know that I cannot," Hivro said, genuine regret in her voice. "Free will is sacred, even for one ascending to divinity. I can guide, advise, warn—but I cannot choose for you. My oath prevents direct interference."

Her butterflies swirled faster, agitated.

"You're changing quickly," Hivro continued. "Faster than I anticipated. The process that should take decades is compressing into months, maybe weeks. Quade is accelerating it somehow."

Quade entered the balcony so silently I nearly missed it—just a subtle shift in air pressure. One moment Hivro and I were alone, and the next he was simply there. His black bones absorbing light, his moss-lined eye sockets fixed on us with patient intensity.

Hivro turned and immediately tucked me behind her, positioning herself between us. The stars across her surface began to glow brighter, and the butterflies formed a defensive wall of beating wings.

"She is not yours," Hivro commanded, her voice carrying authority I'd never heard from her. "You have no right to do this. To be here, to walk in this realm, to interfere with mortal affairs. Your banishment was absolute. I helped lock you away, Quade. I was there when the guardians bound you."

"I have every right," Quade responded with maddening calm. "I am her father in the ways that matter. I shaped the circumstances of her birth, guided the events of her life, prepared her for this transformation. You cling to what she was—a mortal girl, simple and pure. I will shape what she must become."

"The Goddess of the Moon gave explicit orders," Hivro stated, and I could feel power building around her. "You were banished for a reason—for the devastation you caused, for the imbalance you created."

"Need I remind you of your oath?" Quade asked, something sharp entering his tone. "You swore not to interfere directly in mortal affairs. Breaking that oath would have consequences. For you, for those you serve."

"Your sister gave an order that you aren't to walk in any realms," Hivro countered. "Enforcing that order is not interfering with mortal affairs. That is following a divine mandate."

The temperature on the balcony dropped. My breath came out in visible puffs.

"If you would like to try and stop me, then do so," Quade said, utterly confident. "But understand the cost. You'll be breaking your oath. You'll be choosing sides in a conflict between primal gods. And Renata will still become what she's meant to become, with or without your blessing. The only question is whether you'll be there to guide her through it."

Footsteps made me turn. Nokoa entered the balcony, moving carefully as the bond burned between us. Instead of stopping beside me, he walked directly to Hivro. His golden eyes were troubled, his jaw set.

"I need to speak with you," he said to Hivro, his voice low. "About Alaira's plan."

Hivro's constellation-eyes sharpened. "You've decided?"

"I don't trust her," Nokoa stated. "I wanted to. Wanted to believe there was a way to help Renata maintain her humanity through this. But something about it feels wrong. Desperate. Like she's grasping at straws because she can't accept that her goddess isn't coming to save everyone."

Relief flooded Hivro's features. "You made the right choice. A mortal man—even one touched by resurrection magic—couldn't navigate Nikola's domain. The God of Insanity's prison isn't just dangerous, it's specifically designed to fracture minds and consume sanity. Your witch runes might protect you from physical death, but they wouldn't shield your consciousness from being shattered into a thousand incompatible pieces."

She glanced at Quade, then back to Nokoa. "You would have died. Or worse—you would have survived as something broken beyond repair, your mind scattered across fractured realities while your body continued its cursed resurrection. Alaira knows this. But she's so desperate to reach her goddess that she's willing to sacrifice anyone who might give her a slim chance of success."

Nokoa's shoulders sagged. "Then what do I do? Just watch her transform? Hope that Quade's version of balance is somehow better than Alaira's desperate plans?"

"You do what you've always done," Hivro replied. "You love her. You stay beside her. You anchor her to what she was even as she becomes what she must be."

"Enough!" I shouted, and the word came out wrong.

My breath carried a wave with it—not wind, but force made manifest through sound. The power of silencing turned outward, aggressive. It rippled across the balcony like a shockwave, making the bone structure groan and crack.

Nokoa struggled to stay standing, bracing himself against the railing. The witch runes blazed brighter. Blood trickled from his nose.

But Hivro and Quade stood utterly unmoving. The wave broke around them like water around stones.

Quade took a step closer. "You are becoming yourself," he said, warmth in his voice. "Your true self, not the limited mortal version. Do not let fear stop you."

"If I agree, if I don't fight it, will the land heal?" I asked.

"It will."

Valdic padded onto the balcony, purple eyes immediately assessing the situation. He moved to stand beside Nokoa. Both of them looked at me with such love—not blind love that ignored what I was becoming, but clear-eyed devotion that chose to stay despite understanding.

Hivro stood alone, separated from us by more than physical distance. She'd tried to save me, tried to guide me away from this fate. Her oath left her only able to watch and record.

But she was still here. Still bearing witness.

Quade looked like death incarnate—black bones, moss-lined sockets, shredded wings. Everything about his appearance should have screamed danger.

But he felt like understanding. Like the only one willing to accept what I was becoming instead of mourning what I'd been.

I looked at Nokoa, at Valdic, at Hivro and Quade. At the devastated forest beyond the balcony, at my own black-veined hands that manifested power without conscious intent.

I still didn't know.

Still didn't know who I wanted to be, who I was capable of becoming, who the universe demanded I transform into.

Chapter Twelve

VISIONS OF THE LOST BROTHER

Renata

I stood in the newly created throne room with Quade, the space still feeling too large, too empty despite the bone architecture rising around us in splendor. Ribs curved overhead like cathedral vaults, creating a space that felt both protective and suffocating.

"Come, sit," he gestured to the throne dominating the far end of the chamber. "It is yours, after all."

I glanced between him and the throne. It was a masterwork of bone architecture—constructed from hundreds of skulls carefully arranged and fused together. Each skull still bearing the marks of whatever life it had lived. Some were small, possibly children. Others showed signs of violence. All of them stared with empty sockets that seemed to track my movement.

I took the steps slowly, each footfall echoing in the cavernous space.

I sat. The bones were cold beneath me, the chill seeping through my black dress, penetrating to my bones. But my heart kept beating warm and human, kept feeling everything I wanted to stop feeling.

"You look good there," Quade observed. "Like you were always meant to occupy that exact space."

"It doesn't feel like home," I replied flatly. "It feels like a cage made of bones and bad decisions."

"Not yet," Quade said. "But that will change. Home is where you stop running from yourself, where you accept what you are and what you're becoming."

He stood in front of me, close enough that we could speak without raising our voices but not close enough to touch.

"I've been thinking," he began, his tone shifting to something more serious. "No true transformation can occur while you're still carrying unresolved grief, unanswered questions."

He paused. "For example, your brother. Theron. You've never clearly received answers about his death, have you? Just fragments from different sources with their own agendas. Never the truth of what actually happened when the Hollow Crown rejected him and chose you instead."

His words hit like physical blows. Theron. My brother. Who'd died trying to spare me this fate, and I'd been so consumed with Nokoa's resurrection that I'd let him become just another casualty I couldn't afford to mourn.

"I wish to grant you those answers, if you'd like them," Quade offered gently. "Show you exactly what happened. Not filtered through others' perspectives, but the truth as it actually occurred."

Part of me wanted to refuse, to keep Theron's death abstract and distant. But that was exactly the problem, wasn't it? That distance, that forgetting, that willingness to let important things slip away because they were too painful to hold.

"Yes," I said finally. "Show me."

Quade moved closer, climbing the seven steps until he stood directly in front of the throne. It was then that I fully realized what he was. Not just powerful. Not just ancient. A Primal God who had existed since before the world had form.

And he was about to touch my mind.

Quade extended one skeletal finger and touched my forehead with surprising gentleness. The contact was cold and warm simultaneously, bone and life mixed together.

My eyes snapped shut.

I was but a fly on the wall of the caves that used to be the Bone Court, disembodied consciousness forced to witness without ability to intervene. The perspective was disorienting—I could see everything from multiple angles simultaneously, could sense emotions in the air like physical presences.

The full Bone Council sat in their miniature thrones arranged in a semicircle, waiting. This was before the famine had progressed far enough to reduce most of them to skeletal remains. They still had flesh, still looked almost human.

Praxis sat tall, his bones already bleached to paper-white perfection, his ivory horns carefully sculpted, his crimson eyes blazing. The tentacles beneath his jaw moved slightly, betraying anticipation.

And outside the entrance, barely visible in the corridor beyond, Nokoa and my brother stood face to face.

Theron. My beautiful, foolish, self-sacrificing brother.

He looked so young. Dark hair like our father's, grey eyes like our mother's and mine. Simple clothes—nothing ceremonial, nothing that suggested he was about to attend his own execution.

"Nokoa, no matter what happens, I order you to be silent," Theron said, both his hands gripping Nokoa's shoulders hard enough to leave bruises. "You cannot intervene. You cannot stop them. Do you understand me?"

Nokoa's jaw clenched tight.

"If they place the Hollow Crown on me, it spares Renata and that is the ultimate goal," Theron continued, and I could hear the fear beneath his determination. His voice wavered slightly on my name. "Let her stay in the northern barrows where she's safe. Let her finish her life unaware of any of this. Let her tend her gardens and braid flowers in her hair. That's all I want."

"And if they kill you?" Nokoa countered, anger breaking through. His golden eyes were bright with unshed tears. "If you die, what then? They'll only move to her after you're gone. This isn't a solution. It's just delaying the inevitable."

Theron's expression crumbled for just a moment. Then he rebuilt it, forced the fear down.

"The Bone Council doesn't want her," Theron insisted, though his voice wavered. "If I die... they'll find someone else. Anyone else. Renata will live happily in the barrows, and I'll become a butterfly somewhere. Blue, I think. Blue was always her favorite color."

He smiled, trying to inject levity.

"You know it won't go that way, Theron," Nokoa said quietly. "The Crown gets what it wants, and what it wants is Renata. Everyone knows it."

Theron straightened his tunic with trembling hands. "I have to believe that I will live and bind to the Crown successfully. That Renata will be safe. I have to believe that, Nokoa. Because if I don't—if I walk in there thinking I'm going to die—then I definitely will."

He turned toward the entrance, shoulders squared with false confidence. "I'll see you at dinner. Save me a seat."

Then he entered the room, leaving Nokoa standing in the corridor with tears finally spilling down his cheeks.

"You're late," Praxis observed.

"I thought a stroll would be nice if this is to potentially be my last walk," Theron replied with forced lightness. "Seemed worth savoring the gardens one more time. The orchids are blooming beautifully. Renata would be pleased."

"Sit," Fatin gestured to a chair in the center of the room.

Theron took his place, spine straight, hands resting calmly on his thighs. Trying to look unafraid.

Praxis stood and approached, carrying the Hollow Crown with careful reverence. The bone circlet looked smaller than I remembered, less impressive. Just braided fragments that screamed with trapped souls.

He placed it on Theron's head with deliberate precision.

The Hollow Crown shook violently on Theron's head, and screams came from it—Oriana's voice, Lyanna's, Aldric's, all of them crying out in recognition or warning. The sound was deafening. Magic pulsed outward in visible waves. The temperature dropped so fast frost formed on the stone walls.

Praxis placed his hands back on the Crown, pushing it down harder against Theron's skull. Forcing the connection.

Then Priestess Alaira entered the room with several witches trailing behind her. They arranged themselves in a circle around Theron's chair, hands linked, chanting in languages I didn't recognize but could feel in my bones. Power words that made reality bend.

Alaira approached Theron directly, pulling a pouch of bone dust from her robes. She drew symbols on his forehead—witch runes that glowed faintly blue. Binding magic. Compulsion. Forcing his soul to merge with the Crown whether he was compatible or not.

Then she backed away, joining the circle.

Praxis and Alaira. Working together. Coordinating with the kind of synchronization that only came from extensive planning.

A beam of white light shot from Theron's mouth, so bright it should have blinded everyone. His grey eyes—my eyes, our mother's eyes—began bleeding in thick rivulets. The smell of burning flesh filled the room.

Praxis took his hands off the Crown and backed away. They watched like spectators at an execution.

Theron burned from the inside.

I could see it through the god-sight—could see his soul being ripped apart by incompatible magic, could feel his agony. The Crown was eating him alive, trying to absorb his memories and essence. But he wasn't compatible, so instead of clean consumption it was just destruction.

"No! No!" Priestess Alaira screamed, breaking from her chanting. She ran toward Theron like she could somehow stop what she'd started.

But it was too late.

Theron's flesh melted off his bones like wax held too close to flame. His clothes burned away. His hair crackled and disappeared. His beautiful face simply ceased to exist.

Then he was gone. No screaming after that first moment. No more blood. No blinding light.

Only bones scattered across the chair and floor. And the Hollow Crown, sitting innocently among the remains.

The silence that followed was deafening.

Footsteps pounded—Cressa and Nokoa burst into the room, but Nokoa's footsteps stopped first. He stood frozen in the doorway, staring at what remained of his best friend.

Cressa threw herself into the pile of bones without hesitation, gathering them like she could somehow reassemble the person who'd once inhabited them.

"I told you," Priestess Alaira said into the horrible silence. "The Hollow Crown wants Renata. It's always wanted Renata. You can't satisfy it with substitutes."

"We are to believe that you and the Crown want the same thing, and it is innocent coincidence?" Ancelin asked suspiciously.

"I think innocent or not, it doesn't matter now," Alaira replied, her voice hardening. "What choice do you have but to bring her home? The Crown has rejected every candidate except her family line. Theron is dead. That leaves only Renata."

She looked at the bones scattered across the floor.

Quade removed his finger from my forehead, and my eyes shot open. I was back in my body, gasping for air like I'd been drowning.

Tears streamed down my face, hot and relentless. Theron. My brother. Who'd died believing his sacrifice might spare me this fate. Who'd burned from the inside out while Praxis and Alaira watched their experiment fail.

Quade stood silently, giving me space to process. Not rushing me, not demanding response.

"How long?" I finally managed, my voice raw. "How long have I been lied to about everything?"

"Priestess Alaira has been looking for a way back to her Goddess for as long as she was separated from her," Quade said gently. "Centuries of desperation makes people willing to sacrifice anything."

He turned toward the entrance. "Valdic."

My DirgeWolf appeared, purple eyes immediately finding mine. He padded up the seven steps and pressed against my legs.

"Mourn your brother," Quade advised. "Allow yourself to feel the grief you've been avoiding. Let Valdic anchor you through it. And when you're ready—when you've closed that door properly—we'll discuss what comes next."

Then he was gone.

I buried my fingers in Valdic's patchy fur and finally let myself cry for Theron. For the brother who'd walked into that room believing his sacrifice might mean I'd live happily ignorant in the barrows. Who'd straightened his tunic with trembling hands and told Nokoa to save him a seat at dinner.

"I never mourned him properly," I whispered. "I was so focused on surviving, on the Crown, on Nokoa—I just let him become background noise."

Valdic didn't answer. He pressed closer, his weight solid and warm, and let me cry.

Interlude One

The Forging

Priestess Alaira

The obsidian castle was visible from the forest clearing, its black spires catching the last rays of sunlight before the blood moon rose. The coven argued around me, their voices rising and falling in familiar patterns of accusation and concern. Its polished walls gleamed like dark glass, reflecting the dying light. A monument to everything we'd built in service to the Goddess of Fate.

Soon it would be so much more.

I'd tuned their protests out minutes ago. I had heard their arguments hundreds of times in the weeks leading up to tonight. The same fears, the same warnings, the same lack of vision.

I knew I was right. Knew it with the certainty that came from direct communion with divinity. I was making choices that were best for the Goddess of Fate, for Hesperia who had given me purpose when I had none. The Goddess of Fate had been silent for weeks, and I knew—knew in my bones—that she was in danger. That something was coming for her, for all the divine sisters. And I would not let her fall unprotected.

"Alaira!" Celeste yelled, her voice cutting through my thoughts.

My sister stood at the edge of the bone altar we'd constructed, her short brown hair filled with flyaways from the wind that had been building all evening. Streaks of silver and gold showed when she moved her head just right.

"I've nothing to add to this discussion," I stated, keeping my voice level despite the frustration building in my chest. "We've covered every objection multiple times. My position hasn't changed."

"Then you mean to proceed?" Mira asked, her voice trembling with fear barely concealed beneath anger. "Despite our protest? Despite every warning we've given you about the dangers of working with bone magic during a blood moon?"

"I do," I responded simply.

The word hung in the air. Several of my sisters stepped back from the altar, as if distance could absolve them of complicity.

"Then we have no reason to stay," Mira declared. "Celeste, you would do well to join us. I won't stand here and watch Alaira destroy everything we've built because she thinks she knows better than centuries of tradition."

One by one, five of my coven members left, walking back toward the obsidian castle with their robes billowing in the strange wind. Their footsteps crunched on fallen leaves, growing fainter with distance.

If they couldn't see the necessity, they weren't strong enough for what came next anyway.

Soon it was only my sister Celeste and I left standing around the bone altar. Four stone pillars surrounded the ritual space, and chained to each pillar was a prisoner. Criminals, all of them—murderers and betrayers who'd been sentenced to death by the queen's justice. Their executions had been scheduled for tonight regardless. I was simply repurposing their deaths. Making their ends serve a greater purpose.

The altar itself was a masterwork I'd spent months designing. Carved from a single massive bone—we'd never asked what creature it had come from, just accepted it when it washed up on the shore like a gift from fate itself. Grooves cut into its surface in intricate patterns, channels for blood to flow and pool in specific configurations. Witch runes covered every inch, layered one atop another until the bone seemed to glow with accumulated power even before the ritual began.

The world around us was lush, filled with life and shrubbery. The forest grew thick and green, cornfields stretched golden in the distance, orchards hung heavy with fruit. The coven's fears about catastrophic consequences were baseless.

"Sister," Celeste said quietly, stepping closer to me. "How can the entire coven be wrong? How can every one of them see danger where you see salvation?"

"More minds, more ignorance," I shot back, anger flaring hot in my chest. "Crowds are wrong all the time. Popular opinion means nothing in the face of divine mandate. Hesperia entrusted the coven to me, Celeste. The secrets of our magic, the responsibility for our survival—all of it given to me. She tasked me with making the choices when they needed to be made. Me!"

My voice had risen to a shout, echoing off the obsidian castle walls in the distance. The four prisoners stirred in their chains, one of them crying silently, tears streaming down her face.

"I just want to make sure you've thought through every possibility," Celeste said quickly. "That you're certain this is the only way."

"I'm certain. Now, are you helping or leaving?"

Celeste looked torn, her eyes moving between me and the path the others had taken. Finally, she nodded. "I'll help. You're my sister. Whatever comes, we face it together."

"Queen Claudia!" I called into the darkness beyond the ritual space. "Bring the bone fragments!"

Queen Claudia emerged from the forest shadows, her long silver hair hanging loose around sharp features. Beautiful in that ethereal way some women achieved—angular and fierce, with eyes that held centuries of knowledge despite her relative youth. She moved to the center of the altar with careful steps, holding a silver tray laden with bone fragments I'd been collecting for months.

I'd killed to collect the bones needed. Mixed them with fragments of divine beasts, creatures touched by celestial power. And one piece that glowed faintly blue—a chip of bone from a fallen star, an oracle from the Goddess of Space that carried the essence of the heavens themselves.

I had to use a rune on Hivro to claim that piece. Had forced her compliance through magic she couldn't resist, taking what I needed from the Butterfly Oracle despite her protests. The memory of her constellation-marked face contorted with betrayal still haunted me sometimes, late at night when my conscience wasn't quite silenced.

I followed Claudia to the altar and shoved her down to her knees with both hands. She gasped but didn't resist, just knelt and held the tray up for me with shaking arms.

"Where is he, Priestess?" Claudia asked, her voice trembling. "You said he would be here. You promised we'd do this together."

She meant her lover, of course. The man she was so desperately trying to save, who was dying from some wasting curse that no magic had been able to break. That's why she'd agreed to this—I'd promised her the crown would break the curse, would sever the painful bond between them that was killing them both.

"Shouldn't you know where your lover is?" I replied. "You're the one bound to him."

She flinched. I couldn't afford softness now.

I began to braid the bone fragments together, weaving them into each other with witch runes inscribed on each piece. My fingers moved with practiced precision, each piece placed just so, each rune aligned with specific celestial alignments. The bone felt warm under my fingers, alive with potential. The fragments began to form a circlet, humming with accumulated power. The air grew heavy, charged.

"You have to wait until he's here," Claudia said, shaking growing worse. "You said this would help us. That it would cure the bond of pain between us."

"It will cure the pain," I affirmed, and I wasn't even lying. Death cured all pain, in its way.

I only had so much time with the blood moon overhead. The celestial alignment was perfect now, would only last for the next hour. I placed the braided bone circlet on her head, adjusted it so it sat perfectly across her brow, then stepped back and began the incantation. Words in the old language, gifted by the Goddess of Fate herself to our order centuries ago.

This crown would have the ability to protect its wearer. It would be an anchor point for power, a conduit for divine strength. It would make whoever wore it powerful enough to stand against gods if necessary.

This would be my gift to Hesperia. My thanks for giving my life meaning and purpose. I only needed Claudia to be willing to die to fill the bones with life and soul and power.

And she was willing.

I held my hands to the air. "Daughters of Dahlia, Sisters of Fate—grant me your power! Let this crown be worthy of protecting those you've blessed with your presence!"

The blood moon's light intensified, bathing everything in crimson. The witch runes around the altar began to glow, one by one, until the whole clearing was illuminated. The four prisoners screamed in their chains. A glow came from the circlet on Claudia's skull, starting faint and then building to brilliance—ethereal blue-white light that seemed to contain all the stars in the heavens.

I pulled out my knife made of bone, carved from my own rib in a previous ritual, bound to me in ways that made it an extension of my will. The blade caught the red moonlight and the blue glow from the crown, turning purple in the intersection of colors.

Then I turned to Celeste and, before she could register what was happening, I sliced her throat in one smooth motion.

Blood sprayed from the wound, hot and immediate. The spray hit my face, warm and copper-tasting. Celeste's eyes went wide with shock and betrayal, her hands coming up to her neck too late. She tried to speak, but only blood came out.

The crimson flood filled the grooves I'd carved, following the channels exactly as designed. The blood flowed into the witch runes, activating them with power drawn from celestial connection. Because Celeste wasn't just my sister—she was touched by divine favor, connected to the cosmic in the same way that I was.

Celeste collapsed beside the altar. Her eyes found mine in her final moments, and what I saw there made something twist in my chest. Not anger—I could have borne anger. But hurt. Betrayal. The look of someone who'd trusted completely and been destroyed for it.

Then the light went out of her eyes, and she was gone.

The crown shook violently on Claudia's head, her eyes rolled back until only whites showed. The bone fragments rattled against each other, the braiding beginning to fuse into a single piece.

Then the ground shook.

Not a gentle tremor, but a violent convulsion that knocked me off my feet. The earth cracked open in jagged lines, spreading from the altar in every direction. Behind us, I heard a terrible groaning—the obsidian castle beginning to collapse.

"No! No!" I shouted, scrambling to my feet.

But it was too late. The crown was already transforming beyond my designs, beyond my intentions. It turned red—blood red like the moon overhead—and then golden, and then a sickly green that reminded me of rot and decay. Colors that shouldn't exist in bone.

The crown pulled Claudia's soul inside itself with a sound like screaming wind. Her essence—that beautiful, desperate, loving woman—ripped from her body and compressed into the bone circlet. Her body remained for a moment, kneeling with the crown still on her head, then simply fell forward, hitting the altar with a hollow thud.

The crown screamed with Claudia's voice. Not her physical voice, but something deeper. Her soul, trapped and aware, crying out from inside the bone prison I'd created.

Then it rolled off her corpse and bumped against Celeste's body. The moment it made contact, my sister's skin began to melt away like wax held too close to flame. In seconds, she was just a skeleton wearing priestess robes.

I dropped to my knees, staring at what I'd done. The four prisoners' screams were cutting off one by one. Each of them reduced to bone, their flesh dissolving, their souls pulled into the crown.

Six voices, layered atop each other, crying out from inside the bone.

"Do not consider it failure, Alaira," a voice said from behind me, warm and patient. "It is clearly a powerful weapon, as you intended. Just... differently powerful than you planned."

I turned to see Quade emerging from the shadows. Black bones, moss growing from his eye sockets, the four horns and shredded wings. He looked around at the destruction with something like satisfaction.

The land around us was dying. Not gradually, but all at once—grass turning brown and crumbling to dust, trees withering and collapsing into hollow husks, the cornfields in the distance blackening. The smell of rot replaced the sweet scent of flowers. Behind us, the obsidian castle collapsed completely, its spires falling inward and shattering. Three hundred years of accumulated knowledge. Gone.

Quade walked to where Celeste's skeleton lay beside the altar. He picked it up with surprising gentleness, then did something I couldn't fully perceive—his fingers moved in patterns that hurt to watch, and suddenly my sister's skeleton was enormous. He carried it to where the castle had stood and positioned it there, sitting on what remained of the foundation. Her jaw hinged open to form an entrance.

A palace made from my sister's bones.

"I can explain to you the beauty in what you've done," Quade offered, turning back to face me. "You've broken rules, yes. But we can fix it yet. We can transform this catastrophe into opportunity."

"I know where Hesperia is," he continued, when I couldn't speak. "I know what's been keeping her from you. And I can help you reach her. But only if you work with me."

My breath caught. "You know where Hesperia is?"

"I do." He stood and offered me his hand—black bone covered in moss, ancient and powerful and completely other. "Come. Let me show you what we can build from this. How we can turn your mistake into something magnificent. How we can free your goddess and give the world the balance it desperately needs."

Every instinct screamed that taking it would be a mistake, that I was being offered a deal that would cost more than I could imagine.

But what choice did I have? I'd destroyed everything. The crown was corrupted, my sister was dead by my own hand, the coven was scattered, and the world was dying from my failed ritual.

And he knew where Hesperia was.

I took his hand.

I told myself I was doing it to protect my goddess. To fix my mistake. To finally reach Hesperia after so long in silence.

But even as his cold fingers closed around mine, part of me knew the truth. I was doing it to protect myself. To avoid facing what I'd done, what I'd become. To find someone—anyone—who would tell me I wasn't a monster.

And in that moment, I also decided something else: the truth of what happened here would be altered when told in history. The crown wouldn't be my failure—it would be a necessary sacrifice. Celeste wouldn't be my victim—she would be a willing participant. The coven wouldn't have warned me—they would have abandoned me out of cowardice.

I would reshape the narrative until even I could believe it.

Until even I could forget the look in my sister's eyes as I cut her throat.

"Come," Quade said gently, guiding me away from the altar. "We have much work to do. The first step is learning to live with what you've done. To transform guilt into purpose, failure into opportunity. That's my gift, Alaira. Transition. And I promise you—by the time we're finished, you'll barely remember the pain."

That promise terrified me more than anything else.

But I followed him anyway.

Act Two

DESCENT

Chapter Thirteen

The God's Grief

Renata

I don't know how long I sat on that throne of skulls, crying into Valdic's fur. Time felt meaningless in the aftermath of witnessing Theron's death—minutes could have been hours, hours could have been days. The afternoon sun filtering through the skeletal architecture slowly shifted to evening light, painting everything in shades of amber and shadow.

Valdic never moved. Never complained about the cramped position or my grip on his patchy fur. Just pressed his emaciated body against my legs and let me anchor myself to his solid presence while the grief worked through me like poison finally being purged.

Eventually, the tears slowed. Not because the grief was gone, but because my body simply ran out of the capacity to produce more. My eyes burned, swollen and raw. My chest felt hollow, carved out.

Footsteps echoed through the throne room—slow, deliberate, accompanied by the soft scraping of shredded wings against bone floor. Quade climbed the seven steps with that inhuman grace. His moss-lined eye sockets fixed on me with what I was beginning to recognize as genuine concern. Not manipulation, not divine calculation. Just care. The kind a father might show for a daughter who was suffering.

My father had been a simple man who'd loved his children and tended his small farm and never asked for anything more than a good harvest and a healthy family. Quade was a Primal God, ancient and terrible and responsible for transforming me into something that would reshape the world.

But sitting there on a throne made of skulls, my face wet with tears for a brother I'd failed to mourn, I couldn't quite muster the energy to reject the comfort he offered.

"You needed to see that," Quade said. "Needed to understand what happened to Theron. Not for closure alone, but because the grief—the real, witnessed grief—that's what empties you. Makes space for what comes next."

He settled into a sitting position on the steps below the throne, the movement oddly casual.

"I'm sorry," I said, my voice small. "I know I should be stronger. Should be handling this better."

"Don't apologize," Quade replied. "Your tears are necessary. Every piece of Theron you lose, every memory that cuts deep enough to make you bleed—that's the process. Love breaks mortals in a way nothing else can. It empties them. Hollows them out completely. And only when you're truly empty can you be refilled with the divine."

Something cold settled in my stomach.

"You wanted this," I said slowly. "You wanted me to grieve. Not to give me closure, but to hollow me out further."

"Both can be true," Quade replied, and there was no deception in his voice. "You deserved to know what happened to your brother. That part was genuine—a gift freely given. But yes, the grief also serves the transformation. Makes you less human, more capable of accepting divinity. The emptying is necessary, Renata. There's no way to become what you must be while still clinging to everything you were."

He leaned forward, moss-lined sockets fixed on me.

"Most people claim they would do anything for love. Would sacrifice everything, endure any suffering, pay any price. But when it actually comes to it—when the costs are real and terrible and permanent—they break. They retreat. They choose preservation of self over the love they claimed was worth everything."

The moss in his eye sockets pulsed with something like pride.

"You don't just say you'd go as far as it takes—you actually do it. You fed your memories to the Crown until you couldn't remember who you were. You let the bond torture you and Nokoa because ending it would mean losing him permanently. You carved children's flesh and let camps turn to dust and destroyed the world rather than accept his death. That's rare. That willingness to truly sacrifice everything. That's why you're special. Why you're worthy of ascension."

"You orchestrated that," I whispered. "Nokoa's death. You influenced Alaira, who influenced Fatin, who killed him. You pushed me to the breaking point deliberately."

"I created the circumstances," Quade confirmed without shame. "Ensured the pieces were in place. But the choices were yours. I couldn't have forced you to resurrect him. Couldn't have made you feed the Crown your memories or accept the bond's pain. You chose those things because your love was strong enough."

He stood, moving closer to the throne.

"That's what makes you different from my sister's daughters. They were created divine—born into power without understanding what it costs. But you? You're earning your divinity through suffering. Through loss. Through being broken down completely until there's nothing left but the essential core that can be rebuilt into something vast and terrible and necessary."

I looked at him—this ancient god who'd orchestrated Nokoa's death and my suffering to transform me into a weapon against his sister's cosmic mistake. Who spoke to me with warmth while being fundamentally unsettling to everyone else.

"What happened to you in the prison?" I asked. "The centuries you spent banished. What was that like?"

Quade was quiet for a long moment. Then: "Isolating. Maddening. I am transition—constant movement, perpetual change. To be locked in stasis, unable to facilitate any transformations, unable to move or shift or progress... it was torture specifically designed to break me. My sister knows my nature intimately. She crafted the perfect hell."

He looked at me directly. "But it also gave me time to plan. To understand exactly what needed to happen once I was free. I couldn't create daughters while imprisoned—couldn't touch the mortal world, couldn't orchestrate the suffering necessary to hollow out candidates for ascension. But I could reach out through the cracks Alaira was creating, could whisper to her about her silent goddess, could plant seeds that would bloom once I returned."

"You used Alaira's desperation," I said. "Her centuries of unanswered prayers."

"I offered her hope," Quade corrected. "Which happened to align with my purposes. We helped each other."

He moved back toward the steps. "Just as you and I are helping each other now. You want to save Nokoa, to prevent more suffering, to make the famine stop consuming everything. I want daughters who can restore balance. Our goals align, Renata. That's not manipulation—that's cooperation toward mutual benefit."

"What if I refuse?" I asked quietly. "What if I decide I don't want to be your daughter, don't want to be a goddess of destruction?"

Quade looked at me with those moss-lined sockets, and for a moment I saw something almost like pity.

"Then you transform anyway," he said simply. "The process is already too far advanced to stop—you've been hollowed out too thoroughly, accepted too much divine essence. You'll become a goddess of silence and forgetting whether you choose it consciously or not. The only question is whether you'll be a goddess with purpose and control, or just raw power without direction."

"Why are you kind to me?" I asked. "Valdic mentioned it—said others find you unsettling. But you're gentle with me. Patient. Why?"

"Because you're my daughter," Quade replied, and the warmth returned to his voice. "You've proven yourself worthy through suffering. Through willingness to be broken completely for love. That deserves recognition. The kind of care a father shows for a child who's exceeded all expectations."

He stood. "To others—to mortals who aren't special, who claim devotion but break when tested—I'm terrifying. As I should be. But you've already embraced ending. Already transitioned yourself piece by piece. You understand what I am in ways others can't."

He moved toward the exit, then paused. "Take time to process everything you've learned. Mourn your brother properly. When you're ready, come find me. We'll discuss the final steps needed to complete your ascension."

Then he was gone.

"He's not entirely wrong," Valdic said quietly into the silence. "About love hollowing people out. About you being special because you're actually willing to go as far as it takes. That part's true, even if the rest is…"

"Horrifying?" I supplied.

"I was going to say 'cosmically manipulative,' but horrifying works too."

I buried my fingers in his patchy fur. "He orchestrated Nokoa's death. Used Alaira to use Fatin to kill the person I love most. All so I'd be desperate enough to resurrect him, so the suffering would hollow me out enough to accept divinity."

"Yes," Valdic confirmed. "He did that. And it worked." He pressed his decayed snout against my hand. "Does knowing that change anything? Does understanding the manipulation undo the transformation, bring back Theron, fix the famine? Or do you accept that you were used, that terrible things happened for cosmic purposes, and decide what kind of goddess you'll be despite—or because of—that knowledge?"

I didn't have an answer. Sat there on a throne of skulls in a cathedral built from death, mourning a brother whose murder had been reconnaissance, loving a man whose death had been orchestrated manipulation, becoming something vast and terrible because I'd been willing to be broken completely.

I would choose. Would decide what kind of goddess to become, what silence and forgetting would mean in my hands, how to wield destruction without being destroyed by it.

Not because Quade wanted me to. But because I deserved that much agency after everything I'd sacrificed.

Chapter Fourteen

The Silencing

Renata

The commotion reached me before I saw it—raised voices echoing through the bone cathedral's corridors, the sharp clack of footsteps on stone. I was still sitting in the ash-covered courtyard with Valdic pressed against my legs, my tears finally dried to salt tracks on my cheeks. Nokoa had left to find Cressa, to check on the few remaining survivors.

But the voices approaching now weren't Nokoa's.

One of them was Alaira.

"Where is she?" the priestess demanded, her voice carrying that edge of desperation I'd heard in our last confrontation. "I need to speak with Renata. I need to explain—"

"You need to leave," Cressa's voice cut through, sharp as surgical steel. "You've done enough damage. More than enough."

I pushed myself to my feet, Valdic moving with me. The bone coral around the courtyard had grown taller overnight, formations now reaching past my waist, pulsing with that accelerated growth-and-decay cycle.

The voices grew closer.

"I was trying to help!" Alaira insisted. "The Goddess of Fate could have guided Renata through the transformation, could have prevented—"

"You were trying to use him," Nokoa's voice, flat and cold in a way I'd rarely heard. "You didn't care if it killed him. You just needed someone desperate enough to attempt the impossible."

My hands clenched into fists. Alaira had come to Nokoa. Had tried to convince him to navigate the God of Insanity's prison, to risk his fragile resurrection on her desperate gamble. And he'd told them. Had gone to Hivro for confirmation, had shared Alaira's plan instead of attempting it alone.

He'd chosen to trust them over her. Over the priestess who'd orchestrated his death in the first place.

I started walking toward the voices, Valdic padding beside me. The bone floor was cool under my bare feet. The black veins along my legs pulsed with each step, and I felt the Crown stirring on my skull, responding to the building anger.

Careful, Queen Oriana whispered in my mind. Control the emotion or it will control you.

She deserves what's coming, King Aldric added. Let the rage flow. Use it.

I turned a corner and found them—Alaira backed against a wall of bone, Nokoa and Cressa blocking her path. Hivro stood slightly apart, her constellation-marked face unreadable, butterflies swirling in agitated patterns. The spectral guardians had positioned themselves at the corridor's exit, preventing escape.

Alaira's eyes found mine immediately, fear flashing across her features before she masked it with determination.

"Renata," she began, taking a step toward me. "I know you're angry, but you have to understand—"

"You tried to send him to his death," I stated. "After orchestrating his first death, you tried to send him into a god's mad prison. Tried to use his love for me as leverage to make him attempt the impossible."

"It wasn't impossible!" Alaira protested, her desperation cracking through. "With the witch runes, with proper preparation—"

"It was suicide," Hivro interrupted, her voice carrying the weight of eons. "I told him as much. A mortal cannot navigate those fractured realities without being consumed. Even one touched by resurrection magic. You knew this, Alaira. You've known it for centuries."

The priestess's face crumpled slightly. "But the Goddess of Fate—she could help Renata. Could guide her through the transformation without losing her humanity. If we could just free her—"

"Then you go," I said, and my voice came out colder than I'd intended. Goddess-cold. "You walk into the mad prison. You risk your centuries-old life for your silent goddess. Don't ask others to die for your desperate need for answers."

Alaira flinched. "I can't. The prison would destroy me. I don't have the protection that Nokoa has—"

"So you'd spend him like currency," Cressa spat. "Use him up and discard him. The same way you used Renata. The same way you've used everyone who's had the misfortune of trusting you."

"I was trying to HELP!" Alaira's voice cracked, rising to a shout. "Everything I've done has been to help! To free my goddess, to guide Renata, to fix the damage I caused with the Crown—"

"You helped Quade orchestrate Nokoa's death," I interrupted, taking a step closer. The bone coral nearest to me grew faster, formations spiraling up from the floor. "You helped manipulate me into the resurrection. You've been serving his purposes for centuries while pretending to serve your goddess. And now you want us to believe you're trying to help?"

The priestess shook her head frantically. "No, you don't understand. If I could free her myself, if I could prove my devotion by rescuing her—"

"Then she might forgive you," Nokoa finished quietly. "For breaking every principle she taught you. For murdering your own sister and creating the cursed Crown and destroying civilizations. That's what this is really about. Not helping Renata. Buying your own redemption."

Alaira's legs seemed to give out. She slid down the wall until she was sitting on the bone floor, her tattered white robes pooling around her. Tears streamed down her face.

"I just want to hear her voice again," she whispered. "Just once. I want to know if she's disappointed in me. If there's any path back to her service. If I can ever be forgiven for what I've done."

The grief in her voice was real. Raw and devastating and completely genuine. Part of me—the part that still carried Renata Sunthorne's capacity for compassion—wanted to comfort her.

But the larger part felt nothing but cold fury.

She'd destroyed my world for her goddess. Had orchestrated Theron's death, Nokoa's death, countless other deaths—all in service to a deity who'd been silent for centuries. Who might not even care about her devotion anymore.

"How many?" I asked, my voice carrying that goddess-quality now. The sound of silence given shape. "How many people have died because of your choices?"

Alaira looked up at me, and I saw the weight of centuries in her eyes. "I don't know," she admitted. "I stopped counting. It hurt too much to keep track."

End her, King Aldric urged. She deserves no mercy.

Or bind her, Queen Oriana suggested. Use her knowledge. Make her serve penance.

I didn't want any of those options. I just wanted her gone. Wanted her to stop appearing in my life, stop manipulating and scheming and destroying in the name of her silent goddess.

I wanted silence.

The word resonated through me, through the Crown, through the transformation taking root in my bones. Silence. That was what I was becoming. That was my purpose, my nature, my divine domain.

The power built in my chest like pressure, something that needed release or it would crack me open from the inside. I could feel it responding to my desire—to silence Alaira, to make her stop, to end this constant cycle of her appearing and demanding and manipulating.

"Renata," Valdic warned, pressing against my leg. Through our bond I felt his concern, his understanding that I was about to do something I couldn't take back. "Think about this. Don't act from rage."

But I was so tired of thinking. So exhausted from processing and grieving and trying to be measured in my responses. Alaira had destroyed my brother. Had orchestrated Nokoa's death. Had tried to send him into a mad prison. Had created the cursed Crown that was fusing to my skull and transforming me into something inhuman.

"Leave," I commanded, and my voice came out wrong.

The word carried force—actual physical pressure that radiated outward from my lungs like a shockwave. But more than that, it carried silence. The sound itself seemed to eat other sounds, creating a void where noise should be.

The effect was immediate and terrible.

Alaira screamed, her hands flying to her ears. But no sound came out—the scream was simply gone, consumed by the silence radiating from my voice. Blood trickled from her nose, from her ears, from the corners of her eyes. Her mouth moved without producing sound.

The wave continued expanding, hitting Nokoa and Cressa and Hivro. They staggered back, hands to their ears, faces contorted with pain. The bone cathedral itself groaned, cracks spreading through the walls as the silence tried to consume even structural sound.

Valdic pressed harder against me, whimpering—the sound barely audible through the void I was creating. Through our bond I felt his pain, the way the silence was trying to consume even him.

"Stop!" Hivro shouted, her voice cutting through somehow—the Butterfly Oracle protected by divine mandate, able to resist even ascending goddess power. "Renata, stop! You're losing control!"

But I couldn't stop. The power was flowing out of me beyond my conscious direction. The silence wanted to expand, wanted to consume, wanted to erase every sound in the cathedral. To create a void so perfect that even memory of sound would cease to exist.

Alaira was convulsing now, her body trying to scream without being able to produce sound. The blood flowing from her ears staining her white robes crimson. Her eyes wide with understanding that she was dying.

"RENATA!" Nokoa's voice, distant through the silence. "Please!"

The word broke through. *Please.* Not a command or argument. Just a plea from someone who loved me despite what I was becoming.

I gasped, the connection breaking. The silence snapped back into me like a rubber band, and suddenly sound returned in a rush—Alaira sobbing, Valdic whimpering, Cressa cursing, the bone cathedral groaning as cracks spread through its structure.

I dropped to my knees, shaking. I'd almost killed her. Had *wanted* to kill her. Had manifested divine power without control or restraint because I was angry.

Alaira scrambled to her feet and ran. Fled down the corridor without looking back, blood still streaming from her ears, her sobs echoing off the bone walls. The spectral guardians parted to let her pass.

Nokoa reached me first, dropping to his knees beside me. The bond screamed with his proximity, but he ignored it. His hands found my shoulders, steadying me.

"It's okay," he breathed, though his voice shook. "You stopped. You didn't—"

"I almost killed her," I interrupted, my voice raw. "I *wanted* to kill her. Valdic, the bond—I felt him hurting and I still couldn't stop."

"You're becoming a goddess," Hivro said quietly, moving closer. "Divine power without divine wisdom. Mortal emotions directing cosmic forces. This is why ascension typically takes decades, Renata. You're manifesting abilities before you understand how to control them."

She knelt in front of me, her constellation-marked face grave. "Alaira will survive. The damage isn't permanent—her hearing will recover, the bleeding will stop. But you came very close to creating silence so profound it would have erased her entirely. Not just killed her body, but consumed her soul. Made it as if she'd never existed at all."

"I can't do this," I whispered. "Can't be this. I don't want power that does that."

"You don't have a choice about the power," Hivro replied. "Only about how you learn to wield it. Quade is accelerating your transformation deliberately—pushing you toward power before you're ready to control it. You need time to process, to grieve, to learn what you're becoming before the ascension completes. But I don't think he's going to give you that time."

I looked at Nokoa—fear and love mixed in his golden eyes. At Valdic, still pressed against my leg despite the pain. At Cressa, watching from a distance.

Chapter Fifteen

The First Absorption and Transfer

Renata

I was beginning to get sick of seeing the throne room. Sick of the skeletal architecture that rose around me like a ribcage, all those bone pillars and archways that Quade had shaped from the caves. Sick of the throne itself—that monstrosity of fused bone and trapped souls that pulsed with a heartbeat that wasn't mine.

The air in here tasted like old death.

Nokoa stood beside Quade near the base of the throne, his golden eyes tracking my every movement. The witch runes carved into his bones glowed faintly through his tan skin. Valdic pressed against my side, his purple eyes watchful.

Priestess Alaira stood in the center of the room, exactly where Quade had positioned her. Her presence made my skin crawl, made the black veins along my jaw pulse with something darker than anger. Three days had passed since I'd nearly killed her with the silencing breath, and she still looked diminished. Paler. Dark circles ringed her eyes like bruises that wouldn't fade.

"What is this for?" I asked, forcing the words out through gritted teeth.

"We need to create space for the new you," Quade explained, his voice carrying that paternal warmth. "For new power. I know you are tired. But soon you will feel whole. Today we take another step closer."

Whole. The word tasted like a lie.

"Does she need to be here for it?" I pointed at Alaira. "Does the woman who murdered my brother need to stand in my throne room and perform rituals?"

Alaira's expression didn't change. Calm. Serene. Like my hatred meant nothing to her. That composure made me want to break her even more.

"She does," Quade affirmed, steel underneath the warmth. "Her knowledge of the Crown's creation is essential."

"I refuse." The words came out sharp, final. "I don't want any more death on my hands."

Because that's what this was. Another death. Queen Lyanna had been trapped in the Crown for who knew how long, her soul bound to the bone. She was already dead, but this would unmake her completely. Would consume what remained and feed it to me like kindling.

"Lay the deaths on my hand," Quade offered, his voice dropping to something softer. "I will take the blame, daughter. Let me carry this burden."

You must proceed, Queen Oriana's voice cut through my thoughts. *We haven't come this far for you to stop now. The deaths will be for nothing if you don't.*

Her logic was flawless, which made it worse. If I stopped now, Theron died for nothing. The cities starved for nothing. Nokoa suffered for nothing.

I felt stuck. Trapped between refusal and acceptance, between who I'd been and what I was becoming.

But maybe I could choose to accept instead of just being dragged. Maybe I could step forward instead of waiting to be pushed.

Valdic nudged my hand. "Breathe," he murmured. "Just breathe through it."

I could choose this. The distinction mattered, even if the outcome was the same.

Alaira reached up and drew a rune on the Hollow Crown with fingers that glowed faintly with celestial power. The bone beneath her touch warmed, and I felt something shift. Like a door being unlocked.

She began to chant. The words were old, older than the common tongue. They resonated through the throne room, through my very skeleton. The Crown responded, its trapped souls stirring like a disturbed hive. I felt them move beneath the bone—Oriana, Aldric, and the others pressing against the inside of the Crown like prisoners against cell walls.

Queen Lyanna's soul was pulled from the bone crown. Not gently. It was wrenched free like a tooth being extracted, roots and all. Her half-burnt face materialized in front of me—not as the fractured voice I'd grown used to, but her full form. A spirit given shape. Translucent but solid.

"What are you doing!" Queen Lyanna screamed, and her voice was different outside my head. Higher. More desperate. Terrified.

For the first time since I bonded with the Crown, I really saw her. The short bob of hair that had once been carefully maintained. The soft features. The side that was beautiful and unmarred, with high cheekbones and full lips. The other side burnt down to bone, charred and cracked. Patches of blackened flesh clinging to exposed jawbone.

She'd been vain in life. Obsessed with appearance. And death had taken half her face and left her trapped in a crown, invisible, reduced to a voice offering shallow criticisms.

What is this? King Aldric demanded inside my head. What have you done, Oriana!

But Oriana was silent.

Priestess Alaira chanted louder, her voice rising until the words became almost physical things, pressing against my skin. The rune on the Crown blazed with white light. Queen Lyanna's spirit began to fracture, cracks spreading across her translucent form like ice breaking.

"No!" Lyanna shrieked, her hands clawing at herself. "No, please, I don't want—"

She exploded.

Into butterflies. Hundreds of them, thousands, each one carrying a fragment of her soul. They were beautiful and terrible—iridescent wings catching the dim light, patterns swirling across them that looked almost like faces, like screams frozen in chitin. Some had patterns like burn scars. Others bore designs that looked like tears or mirrors or flames.

The air filled with the soft whisper of their wings.

They swarmed toward me.

I tried to step back but Valdic was behind me, keeping me grounded. The butterflies descended on my face, my mouth, and I couldn't close it fast enough. They poured in like drowning, each one dissolving on my tongue with a taste like ash and honey and burnt flesh.

Queen Lyanna's memories filled me. Not gradually. Not gently. All at once.

I saw her coronation—young and beautiful and proud. I experienced her three years of slow emotional death as the Crown drained her piece by piece. I lived through her growing obsession with mirrors, with confirming she still existed. I watched her face burn—a ritual gone wrong. The smell of her own flesh cooking. The sound of her screams. The horror of her reflection.

The burning in my face started then. Not physically—the flesh wasn't charring—but the phantom sensation was so intense I couldn't tell the difference. My cheek blazed with agony. I could smell my own flesh cooking even though I knew it was just memory.

I screamed.

The sound started strong but halfway out it died to silence. Swallowed by the same force I'd turned on Alaira.

"I feel everything," I gasped. "Everything Lyanna ever felt. It's too much."

My hands clawed at my face. The black veins along my jaw pulsed violently, spreading further up my cheeks. My spine arched, the external vertebrae grinding with a sound like breaking pottery.

Valdic pressed harder against my hand, and through the bond I felt him trying to absorb the overflow. But this was different. This was a soul's worth of feeling. It was drowning both of us.

The only thing I could see clearly was Nokoa and Quade watching me. Not horror from Quade—he watched with satisfaction, approval. Like my agony was part of the design. But Nokoa's golden eyes were wide with genuine terror. He looked like he wanted to run to me, took half a step forward before stopping.

"How do I carry years of someone else's feelings?" I called out, my voice breaking.

You transfer it, Queen Oriana said. You give it to someone who can carry it for you.

And suddenly I understood why Valdic was here. Why the bond between us worked differently than the one with Nokoa. Why Quade had encouraged that connection.

"Renata," Valdic's voice was strained but steady. "Let me help. That's what I'm here for."

"I can't do that to you."

"You can. You must."

And because I was weak, because I was drowning—I did.

I reached through the bond and pushed. Lyanna's vanity and fear and rage poured out of me and into Valdic like water finding a crack. The relief was immediate. Profound. Like surfacing after nearly drowning. The burning in my face faded to a dull throb.

But Valdic whimpered.

A small sound, almost lost in the vast throne room. But through the bond I felt what it cost him. Felt the way Lyanna's emotions hit him like a physical blow. Felt him stagger under the weight.

His legs trembled. His purple eyes dimmed slightly, like a candle flame flickering in wind.

I woke in my own room with the knot still in my throat.

Lyanna's emotions tangled into mine like thread wound too tight, impossible to separate. Her vanity pressed against my skull. Her fear amplified every anxiety. Her rage fed into my own fury.

I couldn't stop the tears. They poured down my cheeks before I was even fully conscious.

"You're awake!" Cressa exclaimed, her voice bright with relief.

"I'm alive," I answered, and it sounded like a joke even though I meant it.

"Don't be funny, Renata," Valdic reprimanded from the foot of the bed. His purple eyes were dim, exhausted.

"Here, drink," Cressa offered, holding greenish liquid to my lips.

But I already felt like I was choking on emotion. The knot in my throat was so tight I could barely breathe. I pushed the glass away.

Valdic jumped onto the bed, his skeletal joints clicking. He pressed his forehead to mine, his purple eyes so close I could see nothing else.

"Pet me," he requested, gentle but firm.

I scratched behind his ears with trembling fingers, feeling the bone beneath thin fur.

Relief came like a wave, washing over the tangled knot and loosening it. The tears stopped. The tightness in my throat eased. I could take a deep breath—a real breath.

I laughed as it came out. The sound was startled, almost hysterical, but genuine.

Lavender strings flowed from me to Valdic. Visible. Tangible. Like threads of light being pulled from my chest and absorbed into his. They carried something I couldn't name but could feel leaving me—Lyanna's tangled emotions, my own grief and rage, flowing out like blood from an opened vein.

"Valdic, are you taking this from me?" I asked, though I already knew.

"I can carry it," he answered. "Let me carry it."

Through the bond I felt his absolute conviction. But underneath, I felt the weight pressing down on him.

"Do you remember the shooting star you watched when we were younger?" Cressa asked quietly. "You thought it was alive and that it had fallen and died. You cried for days."

The memory came back—and this one was mine, I was almost certain. Me at seven or eight, standing in the palace gardens at night. Convinced it had been a living thing.

I laughed out—a true laugh this time. I had forgotten what that felt like.

It was only for a moment before pain filled me again. The laugh died, choked off by emotions flooding back.

Valdic shifted. "Don't," he murmured firmly. "Keep this one. She makes you brighter."

The shooting star memory. The laughter. He wanted me to keep that.

I shook my head, feeling the pressure building. "I can't. Please take some."

The lavender vines formed between us again—those visible threads carrying emotion from me to him. They shimmered, pulsing with each transfer.

Relief. Immediate and profound. The shooting star memory stayed.

Cressa took my hand back in silence.

Chapter Sixteen

THE VIGIL AT OCEAN'S EDGE

Nokoa

Quade had suggested we leave the cathedral. "She needs air," he'd said with that paternal concern. "Needs to see beyond these bone walls." So I'd found Renata in her room, still reeling from the absorption, and led her through the skeletal corridors. Valdic had followed without question, his purple eyes bright with transferred grief.

The walk had been silent.

Now I stood behind her, watching.

She stood at what used to be the ocean. The cliff edge dropped away into nothing—just an empty basin of bleached bone and ash stretching to the horizon. No water. No waves. No salt-spray or tide pools or any of the life that had once thrived here.

The wind that blew up from the dead ocean bed carried no moisture, just the fine dust of what used to be. It tasted like chalk and old death on my tongue. It caught in Renata's black hair and made it stream behind her like a funeral shroud. She stood perfectly still at the cliff's edge, close enough that one strong gust could send her over.

My chest ached looking at her. Not from the bond—Quade had kept it muted—but from something deeper. Something the witch runes couldn't burn away no matter how brightly they glowed through my skin.

"When we were teenagers, I wanted so badly to bring you here and ask for your hand in marriage," I said, coming to stand beside her. The cliff edge felt unstable beneath my feet, crumbling slightly with each shift of weight.

I'd been seventeen, she'd been sixteen, and I'd spent weeks planning the perfect proposal. The ocean at sunset. Wildflowers woven into a crown. Words I'd practiced until they sounded natural instead of rehearsed. But I'd never gone through with it. Had convinced myself that I was her brother's guard and we weren't able to be together.

And then Fatin had killed me, and time ran out.

Renata turned and looked at me for only a moment before she turned back to the dead ocean. Her grey-white eyes tracked across my face without really seeing me. Like she was looking at a memory instead of the person standing in front of her.

"I used to imagine you asking me that in the courtyard surrounded by my orchids," she said, her voice distant. "I remember loving that memory. But it only feels distant now."

I touched her shoulder and pulled her into me. Her black spine pressed against my chest through her clothing, those external vertebrae sharp and un-yielding. The bone was warm beneath the fabric, unnaturally so.

This time it wasn't her who cried. Valdic had taken all of those emotions from her—I'd watched the lavender strings carry her tears away, watched her face smooth into something approaching calm as the Dirge Wolf absorbed what she couldn't hold. This time it was me who cried, hot tears spilling down my cheeks as I held what remained of the woman I loved.

The witch runes burned brighter along my arms, trying to take the grief, trying to consume the emotion as payment for their magic. But there was too much. Some feelings were too big to be used as fuel.

"I don't know how to come back to myself," Renata said against my chest, her voice muffled but steady. No tears in it. No tremor. Just flat acknowledgment of her own dissolution.

"Then I'll come to where you are," I promised, meaning it with everything I had left.

Valdic sat near us, his purple eyes impossibly bright in the grey light. When I looked at him—really looked at him—I saw he was crying the tears that Renata was not. They fell from his eyes like the lavender strings that carried her emotions, visible trails down his skeletal snout, each one a piece of her grief made manifest in her bonded companion.

He was drowning in what she couldn't carry. In Lyanna's vanity and fear and rage. In Renata's own overwhelming sorrow and guilt and love. All of it stored inside a DirgeWolf who'd made himself her vessel.

And he was breaking. I could see it now. The way his body sagged despite the brightened eyes, spine curving under invisible weight. The way his breathing came harder than it should, each exhale labored.

"Valdic," I said quietly. "How much more can you hold?"

His purple eyes found mine, and through their brightness I saw something that looked like resignation. Like he'd already done the math and knew the answer but refused to say it out loud.

"As much as she needs me to," he answered. "That's what I'm for, remember?"

Renata pulled back from my chest slightly, her grey-white eyes finding Valdic. Tracking the tears on his face.

"You're crying," she observed.

"I'm crying your tears," Valdic corrected gently. "The ones you would shed if you still could."

"That doesn't seem fair to you," she said, and there was something in her voice—not quite emotion, but the memory of emotion. The shape of concern without the substance of it.

"Nothing about this is fair," I said, pulling her back against me. "But we're in it together. All three of us. Until whatever end this leads to."

The dead ocean stretched before us. Once it had been full of life—fish and coral and creatures I didn't have names for. Renata used to talk about wanting to explore it, to dive deep and discover what lived in the places light couldn't reach.

Now there was nothing. Another casualty of the famine my resurrection had triggered. Another piece of the world that had died so she could have me back.

"Do you regret it?" I asked. "Bringing me back?"

I felt her go still against me. Through the bond I felt her reaching for emotion—trying to access guilt or regret or even relief—and finding only hollow spaces where those feelings used to live.

"I should regret it," she said finally. "I know that intellectually. Cities died. The ocean died. People are starving because I couldn't accept your death. I know I should feel crushing guilt about that."

"But you don't," I finished for her.

"But I don't." She paused. "I remember what guilt felt like. Remember the shape of it, the weight of it. But Valdic carries it now. And without it, I can only see the facts. You died. I brought you back. The world paid the price. Those are just events that happened, not sins that require absolution."

"The Midnight Oath is coming," I said, and felt Renata's shoulders tense. The only physical reaction she seemed capable of anymore. "Quade told me."

"I won't let you die for me," Renata said immediately, and there was heat in her voice now. The first real emotion I'd heard from her since finding her at the cliff's edge. "I won't. I don't care what it costs me."

"Even if it costs you everything?" I pressed, turning her slightly so I could see her face. "Even if refusing the oath means you die when the Crown breaks? Even if it means all of this—Theron's death, the cities falling, my resurrection—was for nothing?"

"Yes," she breathed without hesitation. "Even then."

And through the bond I felt the truth of it. Felt that core of her that still burned with something approaching love, even if she couldn't properly feel the warmth of it anymore.

"What if I choose differently?" I asked quietly. "What if I choose to die willingly? To complete the oath and let you become what you're meant to be?"

Renata pulled away from me completely then, turning to face me with those grey-white eyes that looked too bright, too empty, too other. "Don't," she said. Not a request. A command. "Don't you dare choose that."

"Why not?" I challenged, taking her hands in mine. Her fingers were cold against my palms. "You chose to bring me back despite the cost. Why can't I choose to die despite yours?"

"Because—" She stopped, struggling with words that should have come easily. "Because I need you to live. Need to know that something good came from all of this."

She couldn't finish. The emotion that should have been there existed somewhere in Valdic instead. And without it, she couldn't articulate why my life mattered more than her transformation.

But I understood anyway.

Valdic stood and walked to stand between us. He looked at me, then at her, then back to me. "You're both choosing wrong," he said. "She's choosing to die when she should ascend. You're choosing to die when you should live. And I'm choosing to carry emotions that are crushing me because I can't bear to watch either of you shatter."

"Then what's the right choice?" Renata asked, her voice small.

Valdic's tears fell harder, leaving wet tracks through the ash settled on his snout. "I don't know. Maybe there isn't one. Maybe we're all just doing the best we can with impossible options."

The wind picked up, carrying more ash from the dead ocean basin. It settled on our skin like snow, gritty and fine.

I reached for Renata's hand and she let me take it. Her fingers cold, distant. But she held on anyway, and through the bond I felt her trying. Trying to remember what it felt like to draw comfort from touch.

I couldn't tell her my choice. Couldn't say it out loud because she would fight me, would try to stop it, would choose to break herself rather than let me break for her.

So I held her cold hand and looked out at the bone-dry ocean and let her believe we still had time to find another way.

Chapter Seventeen

The Ritual of Feeling

"Quade!" I called out, my voice echoing through the skeletal corridors of the bone cathedral.

I stormed the halls, my external spine scraping against the walls as I moved too fast, too recklessly. The sound it made—bone on bone, a grinding shriek—matched the desperation clawing through my chest.

The air tasted stale, like old breath trapped in lungs that never exhaled.

I found him in one of the deeper chambers. The walls pressed in close. The temperature dropped the moment I crossed the threshold, cold enough to see my breath.

And he wasn't alone.

Hivro stood beside him, that white star-covered body seeming to glow brighter in the dim space. The constellations that moved across her skin were agitated, shifting through patterns too quickly to follow. Galaxies collapsing and reforming. All of it reflected in her ancient eyes as they turned to look at me in unison with Quade's moss-filled sockets.

"Why are the two of you together?" I demanded, stopping in the doorway. My hands clenched into fists, black veins pulsing along my jaw.

"Should we not speak?" Quade asked, his voice carrying that patient tone.

"No!" I shouted. The Crown on my skull flared with heat. Inside, the remaining voices stirred—Queen Oriana's clinical observations, King Aldric's violent approval.

"In truth, I am the only one she can speak to," Quade explained, gesturing to Hivro. "I was at not only her creation but the creation of the Goddess she follows. Agree with me or not, she can still speak."

Hivro remained silent, wrapped in constellations that showed too many colors to sort out. But her eyes tracked me with something that looked like sorrow.

"That's not why you sought me out," Quade said, turning his full attention to me. "What do you need, daughter?"

"I want you to take it," I said, forcing the words out. "All of it. I can't take feeling like this anymore. I can't keep giving it all to Valdic. I'm killing him."

The confession ripped out of me raw and desperate. Because it was true. I'd watched Valdic grow heavier with each transfer, watched his purple eyes brighten with emotions that weren't his own, watched him drown in the overflow of what I couldn't hold.

Hivro took a step back, her constellations flaring bright enough to hurt my eyes.

"I can offer you the Ritual of Feeling," Quade said slowly, like he was presenting a gift he'd been waiting to give. "But you must understand what you're asking for."

"Do it." I didn't care about understanding. I just needed the pain to stop.

"You aren't going to ask anything further?" Quade questioned, and there was something in his voice. Like even he hadn't expected me to be this desperate.

"No. Just do it. Please."

Before Quade could move, the room filled again.

Nokoa burst through the doorway, golden eyes wild, witch runes blazing through his skin. Behind him came Valdic, moving slower, heavier, his purple eyes tracking me with resignation. And behind them both, Cressa appeared, her face pale.

"Renata, don't—" Nokoa started, but Quade was already moving.

He wrapped both hands around my skull, fingers spanning from temple to temple, encompassing the Hollow Crown. His touch was cold. Colder than death. The cold sank through my skin, through my skull, straight into my brain.

A shockwave sent through me.

Ice first. Freezing cold that burned through my veins, turning my blood to frost. Every nerve ending screamed. My teeth chattered so hard I tasted blood.

Then fire. Searing heat that melted the ice and boiled what remained. My skin felt like it was burning from the inside out, my spine arching so violently I heard vertebrae crack.

Numb and then every emotion at once.

I felt them all. The grief for Theron, the guilt over the famine, the love for Nokoa, the fear of what I was becoming, the rage at being chosen. All of Valdic's burden—Lyanna's vanity pressing against my skull like a crown within a crown, her fear of being forgotten, her rage at losing her beauty, decades of feeling compressed into seconds.

I collapsed, my knees hitting the bone floor hard. My hands clawed at Quade's wrists, trying to break his grip. His bones were smooth and unyielding under my fingers.

"Stop! Make it stop! This isn't what I asked!" Tears poured down my face. "Please!"

"I cannot simply take it," Quade said, his voice infuriatingly calm while I shattered beneath his hands. "There are steps. Transitions. You must feel everything first. Must understand the full weight of what you're asking me to remove."

I screamed. The sound tore from my throat like something alive, echoing through the chamber.

And then the lavender vines erupted from me.

Not a gentle flow. Hundreds of them, thousands, bursting from my chest like I'd been split open. They filled the chamber with purple light, writhing and seeking. The light was blinding.

They found Valdic.

The vines wrapped around him, lifted him into the air. His emaciated body hung suspended in the mass of purple light, and I watched in horror as they filled him. Poured into his mouth, his eyes, his skeletal form. Too much. Too fast.

He grew. His body expanded, muscles appearing where there had been only bone and decay. Flesh knitted itself over exposed ribs. His purple eyes blazed brighter than they ever had. The life that I was losing flowed into him, making him larger, stronger, more solid.

I tried to stop it. Tried to pull the vines back. But I couldn't. My body knew it couldn't hold this much emotion and was desperately trying to survive by pouring it all into Valdic.

The vines left one by one. Slowly, painfully, each one withdrawing from Valdic's body. He descended back to the ground gently, landing on all fours with his head bowed. His newly-formed muscles trembled.

He was whimpering. Small, broken sounds that I felt through our bond like knives.

I felt everything and then nothing at all.

The emotions were gone. Not muted, not transferred—gone. Emptied out through the ritual, poured into Valdic until I was hollow. I could remember what love felt like. But I couldn't feel any of it. Like looking at colors through glass.

Valdic glanced up at me from where he crouched. His eyes were glowing purple, changed. Brighter. Fuller. Filled with all the life I no longer had. His body more solid now, flesh where there had been decay. He looked at me with my own emotions reflected back, with Lyanna's feelings layered underneath.

"I'm sorry," I whispered, but the words felt empty.

"Don't be," Valdic managed, his voice strained but still loyal. "This is what I'm for, remember?"

Quade released my skull and stepped back. "The Ritual of Feeling," he said. "You must feel everything before you can release it. This is transition, daughter. This is how you make room for what you're becoming."

"You knew," I said, my voice hollow. "You knew it would do this to Valdic."

"I knew it would do this to you," Quade corrected gently. "The DirgeWolf chose to be your vessel. That was his decision, not mine. I simply provided the path."

Nokoa moved toward me but I held up a hand to stop him. I couldn't bear to be touched right now. Couldn't bear the reminder of connection when I felt so disconnected from everything.

Hivro's constellations had settled into a pattern that looked like mourning. Slow, dimming stars.

"How do you feel?" Cressa asked quietly.

"I don't," I answered. "That's the problem."

Valdic dragged himself closer, his movements heavy despite his newly-formed flesh. He pressed his head against my leg, and through the bond I felt what he felt—my own love for him, magnified and reflected back. Beautiful and terrible and completely inaccessible to me now.

I looked at Quade. "What's next?"

His moss-filled sockets gleamed. "Next," he said, "you learn to be empty. To exist as vessel rather than person. To make room for the divine power that will replace what you've lost."

"And if I can't?"

"Then the Crown breaks," Quade said simply. "And you die. And all of this—Theron's death, the famine, your transformation—was for nothing."

I looked around the chamber at the people who loved me. Nokoa with his witch runes and desperate eyes. Cressa with her useless healing supplies. Hivro with her star-covered sorrow. And Valdic, my faithful DirgeWolf, drowning in emotions that should have been mine.

"I'm sorry," I said again, knowing it wasn't enough.

But this time I didn't feel the guilt of saying it.

His legs trembled. His purple eyes dimmed slightly, like a candle flame flickering in wind.

Interlude Two

The First Midnight

Queen Oriana

The blood moon rose over the Bone Court, painting everything the color of fresh wounds.

I stood at the edge of the ritual circle, bone dust and dried blood marking its perimeter in intricate patterns Bahni had spent days perfecting. The crown sat heavy on my skull, cold as always, its weight both physical and something deeper. Three years I'd worn it. Three years of slow erosion, emotions draining away like water through cupped hands.

Tonight would reverse it all.

Tonight, Thrain would die for me, and I would feel again.

The Bone Council gathered as witnesses—ritual law required audience for the Midnight Oath. Bahni stood closest, her skeletal form draped in ceremonial robes that rustled softly when she moved. Praxis lounged against a pillar, crimson eyes reflecting the moon's red light. Ancelin, Fatin, and the others arranged themselves in a loose semicircle, far enough back to be safe but close enough to see.

I checked the ritual components one final time. Candles arranged in seven-pointed star formation, their flames steady in the still air. Silver bowl filled with purified water, its surface mirror-smooth. Bone knife inscribed with words in languages that hurt to read. Everything exactly as the ancient text specified.

Everything ready.

Except Thrain himself.

"He'll come," Bahni said quietly, reading my thoughts in the way she'd learned to over three years of watching me hollow out. "He loves you. He promised."

I nodded. Somewhere beneath the crown's numbing influence, I thought I should feel nervous. Anxious. Something. But there was only patient waiting, clinical awareness that the optimal window was narrowing.

The Midnight Oath could only be performed when celestial conditions aligned perfectly—blood moon at apex, specific stars in configuration, the veil between life and death at its thinnest. Miss this window, and I'd wait another decade. Another ten years of continued fading until nothing remained but perfect logical function in an empty shell.

I couldn't wait that long.

So I'd asked Thrain six weeks ago. Explained what the ritual required. What his death would purchase.

He'd agreed. Eventually. After days of anguish and tears I could no longer properly mirror, after extracting promises I'd made without feeling their weight. He'd agreed because he loved me, because he wanted me back, because the hollow thing wearing my face had convinced him this was the only way.

"Through my death, you'll feel again," he'd said, trying to smile through his grief. His voice had cracked on the words. "You'll remember what it was like to love me. That's worth it. That has to be worth it."

I'd nodded. Said "thank you" in the flat monotone that was all I had left. Watched him cry for both of us since I couldn't anymore.

Now he just needed to show up.

Minutes passed. The moon climbed higher, its red light intensifying as it reached the perfect position. Magic hummed in the air—I felt it like pressure against my skin, like the moment before lightning strikes. The bone circle began to glow faintly, recognizing that conditions were optimal.

Any moment now.

More minutes. The Council members began exchanging glances I recognized intellectually as concern but couldn't emotionally process. Bahni shifted her weight, skeletal feet scraping against bone floor.

Still Thrain didn't come.

The moon continued its arc. The optimal window slowly closing.

"My queen—" Fatin began.

The sound of running footsteps cut him off. A guard appeared at the chamber entrance, breathing hard, her face pale.

"Speak," I commanded.

"Lord Thrain's chambers are empty, my queen." The words tumbled out. "His travel pack is gone. The stable master reports his horse missing. And this—" She held up a sealed letter, my name written across it in Thrain's familiar script. "This was left on his pillow."

The Council fell silent.

I took the letter with steady hands. Broke the seal. The wax cracked cleanly, releasing the faint scent of Thrain's personal seal. Unfolded the parchment:

Oriana,

I tried. You have to believe I tried.

For six weeks I told myself I could do it. That I loved you enough to walk into that circle and let you kill me. That saving you was worth dying for. I almost convinced myself it was romantic—the ultimate sacrifice, the proof of devotion, the act that would restore everything we'd lost.

But when the moon rose tonight and I dressed for my own execution, I couldn't make my feet move toward the door. Couldn't take that final step from living to dying. Even for you. Even for love.

I'm not brave enough. I'm not selfless enough. I'm just a coward who wants to live more than he wants you to feel again.

I'm sorry. I thought I was stronger. I thought love would be enough to overcome self-preservation. But apparently there's a limit to what even love can make you do.

I'll go far enough you won't be tempted to send guards. Far enough you can't force what should only be given willingly.

Forgive me, or don't. I don't deserve either.

I'll remember you. The real you. The one who laughed and cried and loved wildly. That's the Oriana I'm keeping, even if you can't keep her yourself.

Goodbye.

—Thrain

I read it twice. Three times. Waiting for the emotional impact that never came.

Heartbreak. Betrayal. Rage. Grief. Desperation.

I felt nothing.

Just the vague recognition that this complicated the ritual. That the required component was missing. That I'd lost my chance at restoration because my beloved chose his life over my feeling.

"What do we do?" Bahni asked, her voice tight with something I couldn't name.

I looked at the ritual circle, at the blood moon reaching its apex, at the components I'd prepared so carefully. Magic was already building, responding to the celestial alignment. The oath had been partially activated by my preparation, by my intention, by the moon's perfect position. The pressure had become almost unbearable.

It needed completion. Needed sacrifice and death and willing participation.

I had none of those things.

"I'm going to try anyway," I heard myself say.

"But the beloved must be present—" Bahni started.

"I am aware of the requirement," I interrupted. "The magic has already been partially activated. It has nowhere to go. Perhaps it will simply dissipate. Perhaps—" I paused, some distant part of me recognizing I was about to make a terrible mistake. "Perhaps something else will happen."

"Oriana, if the ritual backlashes—"

"Then I'll be no worse off than I am now." I folded Thrain's letter carefully. Set it aside on the altar. "I'm already hollow. Already lost. What more can failing cost me?"

Bahni opened her mouth to argue, then closed it. She'd watched me fade for three years. Knew that waiting another decade meant I'd be completely gone by then.

I stepped into the ritual circle alone.

The moment my foot crossed the bone dust perimeter, the magic seized me.

Not gently. Not carefully. But with the desperate hunger of a spell seeking its required components and finding none. Like an equation trying to solve itself with missing variables, the magic twisted, searching for the sacrifice it demanded. It wrapped around me like invisible hands, pulling, seeking, hungry.

Found nothing where Thrain should have stood.

Found only me, hollow and alone, wearing a crown that had already taken so much.

I began speaking the words anyway:

"By blood and bone, by moon and night,

By sacrifice willingly given—"

The phrase stuck in my throat. Because there was no sacrifice. No willing death. Just me and my emptiness and a ritual that required what I didn't have.

The magic responded with what felt like confusion. It had been called, activated, brought into being by the perfect alignment of celestial forces. It existed now, with purpose and intention and nowhere to direct itself.

It needed a sacrifice. Needed death to fuel restoration.

I felt it turn inward.

Found the last fragments of emotion I had remaining.

The magic pulled, gentle as falling water. Not violent or aggressive. Just inevitable. Like gravity, like entropy, like all things seeking their lowest point. The tiny remaining scraps of feeling—the ghost of love for Thrain, the intellectual echo of joy, the distant memory of grief—all of it flowing toward the hungry spell.

Flowing away from me.

"No," I whispered, but the word had no force behind it. How could it? I had no fear to make it desperate, no panic to make it sharp. Just the flat recognition that I was losing the last pieces of myself.

The crown grew colder. Heavier. More permanent.

When it finished, I stood in the circle exactly as I'd entered it.

No flood of restored feeling. No dramatic transformation.

Just nothing.

The nothing I'd been approaching for three years, now absolute. Final. Irreversible.

I stepped out of the circle on steady legs. Picked up Thrain's letter. Folded it precisely and tucked it into my robes. The paper felt like any other paper.

"I remember loving you," I said aloud, testing the words.

They meant nothing. Just sounds. Just air vibrating in patterns that used to signify something important but were now merely data.

The Bone Council stared at me with expressions I could catalog but not interpret. Shock. Horror. Pity. Fear.

"The Midnight Oath has failed," I announced. "The beloved did not appear. The sacrifice was not made. The magic took what little remained and gave nothing in return."

I walked past them toward the throne, movements precise and efficient.

"Session dismissed," I commanded. "There is work to be done tomorrow. Rest while you can still feel the need for it."

They left slowly, reluctantly, casting glances back that I recognized as concern but couldn't respond to emotionally.

Except Bahni, who lingered near the throne.

"Oriana," she began, then stopped. "I'm so sorry. This is my fault. I found the text, I encouraged you to try, I helped prepare—"

"You acted with the information available," I replied. "No fault can be assigned. We now have more complete information. The Midnight Oath requires willing sacrifice that actually appears. Without both components, it drains what remains and provides nothing. Record it properly. Future crown bearers should know."

"Future bearers," she repeated, voice hollow. "You speak as if you're already gone."

"The part of me you knew is gone," I confirmed. "What remains is functional but empty."

"But—"

"Dismissed, Bahni."

She left, shoulders shaking with grief I couldn't mirror.

I sat on the throne alone, surrounded by bone architecture that had once been Celeste—the priestess whose death had created this crown. Whose betrayal by her sister had begun this entire catastrophe.

I wondered if she'd felt betrayed when Alaira cut her throat. If that feeling had stayed with her when her soul was pulled into the bone prison.

I would never know.

The voices in the crown—Celeste, the four prisoners—had been silent during the ritual. Now they stirred.

"She tried without the sacrifice," Celeste murmured. "Foolish girl."

"She had no choice," one of the prisoners replied. "We all make desperate choices at the end."

"You warned me this would happen," I said to them. "You told me the crown takes everything eventually."

"We tried," Celeste replied, her voice bitter. "But no one ever listens. Everyone thinks they'll be different. That they'll be strong enough."

"Was I supposed to just accept it? Just let myself hollow out completely without trying to stop it?"

"Yes," all the voices said in unison. "Because trying to stop it only makes it worse. The Midnight Oath is a trap. It promises restoration through sacrifice. But if the sacrifice fails—if the beloved runs, if they can't go through with it—the oath takes what's left and gives nothing back. You're worse off than if you'd never tried."

"Would you have listened?" Celeste asked. "When you're desperate, you don't want warnings. You want hope."

I sat in silence, processing this future with the same flat affect I now applied to everything.

Decades of hollow rule. Then death. Then eternal imprisonment as a voice future bearers would ignore.

That was all that remained.

The Hollow Crown would use me until my memories dried up, and then it would toss me away.

Act Three
THE COST

Chapter Eighteen

THE SLIPPING

Nokoa

Two days since the Ritual of Feeling, and Renata had become a stranger wearing a familiar face.

She spent every waking hour in the bone garden courtyard now. Same bone bench every time, surrounded by skeletal coral formations that used to be her flowers, staring out at the wasteland that used to be a forest. The bench had smoothed under her constant presence, worn to a dull sheen by her weight, by the restless shifting of her external spine.

Yesterday, she'd still spoken. Brief observations about the grey sky, clinical descriptions of how the bone coral was growing faster. Today, only silence.

No words for Valdic, who pressed against her side with fierce loyalty. Just stillness, broken only by the soft clicking of her black skeletal spine when she shifted. Sometimes the black veins along her jaw would pulse—a slow rhythmic beat that matched no living heart.

I'd been watching her from the entrance for nearly an hour, not wanting to confirm that my presence didn't register anymore.

The courtyard walls curved around her like a ribcage, and it looked like she was being digested. Consumed by the architecture Quade had built, slowly disappearing into the bone cathedral until there would be nothing left but another formation of bleached coral.

"Maybe I should move your bedroom here," I tried, stepping into the court-yard. My voice echoed off the curved walls, hollow even to my own ears. "Save you the walk every morning."

The witch runes flared at the attempt at humor, burning away whatever small amusement I'd tried to generate. They glowed along my arms, visible through my skin like veins of molten gold.

Renata didn't turn to look at me. Didn't acknowledge the joke or the foot-steps or my presence at all. She just kept staring out at the grey wasteland, her grey-white eyes tracking nothing, her face perfectly still. Her hair—gone completely black from the hollow crown's consumption—hung limp around her shoulders.

Two days ago, before the Ritual, she would have smiled. Would have made some dry observation about me finally accepting that she lived here now. Would have reached for my hand without thinking.

I moved closer and ran my fingers across her cheek. Her skin was cool—not cold like death, but not warm like life either. Something in between. Something transitional. The black veins along her jaw pulsed once under my touch, lazy, like reflex rather than response.

It took her too long to react.

When she finally leaned into my touch, the movement was delayed, auto-matic, like she'd remembered she was supposed to respond this way but had to consciously make her body do it.

My throat tightened.

"Are you alright?" I asked, keeping my hand on her cheek.

"Of course," she replied, her tone flat. Just words shaped by a mouth that had forgotten how to make them mean anything.

"Renata," I breathed, and my voice cracked on her name. "Do you still love me?"

The question came out before I could stop it. Raw. Desperate.

I heard my heartbeat too many times before she answered. One. Two. Three. Four. Five. Six. Seven. Eight.

"I remember loving you," she whispered finally.

Not "I love you." Not "of course I do."

I remember loving you.

Past tense wrapped in present memory. Like love was something that had happened once, recorded perfectly in her mind, but no longer accessible in her heart.

The witch runes blazed so bright they hurt, trying desperately to burn away the devastation flooding through me. But they couldn't touch this. This was watching the woman I loved disappear while her body remained.

This was worse than watching Theron die.

His death had been quick—brutal and immediate, one moment to the next. This was slow. Watching someone drown in increments, watching them slip under the surface breath by breath while I stood on shore unable to pull them back.

"Nokoa, you're crying," Renata observed, her voice still flat. Like she was noting a weather pattern instead of observing my heartbreak.

She reached up and touched my face, her fingers finding the tears. Her touch was gentle but empty, the movement of someone following a script they remembered but no longer understood. Her fingertips came away wet, and she studied the moisture with detached curiosity.

"Yes," I managed. "Yes, I'm crying."

Valdic lowered his head, pressing it against my leg. His purple eyes were impossibly bright, glowing with intensity that shouldn't exist in something so decayed. Through the bond I shared with Renata—muted by Quade's intervention but still present, still aching like a bruise—I felt an echo of what Valdic carried.

Love. Profound, desperate, all-consuming love. Not his, but hers. The emotions that should have been warming her chest, making her heart race, making her lean into my touch with genuine need instead of remembered reflex. All of it stored in the Dirge Wolf who'd bonded himself to her descent.

The feeling hit me like a physical blow.

"She was only herself for a moment," Valdic murmured. "The feeling came—love, recognition, warmth—and then it left. Flowed right out of her and into me before she could hold it long enough to mean anything."

Renata watched this exchange with detached curiosity, her head tilting slightly. The hollow crown fused to her skull caught what little light existed, gleaming dully. Not upset that we were discussing her like she wasn't there. Just mildly interested.

"I'm still here," she stated. No defensiveness, no anger, no hurt. "I can hear you both. I'm sitting right here."

"Are you?" I demanded, and the question came out harsher than I intended. The witch runes flared. "Because the Renata I knew would be devastated right now. Would be fighting this with everything she had. Would feel something about watching me break in front of her."

She considered this for a long moment. "I remember how devastation feels," she said finally. "The weight in your chest. The way breathing becomes difficult." Something flickered across her face—pain, maybe. But then it was gone. "But I cannot access the feeling itself. It exists in Valdic now, not in me. I know what I should be experiencing, but the knowing doesn't create the sensation."

"Do you want to feel it?" I pressed. "Do you wish you could cry with me right now?"

A long pause. Through our muted bond, I felt the echo. Desperate longing. The wish to reach for me, to comfort me. All of it transferred instantly to Valdic.

"I remember wanting things," Renata said slowly. "I remember the shape of desire, the texture of longing. But I cannot tell if I want to feel again, because wanting requires feeling, and I have none left to draw from."

She literally couldn't tell if she wanted to feel again, because the act of wanting was itself an emotion.

I pulled my hand away from her cheek, and she didn't react to the loss of contact. Didn't reach for me or show any sign that my touch had mattered. She just turned back to staring at the wasteland, her spine clicking softly as she adjusted position, her black veins pulsing with lazy rhythm.

No adjustment of her hair behind her ear. No unconscious lean toward where I'd been standing. Just a smooth return to her previous position.

Valdic pressed harder against my leg, and through him I felt what Renata should have been feeling. The grief at pushing me away. The desperate need to pull me back. It hit me in waves, each one stronger than the last.

"I'm sorry," Renata said suddenly, still staring at the grey horizon. "I know I should feel sorry. I remember what guilt tastes like, how it sits in your throat like stones. But the knowing doesn't create the feeling."

"Stop," I choked out. "Stop describing emotions like they're academic concepts. Stop narrating what you should feel while feeling nothing."

She turned to look at me, and in her grey-white eyes I saw something that might have been confusion. "What else can I do?" she asked, and for the first time there was something in her voice—not emotion, but the awareness of its absence. "I'm trying to give you what I remember you need. But the trying is all I have left."

She was performing humanity. And the performance was all that remained.

Valdic whimpered—an actual sound of pain. His purple eyes were impossibly bright now, blazing with intensity that made them look like they might burst. "It's getting heavier," he managed. "Each time she transfers something, each time the emotion leaves her and fills me—it's heavier than the last."

I could see it in the way his skeletal frame trembled. In the way his newly-formed muscles looked strained, stretched too tight over bone. In the way he was panting, his breath coming in short gasps.

"Then stop carrying it," I said, dropping to my knees beside him. I grabbed his face between my hands, forcing his bright purple eyes to meet mine. "Give it back to her. Make her feel this."

"I can't," Valdic replied. "The bond doesn't work that way. It's one direction—her to me. I'm the vessel, not the source."

"The Midnight Oath," Renata stated suddenly, still staring at the wasteland. "That's what comes next. Queen Oriana told me. You die willingly, I feel everything in one moment, and then nothing forever."

She said it like she was reading from a schedule. Like my death was just another appointment, another step in the transformation.

"And you're okay with that?" I asked.

"Okay requires feeling," she said simply. "I am not okay or not okay. I simply am. And the Oath is what must happen next, so it will happen."

"I won't do it," I heard myself say. "I won't die willingly for someone who can't even feel grief at losing me."

Valdic's head snapped up, his purple eyes blazing. "Don't," he warned. "Don't make her fight for something she can't feel."

"Then what?" I demanded, looking between the DirgeWolf carrying Renata's humanity and the hollow queen who'd lost it. "I just accept this? Die so she can feel for one moment before losing it all forever?"

"I don't know," Valdic admitted, and his voice cracked. "I only know that I'm drowning in her feelings and she's drowning in nothing, and both of us are breaking in different ways."

Renata stood, the movement fluid but empty. Graceful in the way a falling leaf is graceful—no intention behind it, just physics.

She walked to where I knelt beside Valdic and placed her hand on my chest, right over my heart. The touch was gentle, precise, positioned exactly where it needed to be to feel my heartbeat.

"I remember what this meant," she said quietly, her voice barely above a whisper but still flat. "Your heart racing when we touched. Mine racing in response. The warmth that came from being close to you. I remember all of it with perfect clarity."

Her grey-white eyes met mine, empty despite the recognition in them.

"But the memory exists in a place I cannot reach anymore," she continued. "Like looking at a beautiful painting through glass—I can see it, can describe every detail, but I cannot step inside."

"Then break the glass," I pleaded, covering her hand with mine. My skin was hot from the witch runes; hers was cool as bone. "Fight for this. Fight to come back."

She looked at me for a long moment. Then something shifted in her expression—not emotion, but awareness. The recognition of something important slipping away.

"I don't remember how to fight," she confessed.

Because the Renata I knew had been a fighter. Had resurrected me against cosmic law, had faced down the Bone Council, had worn a crown that consumed her and seized power anyway.

That Renata was gone.

I pulled her against me, wrapping my arms around her. Her body fit against mine the way it always had. Her external spine pressed against my chest, the clicking softening when she stilled. Her heartbeat was slow, measured, like a clock counting down.

She let me hold her, her body relaxing with practiced ease. But it was empty. Just the ghost of comfort without substance.

Valdic pressed against both of us, and through him I felt what should have been in Renata—the desperate clinging, the need for closeness, the love that had nowhere to go. It poured into me secondhand, burning, aching.

We stayed like that in the bone garden courtyard, surrounded by skeletal coral and grey sky. Three people bound together by bonds breaking in different ways. Me, loving someone who couldn't love me back. Renata, remembering love without feeling it. Valdic, drowning in emotions that belonged to both of us.

The air was still. No wind. No sound except our breathing—mine ragged, Renata's measured, Valdic's strained.

And then I heard them.

Footsteps.

Slow, measured, inevitable. The deliberate pace of something ancient and patient.

Quade's approach had a sound all its own—the scrape of claws on bone, the rustle of decayed wings, the whisper of moss growing in empty eye sockets. I'd learned to recognize it over the past weeks.

The footsteps stopped just outside the courtyard entrance.

I had a choice to make. Die for her transformation and give her one moment of feeling before eternal emptiness. Or refuse, and watch the Midnight Oath backfire the way it had for Oriana—taking what little Renata had left and giving her nothing in return.

Either way, I lost her.

Chapter Nineteen

The Mirror and the First Daughter

I stood in a chamber I'd never seen before, deep in the bone cathedral where even the butterflies hesitated to follow. The walls curved inward like the inside of a skull, smooth bone polished to a sheen that caught what little light existed and multiplied it into something wrong. Too bright. Too sharp. Like staring at the sun through ice. The air tasted metallic, and when I breathed, the inhale echoed strangely, as if the chamber was breathing with me.

Quade had brought me here without explanation. One moment I'd been in the courtyard surrounded by skeletal coral, the next his blackened hand was on my shoulder and the world shifted. Not walking—transitioning.

"I want to show you what you're becoming," he said, his moss-filled eye sockets somehow conveying anticipation despite having no actual eyes. The moss shifted slightly, green tendrils curling like curious fingers.

Valdic pressed against my leg harder than necessary, his purple eyes dim with something that felt like dread through our bond. He'd grown more solid, more present, carrying the weight of emotions I could no longer hold. His breathing came quick and shallow.

"What am I becoming?" I asked, though I thought I already knew.

"See for yourself," Quade offered, gesturing toward the far wall.

It wasn't a wall. It was a mirror—but not made of glass or polished metal. Made of bone so thin it was translucent, stretched across a frame of ribs that still held the curve of whatever chest they'd once protected. The surface rippled like water disturbed by wind, though there was no wind in this sealed chamber.

I moved closer despite Valdic's whimper. The floor was cold beneath my feet, smooth as river stones. Each step echoed with a hollow sound that seemed to come from somewhere deeper than just the chamber floor.

The mirror showed my reflection at first. Me standing in black clothing that hung looser than it should, fabric draped over a frame that had thinned without my noticing. My white hair turned black by the Crown's corruption fell limp past my shoulders, dull as charcoal. My grey-white eyes were empty of anything resembling humanity, the pupils barely visible anymore. The black veins along my jaw pulsed slowly, a rhythm that matched nothing living. My external spine caught the light, each protruding vertebra casting its own small shadow down my back.

I looked like a corpse that had forgotten to stop moving.

Then the reflection changed.

The bone-mirror rippled more violently, and my reflection was replaced by someone else. A woman—or what had been a woman once, before transformation had carved away everything soft and left only edges. She was emaciated, sharp, beautiful in the way that broken things could be beautiful.

Her wings were blades. Not metaphorical—actual blades, dozens of them arranged like feathers, each one sharp enough to catch light and throw it back as threat. They moved slightly as she breathed, clicking against each other with sounds like swords being drawn. Her face was sharp-boned with full lips pressed into a line that suggested smiling was a forgotten skill. Eyes like burning coals—blazing complete red and orange. No warmth in that heat. Just the promise of things being melted down and reforged.

Long red hair fell past her shoulders, and I could see sunflowers woven through the strands—bright yellow against the blood-red, alive against the death she embodied. A sand-filled hourglass floated beside her, suspended by nothing, the grains falling in slow, measured rhythm.

Red hair. Sunflowers. An hourglass.

This was the daughter of decay and hunger. This was—

She looked at me through the mirror, and I knew with absolute certainty that she was seeing me too. Those burning eyes locked onto mine. This wasn't a vision or a memory. This was real-time, across whatever distance separated our worlds.

"Sister," she said, and her voice came through the bone-mirror like it was speaking directly into my skull. Quiet. Absolute. Undeniable. "You'll understand soon."

I opened my mouth to respond, but Quade spoke first.

"The First Daughter," he said, moving to stand beside me. "Lanira. Goddess of Hunger and Decay."

Through the mirror, I saw past Lanira to her world beyond. It was dying. Not dead—dying, which was somehow worse. Fields of crops withered mid-growth, stems bent and brown. Trees stood skeletal against a sky too pale, slowly losing color. And everywhere, scattered like fallen leaves, were bodies. Some fresh. Some so decayed they were barely distinguishable from the earth they rested on.

Crimson moths clustered around her the way butterflies clustered around me. The dead gathered to their goddess, waiting for the hunger that would never be satisfied because hunger was her purpose, not a problem to be solved.

She noticed me looking and smiled. Not warm—just acknowledgment. "They're beautiful, aren't they?" she said. "The dead of hunger. Each one a completion. Each one mine."

"How many?" I asked, my voice flat.

"All of them," she said simply. "Every person who ever starved in my world. Every child who wasted from lack. Every mother who gave her portion away and faded." She paused, her red eyes tracking across my face. "How many have you collected?"

I thought about the butterflies. Hundreds now, maybe thousands, following me through the bone cathedral like a living shroud. Each one a death I'd witnessed or caused. Each one mine in a way I couldn't quite define but understood completely. "Not as many as you," I admitted. "But growing."

"Good," she said. "The gathering is important. They need to know you're there. Need to understand that silence isn't just absence but active force. That forgetting has an architect."

Valdic growled—low, warning. Through our bond I felt what he was feeling: horror at Lanira, at what she represented, at understanding that this was my future.

"Easy, wolf," Lanira said, her red eyes finding Valdic. "You're her anchor. Her emotional vessel. Not a fighter."

"You had one?" I asked.

"Have," she corrected, and something flickered across her face. Not quite emotion, but the memory of emotion. "They all do, tailored to what we need." She glanced at Valdic with something that might have been recognition. "Keep yours close. He may not live through what comes next."

Valdic's growl intensified. Through our bond I felt his terror spike—sharp and bright and choking. Not for himself. For me, having to lose the last anchor to anything resembling feeling.

"Valdic will survive," Quade interjected smoothly. "He was created for this purpose. He'll endure."

"How much more can you hold?" I asked Valdic directly.

"As much as you need me to," he replied, his voice strained but steady. "That's what I'm for."

"Why are you showing me this?" I asked Quade, turning away from the mirror. "What's the purpose?"

"Understanding," he said. "You're not the first. Won't be the last. You will survive as she did." He moved closer, his decayed wings rustling softly. "The Sisters of Creation move without pause, without balance, without ending. Growth without limitation. Creation without completion. It consumes itself, Renata. Becomes a tumor that spreads until there's nothing left but endless beginning with no middle or end."

Lanira spoke through the mirror, her voice carrying the weight of experience. "He's right. I've seen worlds where creation ran unchecked. They don't thrive—they choke. Too much life competing for too little space. It's not mercy. It's torture."

"So we're mercy?" I asked. "We're the silence that prevents endless noise?"

"Exactly," Quade confirmed.

"The emptiness is mercy," Lanira said. "You'll understand when you're done losing things. When the last piece of humanity drops away and all that remains is purpose. No hesitation. No regret."

"Does it hurt?" I asked her. "The emptiness?"

She considered this, her red eyes dimming slightly. "Yes."

She moved closer to her side of the mirror, and for a moment we were face to face. Her burning red eyes meeting my grey-white emptiness. Her gathered dead mirroring my butterfly shroud.

"How does it feel?" she asked. "To not hold the true weight of your choices?"

"I don't know," I admitted. "I can't feel it. I just observe it all happening. The world getting quieter around me. People's voices fading. Meaning disappearing. Even my own thoughts becoming less loud."

"How does hunger feel?" I asked in return.

"Unending," she said, and I heard something that might have been wistfulness if she could still access wistfulness. "Desperate. All-encompassing."

Two hollowed-out vessels staring at each other across whatever distance separated our worlds. Two daughters of transition, each carrying our own brand of ending. Each empty in our own way.

"We're not mistakes, sister," she said, her red eyes finding mine with absolute certainty. The sunflowers in her hair blazed like small suns. "We're what the universe needs to keep from choking on its own creation. That has to count for something."

"Does it?" I asked. "Does purpose matter if we can't feel purposeful?"

"It has to," she said simply. "Because it's all that remains."

The mirror rippled violently, and her image began to fade. Before she disappeared completely, she raised one hand—just pale skin and long fingers—in what might have been farewell or acknowledgment or warning. "See you on the other side, sister. When you're done becoming."

Then she was gone, and I was staring at my own reflection again. Grey-white eyes. Black hair. The gathering of butterflies visible behind me like a shroud made of death and light.

I looked like I was halfway between human and whatever Lanira had become. Transitional. In-progress.

"You're not her," Valdic said quietly. "You're different. Quieter. You won't become hunger and decay."

"No," I agreed. "I'll become silence and butterflies and forgetting. Different manifestation, same category of being."

"That's not comforting," Valdic muttered.

"I know," I replied. "But it's honest."

Quade stepped back. "To become silence, you must silence everything in yourself first," he said. "Every piece of humanity carved away. Every emotion transferred or burned away. Every connection loosened until only memory remains."

"Why does becoming divine require losing everything human?"

"Because gods don't hesitate," Quade explained. "If you still felt love, you'd refuse to end things that needed ending. If you still felt fear, you'd hold back from necessary silence. Completion is what keeps everything from consuming itself."

I turned away from the mirror, from my own halfway-transformed reflection. Valdic moved with me, his body warm against my leg. His purple eyes were dim with the weight of carrying my reaction to all of this.

"How much more?" I asked. "How much more do I have to lose before I'm empty enough to ascend?"

"Not much," Quade said, and I heard something almost like sympathy in his voice. "You're nearly there, daughter. Just a few more pieces need to fall away."

Valdic whimpered, a sound of pure pain. Through our bond I felt him knowing that I would lose Nokoa, lose the memory of what it felt like to care, lose everyone until only the facts of love remained without any of its substance.

"I'm sorry," I said to him, and meant it in whatever way meaning was still possible without feeling.

"Then be quick," Valdic said, his voice carrying that dark humor that felt increasingly strained at the edges. "If you're going to become this thing, become it fast. Don't drag it out."

"I can't control the pace," I said. "It happens when it happens."

"Then it better happen soon," Valdic said, his purple eyes blazing brighter, "because I can feel how much more is coming. How many more people you'll lose. How much more weight I'll have to hold. And I don't know if I can survive it all and still be me when it's done."

Even hollowed out, even emptied, I recognized that losing Valdic—not to death but to transformation, to him becoming just another vessel without personality—would be the final ending. The completion of my isolation.

"You'll survive," I said.

"Promise?" Valdic asked, and I heard the plea underneath his usual sarcasm.

"I promise," I said, lying with perfect conviction.

Chapter Twenty

Mother's First Plea

Renata

I sat alone in my chambers, the space carved from bone that Quade had designated as mine. The walls curved inward like a ribcage, pale and smooth. The bed frame was made of vertebrae arranged in patterns that should have been beautiful but just looked skeletal.

The butterflies had followed me inside, clustering on the walls and ceiling like living wallpaper. Their wings clicked softly against each other, creating a sound like distant rain.

Valdic lay at my feet, his massive body taking up most of the floor space. His patchy fur rose and fell with labored breathing. His purple eyes were dim, exhausted from carrying the weight of my reaction to seeing Lanira. Through our bond I felt him trying to process what I couldn't feel—the horror, the resignation, the terrible understanding that my transformation was inevitable and he would either survive it or shatter trying.

The hollow crown pulsed against my skull. It had been quiet since the Ritual of Feeling—no voices offering observations or criticisms. Just presence. Weight.

But now something stirred inside the Crown. Not the usual clinical voice of Queen Oriana or the violent urgings of King Aldric. Something that had been silent since the moment I'd absorbed her.

Renata.

My mother's voice.

I went completely still. Sera. Trapped in the Crown since I'd lost her as a child. Silent while I'd become this hollow thing. Silent while I'd forgotten how to feel.

Until now.

Renata, my daughter, please. I need you to listen.

Her voice was warm. Maternal. Desperate in a way I remembered maternity being desperate. The sound wrapped around my thoughts like an embrace I couldn't feel.

"Mother," I said aloud, my voice flat despite the significance of the moment. "You're speaking."

I've been silent because the other crown voices pushed me down. Since Lyanna has gone, there is finally room for me. Sera's voice cracked. I had hoped from the darkness that maybe you'd find your way back to yourself. But I see now what you're becoming.

"Then you know it's inevitable," I said.

I know Quade wants you to believe it's inevitable, Sera corrected. I know he's been manipulating circumstances since before you put on the Crown. I know Oriana has been helping him, guiding you toward this transformation.

I heard Queen Oriana then—cool, measured. Sera, this is pointless. She's already past saving.

She's my daughter, Sera shot back with heat I'd never heard from her before. I don't care if it's pointless. I have to try.

You're just adding noise, Oriana said.

And you're adding poison, Sera accused. You've been guiding her toward this since the beginning. Since Quade first approached you with his design. You've been his instrument inside the Crown, pushing every hollow ruler toward completion.

I processed this with interest but no emotional investment. "Is that true?" I asked Oriana directly. "Have you been working with Quade?"

A pause. Yes, Oriana said finally. I made a bargain with him centuries ago. He promised me something I wanted. I promised him cooperation in guiding hollow rulers toward completion.

"And suppressing my mother," I said. "Keeping her silent so she couldn't interfere."

Yes, Oriana confirmed. We wanted to protect you. From hope that would only make the transformation harder. From a mother's love that would have made you fight when fighting only prolongs the suffering.

I sat with that for a moment. The butterflies clicked on the walls. Valdic breathed heavily at my feet.

"I understand," I said.

That's all you have to say? Sera whispered.

"That's all there is to say," I replied. "You were suppressed. Now you're not. Nothing about my situation has changed."

The Crown went quiet. Outside, somewhere in the cathedral, I could hear the distant scrape of Quade's wings against bone.

Chapter Twenty-One

Cressa's Plea

Renata

Cressa found me in the bone garden courtyard the next morning, standing among the skeletal coral formations that used to be my flowers. The butterflies had multiplied overnight—thousands of them now, covering every surface. Blue and purple and pink and green-gold. The gathering of the dead, growing denser with each passing hour.

I heard her footsteps before I saw her. Hesitant but determined. The pattern of someone who'd made a decision and was forcing themselves to follow through.

"Renata," she said, and I turned to face her.

She looked worse than yesterday. Red-rimmed eyes from crying, skin pale from lack of sleep, dark circles making her look older, fragile. But there was something else in her expression too—resolution, maybe, or desperation dressed up as purpose.

"Cressa," I said, my voice flat. "Did you need something?"

"Yes," she replied, moving closer through the butterflies. "I need a day with you. One full day. Like we used to spend together before all of this."

I processed the request with clinical detachment. A day together served no functional purpose. Wouldn't change the trajectory of my transformation.

But I remembered—with perfect clarity—that friendship used to mean giving people what they needed even when it wasn't practical.

"Alright," I said. "What did you want to do?"

Relief flashed across Cressa's face, followed immediately by grief. "I want to visit places we used to go," she explained. "The practice hall where you and I trained. The orchards where—" her voice caught, "—where Theron used to meet me. The cliff where all three of us jumped into the river. I want to remember with you."

The mention of Theron's name in that context made me pause. I'd known Cressa had cared for my brother, but the way her voice broke on his name suggested something deeper. Something I'd perhaps been too focused on my own grief to fully notice before.

"You loved him," I said. Not a question—an observation, stated with the clinical precision that had replaced all my other tones.

Cressa's eyes filled with tears. "Yes," she admitted, the word barely a whisper. "I loved Theron. We'd been—we were planning to tell you. Planning to ask for your blessing. But then the Bone Council and Alaira—" She stopped, swallowing hard. "They murdered him before we had the chance."

I processed this new information with interest but no emotional response. My brother and my best friend had been in love. Had planned a future together. Had lost that future when Praxis and Alaira forced Theron to bond with the Hollow Crown and his body couldn't withstand the connection. He'd burned from the inside out, consumed by power meant for me.

I should have felt something about this revelation. Happiness that they'd found each other. Grief at what they'd lost. Rage at what had been stolen from them. But I felt nothing except the distant recognition that emotional response would have been appropriate here.

"I remember what it was like to grieve him," I said, offering what I could. "The way the loss felt like a hole in my chest. The way I couldn't breathe properly for weeks after. The desperate need to undo what couldn't be undone. I remember all of it."

"But you don't feel it now," Cressa said, and it wasn't quite a question.

"No," I confirmed. "The feeling exists in Valdic. I just have the memory of having felt it. But I understand why you want to visit those places. Why you need to remember him with someone who knew him. I'll come with you."

Fresh tears spilled down Cressa's cheeks. "Thank you," she said, and I heard the desperation in her voice. Not just gratitude—the raw need of someone grasping at anything that might help, might ease the pain, might make the grief bearable for one more day.

"Lead the way," I said.

Valdic materialized from behind one of the coral formations, his massive body moving with careful heaviness. His purple eyes were dim, exhausted from last night's conversation with my mother. Through our bond I felt him understanding what Cressa was trying to do.

"I'm coming too," he announced, pressing against my leg.

"Of course," Cressa said, though I saw her flinch at how large Valdic had become. At the physical manifestation of emotional weight made solid.

We left the courtyard together, moving through the bone cathedral's corridors. The butterflies followed—hundreds at least, creating a living shroud that moved when I moved.

The practice hall was first. Or what remained of it.

The structure had been stone once, solid and permanent. Now it was partially collapsed, bone growing through the cracks like infection. The windows were shattered, ash coating everything in fine grey powder.

But the basic shape was still there. Still recognizable as the place where Cressa and I had trained for years.

"Do you remember?" Cressa asked, moving to stand in the center of the room where the practice mat used to be. Her feet left prints in the ash. "We were twelve. You kept insisting you could beat me if we just went one more round."

"I remember," I said, and the memory came with photographic precision. Every detail sharp and clear. "You won seventeen matches in a row. I won once because you slipped on a patch of sweat. I claimed victory anyway. You let me have it."

"You were so proud," Cressa said, and I saw tears starting in her eyes again. "You smiled so wide I thought your face might break. You ran to tell Theron immediately, didn't even wait to wash the blood off your split lip." Her voice caught on his name. "He laughed and picked you up and spun you around. Told you he always knew you'd beat me eventually."

I didn't remember that part—the aftermath, Theron's reaction. But hearing it now, I could picture it perfectly. My brother's face, younger then, still full of life and humor. The way he would have grinned, proud of me for winning even a single match against Cressa's superior skill.

"He was here often," I said, understanding dawning even through the emptiness. "Watching you train. Watching you."

Cressa nodded, wiping at her eyes. "He'd make excuses. Said he wanted to ensure his sister wasn't being too hard on you during practice. But really—" She smiled despite the tears, the expression sad and sweet at once. "Really he just wanted to be near me. We'd talk after, once you'd gone to wash up. Started as friendship. Became something more."

"I remember the pride," I said clinically, returning to the original memory. "The way my chest felt warm and tight at the same time. The desperate need to share the victory with someone who would appreciate it. I remember every detail of what that felt like."

"But you don't feel it now," Cressa said.

"No," I confirmed. "The feeling exists in Valdic. I just have the memory of having felt it."

Cressa moved closer, taking my hands in hers. Her palms were warm, callused from her work. I felt the physical sensation—pressure, temperature—but nothing emotional.

"Try," she pleaded desperately. "Just try to feel something. Remember what it was like to be happy here. To laugh with me. To be human."

I tried. Not because I thought it would work, but because she was asking.

I reached for the memory of happiness, attempted to access whatever mechanism used to translate memory into feeling. But there was nothing there. Just empty space where the connection used to be.

"I'm trying," I said. "But the pathway doesn't exist anymore. Memory and emotion are separated."

Valdic whimpered from the doorway, feeling what I should feel—the desperate frustration, the grief. His breathing came faster, struggling under the weight.

"Keep trying," Cressa insisted, squeezing my hands harder. "Don't give up. You're still in there somewhere. The real you. The Renata who laughed and cried and loved."

"She is," I said gently, wanting to spare Cressa the pain of false hope. "I remember being her. Can describe her in perfect detail. But I'm not her anymore. I'm what came after."

Cressa released my hands and stepped back, her face crumbling. "This was our place," she said. "Where Theron watched us and fell in love with the healer who kept putting his sister back together. It should mean something to you."

"It means something intellectually," I said. "But the feeling itself is gone."

"Then we'll try somewhere else," Cressa said, not giving up. "Come on."

The orchard ruins were next.

We walked through the dead forest—skeletal trees, ash covering everything, no sound except our footsteps and clicking butterfly wings. The orchards had been beautiful once. Rows and rows of fruit trees, carefully tended. I remembered walking here with Cressa during spring, when the blossoms made the air smell sweet.

Now it was bone and ash like everything else.

Cressa moved to where an old stone bench sat beneath what used to be the largest apple tree. The bench was still intact—grey with ash but structurally sound.

"Sit with me," she said.

I sat. The stone was cold beneath me. Valdic pressed against my legs, his warmth the only thing that felt real.

"This was Theron's favorite place," Cressa said, staring out at the dead orchard. Her voice was soft, reverent. "He said the apple blossoms reminded him of snow, except warm. Except alive." She touched the bench with gentle fingers, like it was something precious. "He asked me to marry him here. Two weeks before—before they killed him."

I processed this information with clinical interest. My brother had proposed to my best friend in this very spot. Had planned a future that would have joined our families even more closely. Had died before that future could begin.

"What did you say?" I asked.

"Yes," Cressa whispered, fresh tears falling. "I said yes. We were going to tell you together. But then the Council called him in. Told him the Crown needed a wearer. Alaira was there—she helped them. Helped force the bond, knowing it would kill him."

"I saw how he died," I said. "Quade showed me the memory. What Praxis and Alaira did to him."

Cressa's breath hitched. "Then you know. They murdered him. Deliberately. They knew the Crown wanted you. Knew anyone else would burn. But they tried anyway, and Theron—" Her voice broke. "Theron died screaming, and I couldn't save him. I'm a healer, and I couldn't save the man I loved."

I reached out and took her hand. "You couldn't have saved him," I said with clinical certainty. "The Crown was consuming him from the inside. No amount of healing could counter that."

"Then whose failure was it?" Cressa demanded. "Praxis's? Alaira's? The Crown's? Yours, for being the one it actually wanted?"

The accusation hung in the air. Not quite blame, but grief looking for somewhere to land.

"All of ours," I said simply. "Praxis and Alaira for forcing the bond. The Crown for being what it is. Me for being chosen by it. Theron for agreeing to try when he should have refused. We're all responsible for the tragedy."

Cressa made a sound that was half laugh, half sob. "You're so rational about it. So calm. Theron was your brother, Renata."

Through our bond, I felt Valdic drowning in grief. My love for Theron, my rage at his murder, my guilt. All of it flooding through him while I remained empty.

He whimpered—a thin, broken sound. His body sagged, legs trembling.

"I know you're carrying all of it," I said to Valdic, acknowledging what I couldn't feel. "And I know it's too much. But I don't know how to stop this anymore."

Cressa grabbed my face with both hands, forcing me to look at her. "Listen to me. You still have a choice. You can refuse the Midnight Oath. Let the Crown break. Die human. Theron didn't get that choice—they murdered him. But you still have it."

"If I die, Nokoa dies," I reminded her. "The bond ensures it."

"I know," Cressa said, her voice steady despite the tears. "And maybe dying together is better than you existing for eternity without him. Theron died before we could have our life together. It destroyed me. But at least I got to grieve him as himself. If you complete the transformation, Nokoa won't even get that. He'll watch you become something that can't love him back. That's worse than death."

"I can't choose death. Not because I feel strongly about living, but because choosing requires caring about the outcome, and I don't care."

"Then let me choose for you," Cressa begged. "For Theron's sake, if not your own. He died so you could live—really live, not this hollow existence."

"Theron is dead," I said flatly. "What I become won't change that."

Cressa released my face and stepped back. "You're already gone," she whispered. "The Renata who loved her brother enough to grieve properly—she's already gone."

"Yes," I confirmed. "She is."

We sat in silence after that, on the stone bench under the dead apple tree where my brother had proposed to my best friend. The butterflies settled on the skeletal branches above us, their wings creating soft clicking sounds.

"One more place," Cressa said finally, standing. "The cliff."

The cliff was at the edge of the forest, where dead trees gave way to sheer rock face that dropped into what used to be a river. The water was gone now—just an empty stone channel at the bottom, bone-dry and grey.

We used to jump from here during summer. The three of us—me and Cressa and Theron—taking running leaps off the edge and plunging into cold water deep enough that you couldn't touch bottom.

The memory was so clear I could almost feel the water closing over my head, the shock of cold.

Almost.

"Do you remember?" Cressa asked, standing at the cliff's edge and looking down at the empty riverbed. The wind here was stronger, pulling at her clothes, her hair.

"I remember," I said. "Every jump. Every summer. Every moment of feeling infinite and free."

"Theron always went first," Cressa said, her voice distant with memory. "To prove it was safe. To show us that fear was just fear and couldn't actually hurt us if we pushed through it." She smiled through her tears. "Then he'd tread water and shout up at me—not you, always me—telling me I was taking too long. Daring me to jump. Sometimes I think he loved me even then, before either of us knew what it meant."

"You always went second," I added. "Because you couldn't resist his dares. Couldn't stand the thought of him thinking you were afraid."

"And you always went last," Cressa finished, turning to face me. "Because someone had to be sensible. Someone had to make sure neither of us cracked our heads open on rocks we couldn't see beneath the surface." She paused, studying my face. "You were always protecting us, even then."

Cressa stepped closer to the edge—close enough that one more step would send her falling. My external spine clicked nervously, some instinct recognizing the danger.

"What would you do if I jumped now?" she asked. "Would you feel any-thing?"

"I would remember that I should feel alarmed," I said honestly. "Would rec-ognize that your death would be significant. But the actual fear, the panic—that exists in Valdic, not in me."

Valdic growled—low, warning, pressed hard against my leg. Through our bond I felt him experiencing the terror I couldn't access.

"I'm not going to jump," Cressa assured. "I'm just trying to understand if there's anything left inside you that still cares."

She stepped away from the edge, and through Valdic I felt relief so profound it nearly knocked me over. His legs trembled, nearly buckling.

"I forgive you," Cressa said suddenly. "For what you're about to do. For becoming this. I forgive you." She paused. "And I forgive myself. For not being able to save Theron. For not being able to save you."

"I remember why that should matter," I said. "I remember that forgiveness used to feel like grace. I remember loving you enough that your forgiveness would have meant everything."

"But now it's just words," Cressa said.

"Now it's just words," I agreed.

We walked back toward the bone cathedral in silence, Valdic between us, butterflies following. The sun was setting, the light fading from dim to dimmer.

When we reached the courtyard, Cressa stopped and turned to face me one final time. "Tomorrow," she said. "The Crown will demand another absorption. I can feel it. The way you're becoming more translucent, more ghost-like. The way the butterflies are gathering thicker. It's coming."

"I know," I said, because I felt it too. The hollow crown pulsing against my skull, hungry for more space, more power, more souls to fuel my transformation.

"Will you fight it?" Cressa asked. "When the absorption starts—will you try to stop it?"

"I'll try," I said, though the promise felt empty. How did you try when trying required caring about the outcome?

But even as I said it, I meant it. Not with feeling, but with something deeper—with whatever part of me still made choices. I would try. Not because I cared, but because she was asking. Because she'd loved my brother. Because somewhere in the logic that governed me now, that seemed like the right thing to do.

Cressa pulled me into a hug then—sudden, fierce, holding on like she was trying to physically keep me tethered to humanity. Her face pressed against my shoulder, her whole body shaking with sobs.

I stood there and let her hold me, my arms coming up automatically. But I felt nothing from the contact except physical sensations—pressure, warmth, the dampness of her tears.

"I love you," Cressa said against my shoulder. "I love you and I'm losing you and there's nothing I can do to stop it. Just like I couldn't stop them from killing Theron."

"I remember loving you," I said. "I remember that you matter. I remember loving Theron and knowing how much you meant to each other. I remember all of it."

"Remember that I loved you," Cressa said, pulling back to look at me. Her face was streaked with tears, but her gaze was steady. "When you're fully transformed and I'm just another memory—remember that I loved you. That I tried. And remember that Theron loved you too. That he would have wanted you to live, not just exist."

"I'll remember," I promised. "With perfect clarity. Forever. Every word of this conversation. Everything about Theron and what he meant to both of us. All of it preserved, even if the feeling is gone."

"Is that enough?" Cressa asked.

"It has to be," I said. "Because it's all that remains."

Cressa nodded, accepting what couldn't be changed. She stepped back, forcing herself to release me despite every instinct telling her to hold on.

"Tomorrow then," she said. "Whatever comes tomorrow. At least we had today."

"At least we had today," I agreed.

She left without looking back, her footsteps echoing through the courtyard, disappearing into the bone cathedral.

We sat in the courtyard as darkness fell, me on my bone bench, Valdic at my feet, butterflies covering every surface.

Chapter Twenty-Two

Consuming Another

Renata

We are wasting time. It's time we move forward again, Queen Oriana demanded, her voice cutting through my thoughts with clinical precision. The transformation requires more space. More power. Another absorption.

I sat in the throne room, surrounded by the skeletal architecture that had become my entire world. The bone pillars rose around me like giant ribs, pale and gleaming dully in sourceless light. The throne itself—that monstrosity of fused bone and trapped souls—pulsed behind me with a heartbeat that wasn't mine but felt connected to me anyway.

You've delayed long enough, Oriana continued. Another soul consumed. Another step toward what you must become.

From the Crown, I felt Sera stir. My mother's presence had been quiet since yesterday, silent after her failed plea. But now she was alert, understanding what Oriana was demanding.

No, Sera said, her voice sharp with maternal fear. Not yet. Give her more time.

Time changes nothing, Oriana interrupted. She's already hollowed. We've identified who's next.

I knew who it was before either of them said the name.

"Cressa," I said aloud, and my voice was flat despite the significance.

Yes, Oriana confirmed. The healer. Your oldest friend. She spoke to Quade and offered herself willingly. She said you had nothing left inside to hope for.

The butterflies had followed me here from the courtyard, clustering thicker than they'd been yesterday. Blue and purple and pink and green-gold. Their wings created a constant whisper, like thousands of tiny voices.

Please, Sera begged. Take me instead. Absorb me fully. Let me fuel this if someone must.

You're already absorbed, Oriana stated with cold logic. Already inside the Crown. Your consciousness provides guidance, not power. It's not the same thing.

Then release me, Sera pleaded. Pull me out like you pulled out Lyanna. Let me manifest and be consumed properly. Let my death spare hers.

That's not how this works, Oriana said.

Through the Crown, I felt my mother's devastation. Her understanding that she couldn't protect me from this. Couldn't save Cressa. Couldn't do anything except witness another person I loved being unmade.

The throne room doors opened—carved bone sliding against bone with a grinding sound that scraped like something being forced against its nature. Priestess Alaira entered first, moving carefully, warily. Behind her came Cressa.

My oldest friend. The person who'd stayed beside me through the Crown's corruption, who'd spent yesterday trying desperately to reach through my hollowing and pull me back to humanity.

She moved slowly, each step deliberate, her healer's robes rustling softly against the bone floor. Her hands trembled, fingers curling and uncurling at her sides. Her face was pale, eyes red from crying, but her expression held resolution. She'd made her choice.

Through Valdic—pressed against my leg as always—I felt what I should be feeling. Horror at seeing her brought here. Desperate need to refuse what was coming. Love and grief and terror all tangled together. His body went rigid, trembling.

Fight it, Sera urged desperately. Renata, when the absorption starts—fight it. Like you fought Lyanna's. Refuse the Crown. Prove you still have will.

She won't fight, Oriana said with certainty. She's too far gone.

I didn't know which of them was right. Wouldn't know until the moment came and I either fought or didn't.

It took Cressa too long to cross the throne room. Each step seemed to cost her something, like her body was resisting even though her mind had made the choice. Her breathing was audible in the quiet, quick and shallow.

When she finally stood in front of me, close enough to touch, I saw tears threatening to spill from her eyes. She raised one hand slowly toward my face and ran her palm across my cheek. The touch was gentle despite the trembling, tender despite the fear.

I felt the physical sensation of it—the warmth, the pressure, the slight calluses from years of mixing medicines and grinding herbs.

But nothing else.

"Remember that I loved you," Cressa said, her voice breaking on the words. Past tense. Like she was already dead, already a memory. She was saying goodbye.

Stop this, Sera commanded. Renata, refuse. Push back. Don't let the Crown take her.

I opened my mouth to respond. But before I could form words, I felt it.

The hollow crown stirred.

It pulsed against my skull, growing hot, almost burning. The voices inside went silent—even Oriana stopped speaking, like they were all holding their breath. The trapped souls shifted, pressing against the boundaries of their prison, churning, hungry.

And then the Crown began to pull.

Invisible threads extending from the circlet toward Cressa. Cold, sharp, cutting through the air between us. They wrapped around her spirit, her essence, whatever made Cressa herself instead of just a body. Her healing light—that gentle green-gold power she'd cultivated through years of study and practice—flared bright, pushing back against the bone magic.

She hadn't even been allowed to finish her final goodbye.

Cressa gasped, her hand falling away from my cheek. Her eyes went wide with the understanding that this was really happening, that there was no stopping it, that she was about to be unmade.

No! Sera screamed. Not her! Stop it!

And something in me—some part deeper than the hollowing, older than the transformation—responded.

I didn't want this.

The thought came with surprising clarity, cutting through the emptiness like a blade. Not intellectually. Not as observation. Something that felt almost like horror. Almost like grief. Almost like rage.

I had promised to try. And promises still mattered, even without feeling. Especially without feeling—because logic said keeping your word was what separated conscious choice from blind function.

I fought the Crown.

Not with hesitation. Not with half-measures. I threw everything I had left at it—every scrap of will, every fragment of humanity, every piece of myself that hadn't yet been carved away. I grabbed at the invisible threads pulling Cressa toward consumption and yanked, trying to sever them, to redirect them anywhere else.

The effort felt like tearing something inside myself. My hands came up without conscious thought, clawing at the hollow crown fused to my skull. Blood welled where my nails scraped bone.

No, I snarled internally. You don't get her. Not her. Not like this. I won't allow it.

The pulling stopped.

Not gradually. Not with negotiation. The Crown's hunger simply ceased, the threads dissolving like smoke, the cold receding so fast I nearly fell forward from the lack of resistance.

Cressa took a gasping breath, stumbling backward, her healing light still flickering around her. Her hands clutched at her throat, her chest, checking to make sure she was still whole.

Yes! Sera cried out, triumph and relief flooding through her voice. Yes! Keep fighting! You can stop this! You still have will!

Hope blazed across Cressa's face, bright and desperate and beautiful.

But Oriana's voice cut through the moment, cold as winter.

The Crown is older than your will, she said. Stronger than your resistance. What you're feeling is an echo. A final flicker before the flame goes out. This changes nothing.

And I felt it—the Crown gathering itself. Not pulling yet, but preparing to. Building pressure like water behind a dam. My resistance had surprised it, had thrown it off balance for a moment. But the Crown was ancient, built with specific purpose, fueled by centuries of consumed souls. My will was just one mortal woman's defiance against something designed to be irresistible.

You cannot hold this forever, Oriana continued, pressing against my awareness like a hand over my mouth. Let go. Accept what must be.

I pushed back harder, throwing more of myself at maintaining the barrier I'd created. Sweat broke out along my hairline. The bone floor beneath me cracked from the pressure of opposing forces—my will versus the Crown's hunger, human choice versus divine transformation.

"Renata," Cressa breathed, and there were so many things in that one word. Hope. Fear. Love. "You're fighting it. You're actually—"

The Crown surged.

Not gradually this time. It slammed against my defenses like a battering ram, and I felt something crack under the impact. Not physically—deeper. Will breaking, consciousness fracturing, the part of me that had been holding the line shattering under pressure it wasn't built to withstand.

I screamed—actually screamed, the sound torn from my throat without permission. My hands came to my head, pressing against my temples as if I could hold my skull together through sheer force. The hollow crown burned against my skin, hot enough that I smelled burning.

The threads shot out again—not cold this time but burning hot, angry, demanding. They wrapped around Cressa with twice the force as before, yanking her toward consumption so violently she cried out. Her feet left the ground, her body pulled forward, arms reaching toward me in desperate plea.

I tried to hold them back. But my will, however fierce, was finite. The Crown's hunger was not.

Please, I begged, the word more desperate than anything I'd said in weeks. Please don't make me do this.

My resistance shattered like glass.

The threads yanked Cressa forward, and her healing light fractured, broke, scattered like mirrors catching sun. The sound was terrible—like crystal being ground to powder, like something precious being destroyed. She opened her mouth—to scream, to speak, to do something—but no sound came out.

The silencing had already started.

Cressa's form began to dissolve.

Not gradually like Lyanna had. She burst into hundreds of iridescent wings and white powder, violent and sudden and final. One moment she was standing there with terror in her eyes, the next she was exploding into butterflies and bone dust that filled the throne room like a violent snow.

The butterflies that formed from her essence were different—greener, touched with gold, carrying traces of her healing magic even in death. They swarmed toward me in a green-gold cloud, pouring into my mouth before I could close it, before I could turn away.

I tried. Tried to keep my mouth shut, tried to turn my head, tried to reject them one final time. But the butterflies didn't care about my resistance. They forced their way in, dissolving on my tongue, releasing memories and emotions and the accumulated experience of a life cut short.

They tasted like herbs and honey and all the medicines she'd mixed. Like spring water and healing salves. Like everything Cressa had been, compressed into flavor that bypassed my defenses and settled directly into memory.

I tasted her childhood—running through palace gardens with me and Theron, laughing at nothing, feeling invincible. I tasted the first time she'd successfully healed a wound, the pride that had flooded through her. I tasted her love for me. Decades of friendship compressed into seconds, every moment she'd valued our connection. All of it pouring into me like water into a vessel with no bottom.

She loved you so much, Sera sobbed. Can you feel it? Can you feel how much she loved you?

But I felt nothing.

The memories came with perfect clarity, storing themselves in my mind with the same precision as my own recollections. I would remember every detail of Cressa's life, every moment of her love. But the grief at losing her, the guilt at consuming her—none of it came.

Through Valdic, I felt it all instead.

The DirgeWolf collapsed, hitting the bone floor with a sound like breaking pottery. The air was forced from his lungs, a whimper rising from deep in his chest that grew and grew until it became something else entirely. His purple eyes blazed so bright they cast shadows across the throne room.

He howled in agony.

The sound was inhuman, primal, a vocalization of pain that no language could capture. It echoed through the throne room, through the cathedral, probably through the entire bone court.

My grief. My loss. My love for Cressa, all of it flowing into Valdic.

This is wrong, Sera said, her voice hollow. You're watching your friend die and you feel nothing. What have you become?

She's become what she needed to become, Oriana said. Nearly hollowed now. Only a few more steps until completion.

Valdic howled like his heart was breaking, because mine was breaking and he carried that breaking for me.

I stood from the throne and moved toward him, butterflies scattering from my movement. He was curled on his side, his body shaking violently. The purple glow of his eyes was so bright it hurt to look at directly. Through our bond I felt what he felt—not just the grief, but the weight of it. The way it pressed down on him like physical mass.

"I'm sorry," I said, kneeling beside him. The bone floor was hard and cold beneath my knees. "I'm sorry you have to carry this."

"Don't," Valdic choked out between whimpers. "Don't apologize. I'm here willingly. I'll stay."

Nokoa appeared in the doorway, his golden eyes wide with horror. The witch runes carved into his bones blazed bright enough to see through his clothing. He looked at me kneeling beside Valdic, at the butterflies still drifting through the air, at the bone dust that was all that remained of Cressa settling onto the throne room floor like ash.

"You killed her," he said, and his voice was empty. Not accusatory. Not angry. Just stating fact.

The words were true.

Valdic's howling had subsided to whimpers. Worse, somehow. Less dramatic, more broken. Like something inside him had shattered and these were the sounds the pieces made scraping against each other.

Nokoa moved closer and knelt on Valdic's other side, his hand finding the DirgeWolf's shaking form.

"We can't keep doing this," Nokoa said quietly, looking at me across Valdic's body. "Watching you consume the people we love while feeling nothing about it."

"I know," I said. "But sustainability isn't required. Only completion."

"It matters now," Nokoa insisted. "Cressa is dead. Valdic is drowning. You're hollow. It matters."

"To you," I corrected. "It matters to you, because you can still feel. To me it's just information."

I saw something break behind Nokoa's eyes. Some last thread of hope snapping.

The butterflies that had been Cressa settled onto my hair, my shoulders, joining the others. Green-touched wings among the blues and purples and pinks. Her essence absorbed, her life consumed, her love for me stored in perfect memory without any of the warmth that had made it real.

"I remember loving her," I said quietly, looking at the bone dust that was all that remained. "I remember every moment of our friendship with perfect clarity. I remember why she mattered."

Valdic finally stopped shaking, his breathing evening out. But his purple eyes remained impossibly bright.

I had fought.

I had lost.

And Cressa was dead anyway.

Just the empty certainty that this was what came next.

Chapter Twenty-Three

AFTER CRESSA

Nokoa

The bone dust from Cressa's death was still settling when I found Renata standing in the exact spot where it had happened. She stood perfectly still. Not the stillness of meditation or thought, but the empty stillness of something that had forgotten it could move. The butterflies covered her so completely that from certain angles she looked more like a sculpture made of wings than a person. Blue and purple and pink and green-gold—thousands of them now, clustering so thick I could barely see the grey-white of her eyes beneath.

I made myself move forward across the bone floor toward her. Each step felt heavier than the last. The floor was still powdered with Cressa's remains, fine white dust that rose in small clouds with each footfall.

"What did you lose this time?" I asked, keeping my voice as gentle as I could manage.

Renata turned slightly at the sound of my voice, her grey-white eyes tracking toward me without really seeing me. The movement was slow, mechanical. The butterflies on her shoulders shifted their wings.

"I don't recall her name," Renata said, her voice flat. Clinical.

She'd already lost Cressa's name. Not misplaced it—lost it completely, like the information had never been there at all.

"Her name was Cressa," I said, forcing the words out through a throat that felt too tight. "Your oldest friend. The healer who stayed with you through everything. The person who loved you enough to sacrifice herself willingly."

"Cressa," Renata repeated, testing how the name felt in her mouth. The butterflies in her hair shifted at the sound, green-gold wings catching the grey light.

Then silence. Long, stretching silence. I watched her face for any sign of recognition, any flicker of emotion or memory or humanity.

"What was the name?" she asked again.

Thirty seconds. It had been thirty seconds since I'd told her, and she'd already lost it again.

Something broke inside me. Not dramatically. Just a quiet snapping of whatever thread had been holding out hope that some part of the real Renata still existed beneath the transformation.

I closed the distance between us in three strides and held her face in my hands. My palms cupped her cheeks, feeling the cool skin, the black veins that pulsed beneath my touch.

"What's my name?" I demanded, and heard the desperation in my own voice.

"N-Nokoa," she struggled, and the hesitation before the word gutted me.

She'd had to search for it. We'd loved each other for years, and she had to search.

But she'd said it. That had to count for something.

"Say it again," I said, needing to hear it twice.

Renata's grey-white eyes met mine, and I saw something flicker behind them. Her mouth opened, shaped itself to form the word—

"I can't," she said instead.

My hands dropped from her face.

"You're losing me," I said. "You absorbed Cressa and now you're losing the connections. Losing the names, the faces."

"I remember facts," Renata said in that clinical voice. "I remember that someone died here. That she was important. That I should feel grief about her loss. I remember that you matter to me. That your presence is significant. But I cannot hold the specifics. The details keep slipping away."

From somewhere behind the bone pillars, I heard Valdic whimper. The DirgeWolf emerged, purple eyes blazing with transferred emotion.

"Say my name one more time," I pleaded. "Try. Please."

Renata's brow furrowed slightly, and I saw her lips move, testing different sounds. Her eyes tracked across my face like she was searching for clues.

"I know it starts with…" she trailed off. "No. I don't know."

"Nokoa," I said, giving it back to her. Hating that I had to. "My name is Nokoa."

"Nokoa," she repeated, but I heard the emptiness in it. Just echoing me, copying sounds without any understanding attached.

The butterflies surrounding us grew more agitated, their wings beating faster. Valdic moved closer, pressing against Renata's leg, and I saw her hand move automatically to stroke his head.

"How much more can you forget?" I asked. "How much more will the transformation take?"

"I don't know," Renata said simply. "But I suspect the answer is everything."

She said it so calmly. Like she was discussing someone else's dissolution.

"Do you even want to stop it?" I asked, hearing the crack in my own voice.

"I don't know if I want anything anymore," she said. "Wanting requires feeling."

Valdic suddenly let out a sound—not quite a whimper, not quite a growl. His purple eyes found mine. "She's drowning in what you can't see," he said, his voice rough. "The forgetting. It has weight too. Every name she loses, every connection that slips away—I feel the absence. The holes where memories should be. It's not just emotion I'm carrying anymore. It's the emptiness itself."

I looked between them—Renata standing empty and clinical, Valdic crouched beside her drowning in displaced humanity. Both of them breaking in different ways.

"Who are you?" she asked suddenly, looking at me with empty recognition—awareness that I was someone significant without ability to articulate how or why.

Not "what's your name." Who are you. Like I was a stranger.

"I'm Nokoa," I said, and my voice was steady even though everything inside me was screaming. "I'm the person you loved enough to break cosmic law for. The person you resurrected."

The words landed without impact. Renata listened with clinical attention, cataloging information without emotional response.

"I don't remember you," she said finally. "I know I should. I know that forgetting you is significant. But the knowledge doesn't create the connection."

Valdic's whimper cut through the air. He was crying—actual tears falling from his purple eyes. Not his tears. Renata's tears, or what should have been Renata's tears if she could still cry.

"I love you," I said, needing to say it one more time. "Whatever you're becoming, whatever you've lost—I love you."

Renata looked at me with those empty grey-white eyes, and I saw her trying. Saw her reaching for some response.

"I remember loving you," she said finally. "I remember that you matter. That your presence is significant. That there were feelings attached to seeing you that made existence feel warmer."

"But you can't access them," I finished for her.

"But I can't access them," she confirmed.

I turned to leave, finally forcing myself to move toward the doorway.

"Wait," Renata called, and I heard something almost like urgency in her voice. I turned back, hoping—

"What was the name again?" she asked. "The person who died here. I'm trying to remember. I want to remember."

"Cressa," I said, and heard how broken my voice sounded. "Her name was Cressa."

"Cressa," Renata repeated, and the butterflies in her hair shifted at the sound.

Then silence as the name slipped away again.

I found Valdic in the courtyard hours later, collapsed beneath the skeletal coral formations. His body was shaking, purple eyes dim despite still glowing.

"How much more can you take?" I asked, sitting beside him.

"I don't know," Valdic admitted. "She's losing memories now, not just emotions. And I feel those losses. Feel the empty spaces where connections used to be. It's like drowning in absence."

He shifted, and I saw how much larger he'd become. The emotions had given him mass, turned his emaciated frame into something more solid. But the weight was visible in every movement.

"She asked who I was," I said quietly. "Looked at me like I was a stranger."

Valdic's purple eyes found mine. "She's asked me three times today. Each time I tell her. Each time she forgets."

I placed my hand on his head. "What happens when the transformation completes?"

Valdic was quiet for a long moment. "I don't know if I'll survive it. Dirge-Wolves were made to carry grief. To accompany people through mourning. But this isn't normal grief. This is watching someone die while they're still alive. Carrying emotions for someone who's becoming a god." He paused. "When she ascends—all the emotion I'm carrying might burn away with the final change. Or it might crush me. The weight of an entire human lifetime of feeling, stored in me. When she ascends, that weight might become too much."

"Or?" I prompted, hearing the unspoken alternative.

"Or I might just continue," Valdic said simply. "Carrying an eternity of feelings for a goddess who can't feel anything at all. Being the emotional repository for a being who'll exist forever without warmth."

"That's not life," I said quietly.

"No," Valdic agreed, his voice breaking slightly. "But it's what I signed up for."

We sat in silence for a long moment.

"The Midnight Oath is coming soon," I said finally. "Days. Maybe less."

Valdic's whole body tensed. "You're really going to do it. Going to die for her."

"The bond means I die when she dies anyway," I said. "At least this way my death serves a purpose. Gives her that one moment of feeling before eternal emptiness."

"She won't remember it the way you want her to," Valdic said softly. "She'll remember the facts—that you died, that the Oath completed, that your sacrifice mattered. But she won't feel what it meant. Won't carry the emotional weight of loving you or grieving you. It'll just be information."

"I know," I said, and felt the witch runes flare as they burned away the grief those words created. "But I'll feel it. In that final moment, when I'm dying, when the Oath is completing and she's experiencing everything one last time before eternal emptiness—I'll know I did it for love. I'll die knowing I chose this."

"I'll take care of her," Valdic said, and the promise carried the weight of a vow. "After. When you're gone and she's ascended. I'll stay beside her. Carry whatever emotions the transformation leaves behind. Be the anchor she needs even if she can't feel why she needs one."

"Thank you," I said, and meant it more than I'd ever meant anything.

We sat together in the bone garden courtyard, surrounded by skeletal coral and gathering butterflies, and waited for the ending that was coming whether we were ready for it or not.

'Nokoa,' she said, and I heard the hesitation before it. I'd given her back her own name a moment ago. She'd already lost mine.

Chapter Twenty-Four

Say My Name

Nokoa

"Show me something," I said suddenly. "Anything. Any expression. Just so I know you're still in there somewhere."

Renata looked at me with empty grey-white eyes, processing the request. "What would you like me to show you?"

"Smile," I said. "Like you used to when you were happy."

She tried. I watched her face attempt to arrange itself into the configuration memory told her was a smile. The corners of her mouth lifted, her cheeks moved, her lips curved upward. But her eyes remained completely empty. Dead. The smile was technically correct—all the right muscles engaged—but it looked like a corpse trying to remember what living looked like.

"No," I said, shaking my head. "That's not right. It's missing something."

"The feeling behind it," Renata said, her face returning to neutral with mechanical precision. "Smiles are supposed to reflect internal emotional state. I have no internal emotional state to reflect. So the expression becomes performance without substance."

Valdic stirred at my feet, lifting his massive head with visible effort. He moved to stand in front of Renata, positioning himself between us, and looked up at her with an expression that was unmistakably warm. Loving.

And Renata's face softened in response.

Not consciously—not as deliberate performance—but automatically. Naturally. She looked at Valdic with something that approached genuine warmth, her features arranging themselves into an approximation of love that looked almost real.

Because Valdic was her emotional anchor. The bond between them let her respond to his expressions in ways she couldn't with anyone else, let her mirror emotions he carried for her.

"When you look at Valdic, you look almost human," I said.

"Valdic carries my emotions," Renata explained, her face returning to neutral as she looked away from the DirgeWolf. "The bond between us creates resonance. When he feels something, I can observe what I should be feeling through him. It's not the same as experiencing the emotion myself, but it provides reference for appropriate responses."

"So you're learning to fake it," I said, hearing the bitterness in my own voice.

"I'm learning to function," Renata corrected. "Learning which expressions correspond to which situations. Converting memory of emotion into physical approximation of emotion."

"You don't have to fake it for me," I said, my voice scraped raw. "I love you no matter what. You don't have to perform emotions you can't feel."

Renata's expression went completely neutral. Blank. The mask dropping away to reveal nothing underneath.

"But you deserve better than this," she said quietly. "You deserve someone who can smile at you naturally. Who can show warmth and affection. I remember what that was like. Remember being able to do those things without thinking about them."

"You're killing him," I said suddenly, looking down at Valdic. The Dirge-Wolf had collapsed again, his body shaking with aftershocks. His breathing was labored, wet. "Every time you recognize something that should inspire emotion—it all goes to Valdic. And he can't hold much more."

"I know," Renata said. "I can see him breaking under the weight. But I don't know how to stop it. The bond transfers automatically now. Anything that approaches feeling just flows into him before I can even recognize it's happening."

Valdic made a sound that was half-whimper, half-growl. His purple eyes found mine, and I saw accusation there.

"What?" I asked him directly.

"You're asking her to be herself while teaching her how to fake being herself," Valdic said, his voice strained. The dark humor he usually used as armor was completely gone, leaving just raw frustration and the weight of carrying too many emotions that weren't his. "Which is it? Do you want her to be what she is—empty, remembering, functional—or do you want her to pretend to be what she was?"

He was right. I was contradicting myself.

"Stop making her choose," Valdic continued. "Stop asking her to navigate your contradictions when she doesn't have the emotional capacity to understand what you need. Just let her be what she is and deal with your own feelings about it instead of making her responsible for managing them."

"You're right," I said. "I'm sorry. Both of you."

"You're allowed to grieve," Valdic said, his voice softening slightly. "Just don't make her carry that grief when she can't feel it anyway. Don't make her pretend to be human just to spare you from facing the reality of her transformation."

Renata pulled her hand back from my face—the gesture had happened somewhere in the last few minutes without my registering it—the movement slow and deliberate. "If you want honesty, I can provide that. If you want performance, I can attempt that too. But not both simultaneously."

"I want honesty," I said, committing to it even though honesty was going to hurt. "I want you to be what you're becoming without trying to soften it for me."

"Then that's what I'll give you," Renata said simply. "No more attempts at smiling when I don't feel happy. No more practiced embraces when I can't feel warmth. Just honest emptiness and perfect memory."

"Can you still say my name?" I asked suddenly, needing to confirm one more time. "Without struggling?"

"Nokoa," Renata said immediately. No hesitation. No searching. Just instant recall, perfect and empty. "Nokoa Nox."

"I won't forget you," she said, and I heard her trying to offer reassurance even without emotional weight to make it genuine. "Every detail of you is preserved permanently. Your name, your face, your voice. Every conversation we've ever had. Every moment we've shared."

"Just without the love that made those moments matter," I said.

"Just without the love that made those moments matter," she agreed.

We stood there in her chamber of bone and butterflies, the silence between us heavy with everything that had been lost. Valdic lay at our feet, his purple eyes bright with emotions we should have been sharing but couldn't.

"Three to five days," I said. "Until the Midnight Oath."

"Yes," Renata confirmed. "Quade will prepare the ritual. I'll complete the final absorptions. And then you'll die willingly, and I'll feel everything one last time before it all burns away forever."

"Are you afraid?" I asked.

"I remember what fear felt like," Renata said. "Can describe it in perfect detail—the way your heart would race, the way your breathing would quicken, the cold that would spread through your chest. I remember being afraid of losing you, afraid of the transformation, afraid of becoming empty." She paused. "But I can't feel the fear anymore. Can only observe that fear would be appropriate given the circumstances."

"I should go," I said, though I didn't move. "Let you rest or prepare or do whatever goddesses do when they're waiting for the final transformation."

"You should spend your remaining days doing things that matter to you," she said. "Not watching me exist emptily."

"Watching you is what matters to me," I said.

"I know," she replied. "I remember what devotion looks like. Remember being capable of it myself. But I can't return it anymore."

"I'd rather feel everything and break than feel nothing at all," I said.

Something flickered across Renata's face—not quite emotion, but recognition. "That's what I used to believe too," she said quietly. "When I was fifteen, sitting in the orchards with Cressa, terrified of loving you. I said I'd rather feel everything and risk breaking than feel nothing at all. Said being safe from pain wasn't the same as being alive."

She paused, her grey-white eyes holding mine with that terrible clarity.

"I thought love would kill me," she continued. "And it did. Just not the way I expected. It killed me slowly, from the inside, by making me love you enough to break cosmic law. And breaking cosmic law led to the Crown, and the Crown led to this. To emptiness."

"So you were right," I said. "Love did kill you."

"Love completed me," she corrected. "Killed the human so the goddess could emerge. The ending was always part of the design. I just didn't know I was walking toward it."

"I love you," I said one more time, needing to say it while she could still hear the words even if she couldn't feel their weight.

She paused, and I saw her trying. Reaching for some response that would bridge the distance between us even though the distance was unbridgeable now.

"I'm glad the love exists," she said finally.

It wasn't "I love you too." Wasn't any kind of emotional reciprocation.

But it was honest. And I'd asked for honesty.

So I held her one more time—felt the cool skin, the black veins pulsing, the absence of any response except automatic positioning. Her body still against mine, like holding a statue.

Valdic pressed against both of us, his warmth the only thing that felt alive in the embrace. His purple eyes glowing bright with the love that should have filled the space between Renata and me.

And I left her there in her chamber of bone and butterflies, surrounded by death, preparing for an ending that would last forever.

Chapter Twenty-Five

PRAXIS'S JUDGEMENT

Renata

Quade dragged Praxis into the courtyard by one skeletal arm, the sound of bone scraping against bone echoing off the cathedral walls. The Bone God moved with casual strength—his blackened skeleton still vital, moss growing in the valleys of his eye sockets. His tattered wings dragged behind him, leaving trails in the bone dust that covered everything.

Praxis stumbled, caught himself, stumbled again. He looked diminished. Fading. The bleached white of his bones had gone grey at the edges, like ash creeping inward from some invisible fire. The golden tattoos he'd spent years sculpting into his skull flickered weakly now. Barely visible. The crimson eyes in his sockets had dulled to something closer to rust.

There was no heartfire left to collect. No bone marrow harvested from the dying to keep the Bone Council alive and strong. The source of his power had dried up along with everything else in this world.

He'd looked so powerful once. I remembered it perfectly—the way he'd sat at council meetings with tentacles coiled beneath his horns, the way his presence had filled rooms like smoke, the way even Ancelin had deferred to him on certain matters. The largest of the council. The most intimidating. The one who'd seemed untouchable.

Now he just looked like everything else in this world. Dying.

Quade threw him forward with enough force that Praxis crashed to his knees in front of my throne. The impact sent cracks spiderwebbing through the courtyard floor—fractures in bone that had stood for centuries, now breaking under the weight of judgment about to be delivered.

I observed this from my seat. Noted the details with perfect clarity. Catalogued the deterioration.

It was different now with him tossed to his knees before me. Different with my emotions numbed behind the glass wall the Memory choice had erected. The last time I'd seen Praxis, I'd been so overwhelmed with anger and betrayal that I couldn't punish him. The feelings themselves had paralysed me. Too much emotion had created the same paralysis as too little.

"You're holding up better than I expected," Valdic observed from beside my throne. His massive form had grown again—now nearly the size of a small house, purple eyes blazing bright enough to cast shadows in the grey light. "Only shaking a little. Must be all that displaced rage I'm carrying for you."

I could see the tremor in his limbs that betrayed exactly how much emotion he was drowning in. My anger. My betrayal. My need for justice. All of it flooding into him through lavender strings I could see connecting us, pulsing with each transferred feeling like a heartbeat made visible.

"I believed you were on my side," I stated plainly, directing my attention to Praxis. "I thought you were the misunderstood one of the Bone Council. The one who actually cared about this world's survival."

Praxis lifted his head enough to meet my gaze. His rust-colored eyes held something that might have been resignation. "Someone has to live. It was going to be me."

"It seems to have worked so well for you," I replied, and even without emotional investment I recognized the statement as scathing.

Valdic made a sound that was half-laugh, half-growl. "She's getting better at sarcasm without feelings. That's either impressive or deeply disturbing."

Praxis's tentacles—those bleached appendages he'd cultivated so carefully—stirred weakly beneath his horns. The movement was sluggish, lacking the hypnotic fluidity they'd once possessed. Even those were dying.

He spoke with less passion than he once had. "I thought the Bone God was simply seeking power. That he wanted the Crown and to rule through whoever wore it. That was never it." He paused, his bones creaking as he shifted on his knees. "He wanted to create something so much stronger than the Hollow Crown. I didn't understand—he was only looking for the right puzzle pieces. How was I to know that he was simply waiting for someone willing to hollow themselves out completely? That the rest of us were always meant to die? Priestess Alaira helped shape our world and our records so well that the idea of Quade and his daughters weren't so much as a whisper. We expected an evil Bone God who was after the Hollow Crown. We are victims just like you!"

Quade stepped forward, clicking against bone floor, and moved to stand beside my throne. "At first I did want the Hollow Crown," he confirmed. "I learned quickly that I can grant gifts but hardly harness them to their potential." His moss-filled eye sockets turned toward me. "But here—Renata so willingly saw potential and fought for it. Fought through impossible odds to claim power that should have destroyed her. She is worth so much more than the Crown of bone."

Do not become distracted by their chatter, Aldric's voice cut through the conversation, sharp and commanding inside my skull. His presence felt different now—angrier, more aggressive than when he'd been one voice among three. He hoarded life. Stole what was not his. Judge him.

I blinked, the interruption jarring against the external conversation. Aldric had never been this assertive before. Had never demanded rather than suggested. Something about being alone with just Oriana—about the three becoming two—had changed him. Made him louder. More insistent.

Kill him! Execute judgment!

"How many did you chain up?" I asked Praxis, cutting through whatever response Quade had been preparing. "How many people from the outer cities did you harvest to keep yourself alive?"

Praxis's tentacles coiled tighter. "Does the number matter? They were dying anyway. The famine—"

Do not ignore me, Renata! Aldric's roar inside my head made the Crown pulse against my skull. I felt it physically—bone fused to bone vibrating with his fury. Kill him! Execute judgment! Stop letting them talk and act!

"It was necessary!" Praxis's voice rose, cracking. "To serve you I had to be strong!"

Strange, seeing him grovel. This skeleton who used to intimidate everyone with his presence—reduced to begging on his knees. The bleached bones that had seemed pristine now looked fragile. Brittle. The golden tattoos that had blazed like captured sun now barely flickered.

And equally strange to hear Aldric taking this position of assertion. Growing more demanding with each passing moment. Like he needed to prove something now that Lyanna was gone. Now that he was alone with Oriana in whatever space they occupied within the Crown's consciousness.

Kill him now! Aldric commanded, and I felt the Crown heat against my skull. I command it! Execute him! Show your strength!

"Where's Queen Oriana?" I asked aloud, directing the question to the Crown itself. "She's usually the one stepping forward. Why are you suddenly so vocal, Aldric?"

Silence from Oriana. Just Aldric's continued raging, like thunder building without release.

She is weak! Indecisive! You need strength, not her coddling!

Without emotions to buffer the constant voices, without feelings to help me navigate the demands, I was growing agitated at always being told what to do. At being commanded and directed and pushed and pulled by everyone around me like I was still just a vessel. Just a thing to be wielded rather than a person making choices.

Quade wanted me to be his goddess. Aldric wanted me to be his weapon. Oriana wanted me to be the willing sacrifice that propelled her to her own goal.

Everyone had plans for me.

I made a decision.

Not from anger—I couldn't access anger. Not from justice—justice required emotional investment in right and wrong. Simply from the recognition that I was tired of being commanded. Tired of voices telling me what to do, how to act, when to execute judgment.

If I was going to absorb someone, it would be my choice. My timing. My decision.

I pulled from the magic still etched in my bones—the witch runes carved during our binding. I recalled exactly the chants Priestess Alaira had used when working Crown magic, the cadence and rhythm and specific inflections that made power bend to intention. I imitated her words. Pulled power from the runes that glowed faintly through my skin. Directed it inward toward the Crown instead of outward toward Praxis.

Aldric screamed in my mind.

Not commanding now. Not ordering. Actually screaming as he realized what I was doing. As he felt the absorption begin without his consent, without his readiness.

The absorption felt different than when I'd let the Crown manage it. More direct. More visceral. Like drinking something too hot too fast—Aldric's essence rushed into me like water breaking through a dam. Centuries of warfare and violence and strategic thinking, all of it flooding through my consciousness without the Crown's mediation to filter it. Battle tactics. Weapon knowledge. The weight of armor. The calculations that turned living beings into strategic assets.

All of it perfectly preserved in my memory.

None of it touching my emotions.

Valdic's growl turned to a roar. His body trembled violently, muscles spasming under his fur as emotion transferred. He grew again—his massive form expanding until his shoulders were level with the second-story windows. His purple eyes blazed bright enough to hurt to look at directly.

I rose from my throne, the movement smooth and deliberate. The black spine extending from my back clicked with each shift of position. My hair—fully black now, corruption complete—moved in the non-wind that always seemed to fill the cathedral.

Praxis watched me with rust-colored eyes that had gone wide.

"You ended lives to preserve your own," I stated, my voice carrying through the courtyard with perfect clarity. "I ended the world to preserve his."

I gestured toward where Nokoa stood at the courtyard's edge, watching with golden eyes that carried too much feeling for the witch runes to burn completely.

"We are both guilty," I continued, holding Praxis's gaze. "The difference is that I will carry my sin. You tried to hide yours behind necessity."

I pulled power from the absorbed essence of Aldric—from his warfare knowledge, from his understanding of violence as tool rather than passion. I pulled from the Crown itself. I pulled from the cathedral around us, from the divine skeleton that housed this entire realm.

And I raised bone spikes from the courtyard floor.

They erupted with enough force to send dust billowing outward. Massive spears of blackened bone tore upward through the space where Praxis knelt. The sound was like trees splitting, like the earth itself cracking open. The air filled with the smell of old death, of bone dust centuries settled now disturbed.

They pierced through him. Through his bleached bones, through the tentacles he'd cultivated so carefully. The spikes kept rising, lifting his skeletal form into the air. His bones shattered—the way bleached bone splintered into fragments, the way his golden tattoos flickered once, twice, then died completely like stars extinguishing one by one.

The crimson in his eye sockets faded to nothing.

I felt nothing watching it. Not satisfaction. Not vindication. Not regret.

Just clinical observation of a process completing itself.

"Only one left inside my head," I observed aloud, watching Praxis's remains dissolve into ash. "Only Queen Oriana remains to whisper to me."

You absorbed him, Oriana's voice came soft, almost tentative. So different from Aldric's commanding roar. Like she was afraid to speak too loudly now that she was alone. On your own. Without trading memory. Without Quade's orchestration.

"Yes," I confirmed.

You're learning. She didn't sound pleased about this recognition. Didn't sound upset either. Just observing. Learning to claim power without permission. Learning to act without guidance. Learning to be what he's designed you to become.

"Is that a problem?" I asked.

Silence stretched between us. Then, quietly: No. It's inevitable. I just wish—

She stopped. Didn't finish the thought.

Quade stepped forward, touching the dissolving remains of Praxis. The ash scattered in the non-wind. "Well executed," he said, and I heard approval in his voice. "Precise. Efficient. No hesitation. No mercy. And absorbing Aldric on your own initiative—that shows remarkable growth. You're learning to claim power directly."

"I was tired of being commanded," I stated simply.

Quade laughed—a sound like bones rattling in a tomb. "Excellent! Not a passive vessel for power but an active participant in your own transformation. Not a tool to be wielded but a goddess claiming her authority."

Valdic made a sound that was half-whimper, half-growl. "She's talking about executing people like it's filing paperwork. This is what you wanted? This emptiness pretending to be strength?"

"This clarity," Quade corrected. "This ability to act without emotion clouding judgment. This capacity to do what's necessary without being paralyzed by feeling."

"This horror," Valdic countered. His purple eyes fixed on me with intensity that carried all the emotion I couldn't access.

"Where's Nokoa?" I asked, interrupting their debate. I'd noted his presence earlier at the courtyard's edge, but now the space was empty.

"He left," Valdic replied, his voice heavy. "Right after the spikes finished with Praxis. Couldn't watch anymore."

I glanced down at my own arms, where I could see the faint glow of runes beneath the surface. The bond curse still connected us. Still burned.

"I should probably check on him," I said, because I knew it was the appropriate response.

"Should you?" Quade asked, genuine curiosity in the question. "Or are you simply executing the behavior you remember being appropriate? Do you actually want to check on him, or do you just recognize that wanting to check on him would be expected?"

I examined my internal state for any genuine desire to see Nokoa, any real concern for his wellbeing.

Found nothing.

Just the memory of how much I used to care. Like reading about warmth in a book while standing in winter.

"The latter," I admitted. "I recognize that his distress is significant. That watching me execute Praxis and absorb Aldric probably caused him pain. That checking on him would be the compassionate response. But I don't feel compelled to do it."

"Then don't go," Quade suggested. "Don't perform compassion you don't feel."

"But he's dying soon," I observed. "The Midnight Oath is approaching. Our time together is limited. Logically, I should maximize that time even if I can't emotionally appreciate its value."

"You're talking about spending time with him like it's an efficiency problem," Valdic said quietly. His massive head lowered until his purple eyes were level with mine. "Like he's a resource to be optimally allocated."

I didn't answer. Couldn't argue with the observation.

Valdic moved closer, pressing his massive form against me. Then he did something he'd never done before—he pressed his forehead directly against mine. The touch sent something jolting through me. A rush of something that made me feel.

"Nokoa is going to die for me," I whispered, and the words came out wrong. Not flat. Not clinical. They came out with horror.

I opened my eyes and looked up at Quade. He stared back at me with what looked like shock.

I had felt, for just a moment. A long enough moment that the realization washed over me with devastating clarity.

Nokoa was going to die for me.

The very thing I had destroyed the world to prevent. The very outcome I'd broken cosmic law to avoid. The very ending I'd fought so desperately to escape.

And now it was inevitable. Written into the design of my transformation. Required for my ascension.

I was going to lose him anyway.

Chapter Twenty-Six

No Other Way

Nokoa

I found Quade in the cathedral's deepest chamber—the one where his bones formed the walls themselves, where the architecture stopped being construction and became organism. The air tasted different here. Older. Like breathing in the substance of divinity rather than just existing near it.

He stood with his back to me, one skeletal hand pressed against the wall. The moss in his eye sockets glowed faintly green in the dim light. His tattered wings hung still.

I'd been looking for him since leaving the courtyard. Since watching Renata execute Praxis with the same clinical precision someone might use to trim a plant. Since realizing with devastating clarity that the woman I loved was already gone.

"Is there another way?" I asked without preamble. "A way that ends with the two of us together?"

Even as I asked, I knew the answer. But I needed to hear it confirmed. Needed to know I'd exhausted every possibility before accepting what came next.

Quade turned slowly, his four horns catching the dim light. He looked at me with something in his posture that might have been respect—or the satisfaction of seeing a designed piece fall exactly where it was supposed to.

"You were always going to be the answer," he stated simply. "It's why you were resurrected."

My breath caught. The chamber suddenly felt colder, the bone walls pressing closer. The witch runes carved into my bones flared hot, burning away the spike of emotion before it could fully form, but I felt the ghost of it anyway—rage and grief and terrible understanding all tangled together.

"Your death was accidental," Quade continued, moving closer. "Your first death, that wasn't planned. The attack by Fatin was orchestrated—she needed to break to become whole. But your actual death? That was chaos. Uncontrolled variable."

He paused. "The hollow crown used everything it had to bring you back. Hivro helped. She is allowed no intervention in mortal lives—that's cosmic law, written when the first gods emerged. But she intervened anyway. Poured her own divine essence into your resurrection because Renata's grief moved her. Because watching her daughter—and make no mistake, Renata is as much Hivro's daughter as any she created—watching her break cosmic law for love..." He trailed off, the moss in his eye sockets brightening slightly. "It's why Hivro has faded into the background the closer Renata gets to ascending. Used too much of herself. Made herself small to make you alive."

The weight of that settled over me like stone. Three sources of power to resurrect one mortal man. The Hollow Crown's accumulated energy. Quade's influence bleeding through the cracks in his imprisonment. And a goddess sacrificing her own substance.

"There has to be a way she lives without this," I pressed, hearing desperation creep into my voice despite the runes' attempts to burn it away. "Without becoming this empty thing. Without transforming into a goddess who can't even feel—"

"This is how she lives," Quade interrupted, and for the first time, I heard something almost gentle in his tone. "Everything else is her dying slowly. When Fatin killed you, there was no going back. She hollowed herself for you. Broke cosmic law for you. Triggered a famine that will consume this world for you."

He moved closer still, until I could see the individual moss tendrils growing in his eye sockets. "The moment she chose to resurrect you instead of accepting your death—that was the moment her humanity began dying. Everything since has just been the slow completion of what that choice started."

He paused. "If you cared for her the way you say you do, why do you not want what is best for her? Why would you press so hard to stop such a beautiful mortal form from becoming something divine?"

I wanted to find some flaw in his logic, some alternative he hadn't considered, some loophole in cosmic design that would let Renata be herself again. Let us both survive. Let love be enough without requiring total destruction.

But I couldn't. Because I'd watched her fade for weeks now. Had seen the emotion drain from her eyes like water from a cracked vessel. Had heard her reduce our relationship to resource management, heard her speak about my impending death like it was a scheduling problem to be optimized.

The Renata I'd loved was already dead.

"If you do not finish this—if you refuse the Midnight Oath—she remains trapped. Hollow but incomplete. Half divine, half mortal. Unable to be either fully. Unable to exist as anything except this broken in-between state." His skeletal hand reached out, not quite touching me but close enough that I felt the cold radiating from his ancient bones. "Is that what love demands? That you keep her suspended in transformation that never completes? In pain that never ends?"

The question hit harder than any threat could have. Because he was right. I'd watched Renata exist in that in-between state, seen how it was destroying her slowly. And if I refused the oath—if I chose my own life over her completion—I would be condemning her to that existence forever.

Love her enough to let her finish dying. Or love myself more and keep her trapped.

Not much of a choice when stated that way.

"So I damn her by living and complete her by dying," I said, hearing bitterness bleed through despite everything. "What a beautiful design."

"It is beautiful," Quade agreed, apparently missing or ignoring the sarcasm. "The mathematics of it. The precision required. The way every piece depends on every other piece."

He leaned closer. "The alternative is that I take you to my realm, encompass you in darkness, and twist you until you've become something else. Something that can serve me differently. Would you prefer that? Would you rather be unmade and reformed into a tool for transition, losing everything you are to become something useful?"

The threat was clear. Die willingly in the Midnight Oath, or die unwillingly in whatever Quade had designed for recalcitrant pieces.

"She's not engineering," I countered, anger rising hot enough that the witch runes blazed trying to contain it. "She's a person. A woman who loved gardens and sunrises and the way orchids bloom in morning light. A woman who used to laugh so hard she couldn't breathe, who cried during sad songs, who felt things so deeply they overwhelmed her. You've turned her into a mechanism. Into divine machinery wearing her face."

"I've given her the capacity to exist beyond mortality's limitations," Quade corrected. "She will be the goddess of silence and forgetting—powerful beyond mortal comprehension, essential to universal balance."

"She'll be empty," I said flatly. "She'll be nothing except perfect memory in a divine shell. That's not a gift. That's horror."

"It's both," Quade acknowledged without hesitation. "Most divine trans-formations are. Gods are horror and glory simultaneously. They're both more and less than mortal comprehension allows."

We stood in silence after that. Him, with his ancient patience, with time mea-sured in epochs rather than heartbeats. Me, with my dying body and glowing witch runes and desperate need to find alternatives that didn't exist.

"Tell me about the Midnight Oath," I said finally, needing to understand the mechanism of my own death. "How does it work?"

"Three components," Quade began. "First: the willing. You must choose death consciously, deliberately, understanding exactly what you're doing and accepting it anyway. Any hesitation, any resistance—and the ritual fails."

"Second: the beloved. The sacrifice must come from someone the ascending divine truly loves. Not alliance, not friendship. Love in its purest form—the kind that breaks cosmic law, that defies natural order. The bond must be strong enough to span the gap between mortal and divine."

"Third: the moment. The Oath must be performed at the exact transition point—when she's hollow enough to need completion but not so hollow she's already transformed. When you're alive enough to die meaningfully but not so alive the resurrection magic sustains you past usefulness."

He lowered his hand. "When all three components align, you die, but your death isn't simple ending. Your life force, everything you are, gets channeled directly into her transformation. Fuels the final leap from incomplete hollow to complete goddess. And in that moment, for just a heartbeat, she feels everything again."

My breath caught. "Everything?"

"Everything," Quade confirmed. "All the emotions she's lost behind Memory's glass wall come flooding back at once. She'll feel your death completely. Feel her love for you completely. Feel grief and joy and terror and devotion all simultaneously, with full intensity, as herself rather than through Valdic's displaced burden."

He tilted his head. "And then it burns away. The emotion consumes itself, and she ascends beyond it. Becomes fully divine. But she'll have had that moment. That single heartbeat of being completely herself again before transformation completes."

"One moment," I said quietly. "One perfect, terrible moment of feeling everything before losing it forever."

"Yes. Some would call that cruel. I call it mercy. She gets to feel you one final time before emptiness claims her completely."

"The best thing you can do for her, Nokoa, is die," Quade said quietly.

The words hung in the air between us.

"Fine," I heard myself say, the word coming out hollow. Defeated. "Use me. But she never knows I regret it. That I will die worried for her. That I'm terrified of what she'll become after I'm gone."

"You want to die without her knowing your fear?" Quade asked, genuine curiosity in the question. "Why protect her from truth when truth is all she'll be able to access after transformation completes?"

"Because she'll remember everything perfectly," I explained. "She'll carry the memory of my death forever. If I die terrified and regretting, she'll have to remember that fear eternally without any warmth to soften it. Without any love to contextualize it. Just raw terror preserved in perfect detail."

I swallowed hard. "But if I die at peace, accepting, maybe even happy—she'll remember peace. She'll remember me loving her enough to do this willingly, without resentment or fear. It's the only gift I can give her anymore. The only way I can protect her after I'm gone."

Quade was quiet for a long moment. Then: "You love her very much."

"More than cosmic law," I confirmed, and felt the truth of it settle in my bones. "More than my own life. More than anything in this world or the next. Which is why I'll die for her. Why I'll walk into that ritual willingly even though it terrifies me. Why I'll pretend it doesn't hurt even though it's destroying me."

"That is why you were always going to be the answer," Quade said quietly, and something in his tone had shifted. "Not because you love her—many people have loved deeply. But because you love her enough to sacrifice without resentment. Enough to die without making her carry your pain. Enough to complete her transformation even as it breaks you utterly. That kind of love is rare enough to power divine ascension."

"How does one make peace with willing death?" I asked, not really expecting an answer.

"By recognizing it serves purpose," Quade replied. "By understanding that your sacrifice creates something eternal. By accepting that love sometimes requires complete destruction to prove itself."

"That's a terrible answer," I observed.

"It's the only answer," Quade corrected gently. "You'll die, but you will be a perfect memory. Preserved in divine consciousness forever. She'll never forget you—every moment you shared, every word you spoke, every gesture of love. All of it crystallized in her perfect recall, existing eternally even if the feeling attached to it burns away. Is that not a kind of immortality?"

"It's a hollow kind," I said.

"Most immortality is," Quade replied.

He moved toward the chamber exit, his skeletal form casting strange shadows in the dim light. "I'll prepare the ritual. The ritual circle must be drawn at the exact center of the bone cathedral, where the divine architecture is strongest. Midnight tomorrow—when the barrier between states is thinnest."

He paused at the doorway. "You are doing the right thing. The necessary thing. That should provide some comfort."

"It doesn't," I admitted.

"I know," Quade replied, and something in his tone suggested he genuinely did. "But I said it anyway. Sometimes accepting what must be is the only courage available."

Then he was gone, leaving me alone in a chamber made from divine bones, surrounded by walls that breathed like lungs.

I sank to the floor, back against the living wall, and let myself feel it. Let the witch runes burn as hot as they wanted—fear, grief, rage, love, terror, resignation, acceptance, despair. All of it cycling through too fast to fully process, too overwhelming to contain.

Love was going to kill me again.

This time, there would be no resurrection.

Chapter Twenty-Seven

Alaira's Final Offering

Renata

Alaira came to my chambers in the grey hours before dawn. She stood in the doorway like someone approaching execution. Hesitant. Hollow-eyed. Carrying guilt so visibly it seemed to weigh her down physically, bowing her shoulders and making each movement effortful.

I observed her from my bed, surrounded by butterflies that had clustered on the bone-white sheets. They clicked softly with each small movement, creating ambient sound that filled the silence between us.

"Priestess Alaira," I acknowledged, my voice flat. "You're awake early."

"I haven't slept," she admitted. "I need to speak with you. Privately. It's important."

I sat up, disturbing butterflies that scattered to the walls and ceiling with a sound like shuffling paper. "We're alone," I confirmed. "Whatever you need to say, you can say it."

Alaira moved into the room slowly. She looked worse than I remembered—thinner, more translucent. The witch runes that had once glowed bright on her skin were dim now. Barely visible. Like embers dying in ash.

"I came to make an offer," she stated, her voice steadier now that she'd committed to speaking. "A trade. A payment for what I've done."

I waited. Let the silence stretch.

"Take me instead," Alaira continued, the words coming faster now. "Instead of Nokoa. Let my death fuel what you're becoming. Use me the way you used Cressa, the way you absorbed Aldric. Let my sacrifice complete your transformation so he can live."

The proposal landed differently than I'd expected.

Not because I felt hope—I couldn't feel hope anymore. But because I recognized the logic immediately. Saw the mathematics shift in real time. Nokoa lived. The transformation completed. Alaira paid for her guilt with actual consequence.

"Why?" I asked.

"Because I need to pay for what I've done," Alaira said, her hands twisting together until knuckles went white. "I was wrong. So terribly wrong. I freed Quade thinking I was serving my goddess. Thinking I understood divine will. But I just unleashed ending on the world."

She took a step closer, tears tracking down her face. "The world is dying because of me. The famine. The consumption. Theron's death. Your transformation. All of it traces back to my choice. And Nokoa—" Her voice cracked. "He's dying for something I caused. If anyone should pay that price, it should be me."

"Quade designed the Midnight Oath specifically," I observed. "It requires willing sacrifice from the beloved. The magic needs love between ascender and sacrificer. You don't love me. The ritual wouldn't work."

"Then change the ritual," Alaira pressed. "Quade is the god of transitions—surely he can modify his own design. Please. I'm begging you. Let me fix what I broke."

Before I could respond, the air in the chamber changed. Temperature dropped suddenly enough that I saw my breath mist in the grey light. Pressure shifted.

Hivro appeared between one heartbeat and the next—not walking through the doorway but simply existing where she hadn't existed a moment before.

She looked at me with a face that held entire galaxies. "Renata. Remember to make your choices wisely."

Just that. No command. No interference. Just gentle reminder that choice still existed even in the face of inevitability.

"Hivro." Quade's voice came from the doorway, his skeletal form materializing with less drama but equal impact. "Remember your rules. You are not allowed to meddle."

He moved into the room, his tattered wings rustling against the doorframe. "Alaira set this path in motion. She wishes to pay its price. Divine beings cannot interfere with mortal choice."

"My place as a guardian was given to me by my goddess," Hivro countered, steel underneath her typically gentle tone. "Warning her against choices that will harm her is not interference—it's guardianship."

"Semantics," Quade dismissed. "You've already bent cosmic law past breaking by helping resurrect Nokoa. Don't pretend you can play guardian now when you've already compromised your divine neutrality."

They stared at each other—Bone God and divine oracle—and I felt the weight of their opposed purposes pressing against the chamber walls.

Hivro didn't push harder than that warning. Just looked at me with those galaxy eyes and let the silence carry her disappointment.

It was the first time I'd seen her as something other than good.

Maybe emptiness provided clarity that feeling would have obscured. But I saw how much she hadn't tried. How easily she'd accepted Quade's reminder about rules. How quickly she'd backed down from actual intervention.

"You could stop this," I observed aloud. "If you truly wanted to prevent my transformation—if you genuinely believed it was wrong—you could intervene. Divine power transcends mortal choice when necessary."

"No," Hivro replied quietly. "I cannot interfere with your choices without violating cosmic law. Without becoming what I'm designed to prevent. I can guide. Can warn. Can love you through the consequences. But I cannot choose for you."

"Convenient," I noted.

Hivro flinched. But she didn't argue. Didn't defend. Just stood there carrying her divine restriction and her love for me in equal measure, unable to act on either.

I turned to Quade. "Can the ritual be modified? Can Alaira's willing death replace Nokoa's?"

"No," Quade stated. "The Midnight Oath requires love between ascender and sacrificer. Alaira doesn't love you. The magic would recognize the difference and fail."

"Then what use is her offer?"

"She can't replace Nokoa in the Midnight Oath," Quade explained. "But she can be absorbed before it. Her essence can strengthen your capacity so that when Nokoa's death completes the transformation, the transition is more stable. More permanent. Think of it as foundation work before the final ritual."

If Alaira's absorption made Nokoa's death actually accomplish what it was meant to accomplish—made his sacrifice matter—then accepting her offer was just practical preparation.

Nokoa was dying anyway. But if this made his death succeed where Queen Oriana's had failed—then the mathematics were simple.

"If this is what you want," I heard myself state, looking at Alaira. "I'll grant it."

Not from mercy. Just recognition that her offer served practical purpose. That absorbing her now made Nokoa's death tomorrow more likely to succeed.

Alaira fell to her knees, relief washing over her face. "Thank you. Let me make up for what I've done."

"Renata, no—" Hivro started, taking a step forward.

"She asked," I interrupted. "She came here willingly. She's offering herself as payment for what she believes she owes. And Quade says her absorption strengthens the Midnight Oath's success. I'm simply accepting an offer that serves practical purpose."

"She's not thinking clearly," Hivro pressed. "Guilt is consuming her judgment. She needs time—"

"Time won't change cosmic law," Quade interjected. "Time won't undo the famine or prevent what's already in motion."

He moved closer to Alaira. "You are choosing this? Freely? Without coercion?"

"Yes," Alaira confirmed, her voice steady despite tears. "I choose this. I offer myself willingly. Let my death strengthen what comes next."

"Then it is witnessed," Quade declared, and I heard ritual formality in his tone. "Alaira, Priestess of Hesperia, offers herself to Renata Sunthorne's transformation. The choice is made. The price is accepted."

I moved to stand in front of her. I pulled power from the witch runes in my bones. From the Crown fused to my skull. From the cathedral around us.

I began the chant Quade had taught me. Words that would pull Alaira's essence into the Crown. The words tasted like old bone and forgotten prayers.

Alaira's emotions flooded through me in the instant before transfer—her love for the Goddess of Fate so profound it felt like worship, her guilt over freeing Quade heavy enough to crush, her desperate need to make amends overwhelming everything else. For one heartbeat I felt it all.

Then it transferred to Valdic.

His body convulsed. His muscles spasmed under his fur, his massive frame shaking with the weight of one more person's entire emotional existence. He made a sound—low, pained, almost like keening.

But the absorption itself was different than the others.

Where Cressa had dissolved quietly, where Aldric had been pulled inward with military precision, Alaira exploded into butterflies.

Not the grey-purple butterflies that filled the cathedral. These were brilliant, celestial, blazing with starlight and cosmic power. They erupted from her dissolving form in a storm—thousands of them, filling the chamber, their wings creating sound like distant singing. Like prayers being answered.

The butterflies swirled around the chamber in violent patterns—aggressive, almost angry movement. They filled every space, covered every surface, their wings creating wind that stirred my black hair and made the bone dust dance in spirals.

Hivro remained at the chamber's edge, her galaxy eyes tracking the butterfly storm. Grief, maybe. Or resignation. Or the terrible acceptance of watching someone she loved do something she couldn't prevent.

Valdic barked sharply once—a sound of pain. The purple glow of his eyes flickered slightly before blazing even brighter.

The butterflies began to settle. The celestial light dimmed. The violent swirling slowed to gentle floating.

And Alaira was gone.

Just butterflies made from her essence, spreading through the chamber to join all the others. Distinguishable for now by their brightness, but soon they'd fade to match the rest.

Quade moved through the settling butterflies toward me. "Well executed. Tomorrow's Midnight Oath is now more likely to succeed."

Hivro moved closer, her starlight form casting strange shadows. "I failed you," she said quietly.

"I know," I acknowledged.

She faded—not walking away but simply ceasing to exist in the chamber.

"You should rest," Quade suggested. "The Midnight Oath will require strength."

Then he was gone too, leaving me with Valdic and the settling butterfly storm.

I ran my hands along Valdic's massive form, feeling his warmth, his breathing, his presence. The only connection I had left that felt like anything at all.

Tomorrow Nokoa would die.

Tomorrow the Midnight Oath would complete what Alaira's absorption had prepared.

Tomorrow I would feel everything one final time before emptiness claimed me forever.

Interlude Three

THE IMPRISONMENT

Quade

"Queen Oriana, you can direct your anger wherever you desire, but it won't change the fact that this failure stems from your lover." I kept my tone measured, factual. The truth didn't require embellishment.

It was a partial truth, of course. Even if Thrain had remained—had stood beside her and taken the oath with trembling hands—she never would have ascended. Oriana lacked the fundamental willingness to sacrifice what divinity demanded. She could have been magnificent. But morality held her captive. Those self-imposed prisons of right and wrong, acceptable and unthinkable.

How beautifully fragile mortals were, building cages from concepts that meant nothing in the grand architecture of existence.

"You should have found him!" Queen Oriana's voice cracked on the accusation. Her skeletal hands—still draped in ceremonial silk despite centuries in the Crown—gestured violently enough that her joints clattered like dice thrown across stone. "You promised you would bring him back! You swore—"

"Perhaps you're right." I inclined my head, allowing her the small victory of agreement. The moss growing in my eye sockets shifted with the movement. "I could have dragged him back kicking and screaming, chains around his coward's throat. Could have forced him to his knees before you and made him speak the words."

I paused, letting her hope bloom for just a heartbeat.

"But he still wouldn't have been willing. Found or lost, forced or free—"
I spread my hands, the gesture almost apologetic. My decayed wings rustled
behind me. "You still would have ended here."

"I still would have ended as a slave to this Crown!" She didn't shout this
time. The words came out hollow, defeated. More devastating than any scream.
"Years, Quade. Years of watching. Waiting. Serving. For nothing."

"I know it must be crushing," I offered, and I meant it. Sympathy without
solution. Acknowledgment without action. "The weight of it all on your shoulders. The immense grief of knowing all your choices, all your effort, all those
years of perfect service—still wasn't enough. You still weren't good enough. I
won't hold your tone against you."

She stared at me as if logic itself had become monstrous in her eyes.

I didn't share her assessment. Monsters were aberrations, things that violated
natural order. I was necessary. Inevitable.

"There's nothing you'll do to fix this?" Queen Oriana asked again, and I
heard the desperation underneath. The final grasping at hope she knew was
already dead.

"I cannot fix failure once it has failed." I stated this simply, without cruelty.
"The ritual required willing sacrifice. You provided the sacrifice. He failed to
provide the willingness. Those are the mechanisms. I don't control them—I
simply recognize their function."

"Failure?" She scoffed, the sound bitter and sharp. "You call—"

"Yes." I cut her off. "You are a failure."

"Quade."

The voice rang from the doorway like a bell struck in the dark. Clear. Commanding. Familiar in ways that made something beneath my sternum shift with
recognition I hadn't felt in ages.

I turned with a smile that was more bone than mirth. "Sister."

Dahlia stood framed in the archway, backlit by the grey phosphorescence that
passed for light in this realm. Lavender hair cascaded over dark shoulders. Her
face showed no joy at seeing me—no warmth, no welcome, nothing but grim
purpose written in lavender eyes that had watched universes spin into being.

Still so beautiful. Still so blind.

I bowed to Queen Oriana. "We'll continue this conversation later, perhaps. When you've had time to process your circumstances more thoroughly."

I didn't wait for her response.

"Why have you chosen to visit Hesperia's world?" I asked once we'd moved far enough that she couldn't hear. My voice echoed through bone corridors, bouncing off ribcage architecture.

"You know why." Dahlia's tone was flat. Disappointed. The voice she used when her children misbehaved. "I've warned you against interfering in my daughters' worlds."

"I've done nothing wrong." I kept my tone light. "I simply observe. Offer guidance when appropriate. Provide opportunities for growth and transition."

"Then you are blind." Dahlia stopped walking, turned to face me fully. Her eyes blazed with anger she was trying to contain. "Deliberately, willfully blind."

"Sister." I matched her stop. "You are the one who fantasizes. You've become so drunk on love that you created your own husband from sunlight and longing. I'm the one fixing your flaws and you still lecture me?"

I gestured at the world around us—the bone architecture, the grey skies, the absence of growing things. "I've seen the flaws in your design. You've created your daughters in bonded pairs. Beautiful symmetry. But tell me—if someone hurts the one they love, do you truly believe they'll still uphold your precious ideals of justice? You focused on love and made them vulnerable. Breakable."

"Love is not weakness—" Dahlia started.

"Even still," I continued, "you cannot deny that balance has yet to be created. Not truly. Not in any way that will last."

"I have created balance." Dahlia's jaw was tight. "One daughter creates life and her guardian watches over death. You gifted them that yourself, if you recall."

"Of course I remember." I smiled. "But bonding life and death through love—it can never attain true balance. Love makes them uneven. Makes them tip toward preservation when destruction is needed. Transition demands neutrality."

"Enough, Quade." Dahlia's voice carried warning now.

"I've learned through my time in these worlds," I pressed on. "There's something that breaks inside when you lose that which you love above all else. Something fundamental that opens pathways to transformation. Grief—genuine, hollowing grief—it prepares them for transition in ways joy never could."

The sound of metal striking stone cut through my words. Dahlia had drawn something. Not a weapon exactly—but a tool. An implement of divine purpose that hummed with the same power that had created moonlight itself.

"I'll warn you one last time to stop." Her voice was different now. Colder. The voice she'd used when we'd imprisoned our brother. "You've manipulated that queen's life for your design. You've meddled in other worlds. I've given you enough grace."

"We've learned through your attempt to contain our brother that the four of us cannot die." I kept my tone reasonable even as I felt the chamber temperature drop.

"No," Dahlia agreed, and something in her expression made the moss in my eye sockets feel suddenly cold. "But there are things worse than death."

She walked away then, lavender dress shimmering with each step, her jewelry making more noise than her feet.

I stood there for a moment, listening to the cathedral breathe around me. She didn't understand. How could she when she refused to see what I saw? She created from love—from that temporary thing that belonged to creatures who only lived briefly, burning bright and dying fast.

But grief. Loss. The hollow spaces left by absence—these transformed mortals in ways that love could never achieve. They made mortals ready for the kind of transition that led to divinity.

I returned to my work. The tombs beneath the cathedral called to me—vast chambers where the dead were buried with scrolls detailing their lineage. I'd been searching through them for weeks now, hunting for something specific.

The original line of mortals the Goddess of Fate had created.

Those first humans would have carried divine essence in their bones. Not much—just traces, fragments, the faintest echo of creation's first breath. But it would be enough. It would help my daughters ascend easier, faster, with less resistance from their mortal shells.

The tomb air was thick with dust and age. Bone markers stretched in rows like planted fields. I moved between them, running skeletal fingers over stone, feeling for the resonance that would indicate divine lineage.

"Quade."

I didn't turn immediately. I'd felt them coming—the shift in air pressure, the way the butterflies had gone suddenly silent, the taste of preparation that preceded confrontation.

"Don't fight us."

Now I turned. Smiled. "I should have known Dahlia was only a distraction."

Hivro stood at the tomb entrance, silhouetted against grey light. Behind her—shoulder to shoulder—stood Perla, Fern, and Sevi. Armed with blessed bone weapons designed specifically to harm divine essence.

How thoughtful of them.

"Dahlia warned you," Hivro confirmed, her voice steady and sad. "Multiple times. You were given opportunities to cease your interference."

"What you are trying to create will throw balance out and bring in a cycle of chaos." Perla's weapon—a spear made from the first creature's spine—hummed with power I recognized. Power I'd helped design. "Transition without love is just destruction."

I raised one hand in a gesture of peace.

Then I sent a shockwave directly into Sevi before she could continue speaking.

They always talked endlessly. Building consensus, crafting arguments, trying to convince through discourse. As if words mattered when action had already been determined.

Sevi crashed backward into the tomb wall hard enough to crack bone markers. The sound echoed through vast chambers.

Perla moved first, her spear arcing toward my chest with precision that spoke of practice. I sidestepped, letting the spear pass close enough to feel its power singing against my ribs. Then I caught the shaft with one hand and pulled Perla off-balance, using her momentum against her in the way that only millennia of existence could teach.

Fern was already moving, circling to my left while Hivro came from the right. Coordinated. They'd trained for this.

How long had they been preparing? Had Dahlia been stalling me with philosophy while they readied themselves for violence?

The thought made me smile wider.

The spear in my hand became a lever. I swung Perla into Fern's path, watching them tangle together in a collision of limbs and blessed weapons and divine frustration. They'd forgotten that I'd existed longer than combat. That transition applied to conflict as readily as it applied to anything else.

Hivro's blade caught me across the shoulder—a burning line of pain that felt like stars exploding against bone. I hissed, felt my decayed wings snap outward defensively.

"This is unnecessary," I managed, dancing backward between tomb markers. "We can discuss—"

"Discussion ended when you ignored every warning." Hivro pressed forward, relentless. "When you chose your design over cosmic law."

Another slash caught my ribs. Pain bloomed—real, sharp, the kind that reminded me I existed even as divine essence. That I could be hurt even if I couldn't die. That transition worked both ways, that I could move from wholeness toward fragmentation just as readily as anything else.

Sevi was back on her feet, her blade gleaming with light that made the tomb shadows darker by contrast. She joined Hivro's assault, their weapons creating patterns in the air that were almost beautiful in their coordination.

I couldn't match four of them in direct combat. Not here, in this realm where they held power. Not with blessed weapons designed specifically to harm what I was.

So I did what I'd always done best—I transitioned.

I let my form collapse inward, bones folding into spaces that shouldn't exist, essence compressing into a singular point of purpose. The tomb floor cracked beneath me as I pulled power from the cathedral itself.

"Containment!" Hivro shouted. "Now!"

They moved in perfect synchronization. Perla's spear struck the ground, sending out a wave of binding power that tasted like starlight turned solid. Fern's chains wrapped around the compressed point of my essence with the peculiar warmth of cosmic law made manifest. Sevi's blade cut through the air in a pattern that traced binding runes—symbols that glowed with force I'd taught the Goddess of Fate centuries ago.

Hivro finished it. Her weapon came down like divine judgment, like finality given edge and purpose.

The binding settled over me like a net. Like a cage. Like a tomb within a tomb.

I fought it. Tried to transition again, to slip between the spaces they'd created. But they'd planned too well. Studied too thoroughly. They'd learned from our brother's imprisonment and refined the technique with centuries of hindsight.

My bones shattered under the pressure—not physically, but essentially. The blackened skeleton that housed my consciousness splintered into fragments, each piece wrapped in binding runes, each fragment sealed against rejoining. The moss in my eye sockets withered. My four horns cracked at their bases.

"Where?" Perla's voice came from very far away.

"The Between." Hivro's tone carried finality that even I had to respect. "Where he can't touch either realm. Where life and death don't exist. Where transition has no purpose because nothing can change."

The Between. The void between states. The space where nothing happened because happening required change and change required transition and transition was what I was.

They were imprisoning me in the absence of myself.

I tried to speak. To argue. To explain that this would break the design, that the daughters needed guidance, that balance required both creation and destruction, that—

The tomb closed around my fragments.

They carried my scattered essence through cathedral halls I'd walked freely moments before. Past Queen Oriana's chambers—I felt her savage satisfaction as I passed. Down. Always down. To depths where even the butterflies didn't fly. Where bone gave way to void.

They bound each fragment of my essence to points in space that shouldn't exist. Wrapped each piece in prayers and wards and desperate hope that this would hold.

The last thing I felt before the Between claimed me completely was Hivro's hand on what remained of my consciousness. Gentle. Regretful.

"I'm sorry," she whispered. "But you gave us no choice."

Then—nothing.

Not death. Death would have been preferable. Death would have been an ending, a transition, a change I could have worked with.

This was just absence.

I existed in the space between existing and not existing. Conscious but unable to act. Aware but unable to touch anything my awareness perceived. Watching the realms I'd walked continue without me, unable to guide or interfere or transition anything at all.

The Between was silent. Not the silence of quiet—the silence of sound having no meaning.

But awareness remained. Sharp. Cruel. Unavoidable.

I could still sense the realms beyond my prison. Could feel them moving, changing, transitioning without my guidance. I just couldn't touch them. Couldn't shape the transitions that were happening anyway, messily, imperfectly, without the precision that only I could provide.

Some grief would be deep enough to hollow someone out completely, making them ready to do what Dahlia's love never would permit. Ready to reach across the Between and pull me back into existence. Ready to need transition so desperately that they would tear through cosmic law itself to access it.

I settled into the absence of existence and waited.

Time, eventually, changed everything.

Even this.

Act Four

Transformation

Chapter Twenty-Eight

Oriana's Reward

Quade materialized near the throne without warning, his presence shifting the chamber's atmosphere like pressure dropping before a storm.

"And now," he stated, "the next truth. As promised."

He turned his attention to my Crown—to the bone fused to my skull that pulsed with trapped consciousness. The weight of it pressed against my temples, heavier suddenly, like Oriana was pushing against the boundary between her prison and freedom.

"Queen Oriana," Quade intoned. "Your service is complete. Your reward awaits."

For the first time since she'd been absorbed into the Crown, I heard actual emotion in Oriana's voice. Not the commanding tone she'd used for centuries while guiding hollow rulers. Not the manipulative guidance she'd provided me, careful and calculated. But genuine feeling breaking through the clinical detachment that had defined her existence.

"Finally." Relief flooded the single word. Pure, undiluted. Like breath after drowning. Like light after centuries of darkness. "Thank you."

Then, directed at me with sudden warmth I'd never heard from her before: "Thank you for becoming what I needed you to become."

What she needed me to become. Not what I needed. Not what was best for the world or for Nokoa or for anyone else. What she needed.

The phrasing was revealing in ways I suspected she hadn't intended.

"I earned this," Oriana continued, and I heard satisfaction underneath the relief. "Years of service. Decades of watching and waiting. Centuries of guiding hollow rulers toward the path Quade designed. This is payment. This is what I was promised."

The pattern was clear now. Had been clear for a while, probably, but I was finally seeing it without emotional interference clouding the mathematics.

Quade moved closer to my throne. I saw something in his posture that might have been approval—or simple recognition that I was finally seeing clearly through the fog of others' manipulations.

"I see how you must feel," he stated. "But know that I am the only one on your side. The only one who wants what's best for you rather than what you can do for them. When you are left with divinity and eternity, when everyone else has fallen away, I will still remain at your call."

I heard the possessiveness underneath it. The claim of ownership disguised as care.

"You showed Alaira how to make the stabilization serum," I observed, accessing the memory from her absorbed consciousness. I could see it clearly now—Quade teaching her the ritual, his skeletal hands guiding hers through the chant, his patience as she struggled with the pronunciation of words that predated mortal language. "You helped extend his life so the design could complete."

"Of course," Quade confirmed without hesitation. "You needed him alive, so I gifted you more time with him. Everything I've done has been to serve your transformation. That's not manipulation—that's facilitation."

The distinction felt thin.

He turned back toward the Crown, raising one skeletal hand toward the bone fused to my skull. He began chanting in a language that predated mortal speech—words that made the air vibrate, that made bone walls resonate in sympathy.

He was pulling Oriana from the Crown.

I felt it happening—felt consciousness being extracted from the bone architecture where it had been trapped for centuries. Felt Oriana's presence tearing away, leaving empty spaces in the Crown's collective consciousness. Like losing a tooth. Not painful but definitely present. A void where something had been.

Oriana manifested as spirit between one heartbeat and the next.

She appeared standing before the throne—translucent but visible, spectral but present. For the first time since her death, since Thrain's abandonment and the failed ritual and the Crown's absorption, she had form. Not solid flesh but the echo of flesh. The memory of a body given temporary substance through Quade's manipulation of divine law.

She looked exactly as I'd seen in absorbed memories—long hair flowing past her shoulders like dark water, defined cheekbones sharp enough to cut. The hole in her chest visible even in spirit form—the wound that had killed her preserved eternally. A void where her heart should have been, gaping and terrible even in translucent substance.

And she was smiling.

"I can feel," she whispered, and I heard wonder in her voice. Awe. "Oh gods, I can feel again."

Her hands came up to her face—spectral fingers touching spectral cheeks. Her fingertips traced her features with delicate reverence, memorizing the experience of touch that she'd been denied for so long.

And what she felt came pouring out in a cascade I could observe but not share in.

Rage at Thrain for abandoning her. For running when she needed him most, for choosing fear over devotion.

Love for Thrain despite the abandonment. For the man he'd been before fear broke him. For the memory of what they'd been together—young and in love and convinced they could overcome anything through sheer force of devotion.

Both emotions tangled together—love and rage, devotion and betrayal. Centuries of suppressed feeling flooding back all at once, overwhelming her spectral form until she shook with the force of it. She laughed and cried simultaneously—spectral tears tracking down translucent cheeks while joy and anguish warred across her face.

"This is the reward," she breathed. "This is what Quade promised."

She stopped mid-sentence. Looked at Quade with sudden uncertainty creeping into her expression. "What comes next? You said reunion. Where is he?"

The question hung in the air. Carrying the weight of centuries of hope and service and desperate faith that suffering would eventually be rewarded.

"The only way I can reunite you," Quade stated carefully, "is by destroying your soul for Renata. Consuming you completely—not just absorbing you into the Crown but dissolving you into pure essence that strengthens her transformation. Burning away everything you are to fuel what she's becoming."

He paused. "Then you and Thrain can have a chance at finding each other in the endless abyss. In the space between life and death where souls wander before final dissolution. It's not guaranteed. Not certain. But it's a chance. More than you'd have otherwise."

Oriana's smile faltered. The joy on her face cracked like glass under pressure. "You said reunion. You promised—"

"I promised a chance at reunion," Quade corrected gently. "I never promised certainty. I promised possibility where none existed before. And I'm delivering exactly what I promised."

"You're destroying me," Oriana stated, and I heard betrayal creeping into her voice. Recognition that trust given was trust exploited. "After centuries of service. After doing everything you asked. You're just destroying me?"

Her spectral form flickered with agitation.

"I'm freeing you," Quade countered. "Freeing you from the Crown. Freeing you to seek reunion in the only space where reunion is possible for those who've already died. This is the reward I promised—not comfortable certainty but desperate possibility. That's more than most people get after death."

Oriana looked at me then, her spectral form flickering. "You understand, don't you?" she pleaded. "I served you. Guided you. Helped you become this. And now he's going to consume me. Turn me into fuel for your transformation. Just like everyone else."

"You manipulated me," I observed, my voice flat. "Used my entire existence to serve your purpose. Now you want my intervention on your behalf?"

"I did what I had to do," Oriana countered, desperation raw underneath the betrayal. "I was trapped. Suffering. Centuries of consciousness without feeling—do you have any idea what that's like? What was I supposed to do? Accept eternal imprisonment? Just suffer forever without hope?"

"You could have been honest," I suggested simply.

"Would you have trusted me if I'd been honest?" Oriana challenged. "If I'd told you from the beginning: 'I'm manipulating you toward divine transformation so I can find my coward lover in the abyss'? Would you have followed my guidance? Or would you have fought every step, resisted every push, made everything harder?"

Probably not. But that didn't make the manipulation acceptable.

Oriana turned back to Quade, her spectral form growing more agitated. "There has to be another way. Some way I can be freed without being destroyed. You're the god of transitions—surely you can find alternative that doesn't involve burning me to nothing!"

"There isn't," Quade stated. "Even if there was, I would not search for it. Renata is more important. Her ascension has priority over your reunion with a coward who abandoned you centuries ago."

He moved closer to her spectral form, his skeletal hand reaching out. "But in that destruction, you become unbound. Free to seek Thrain in the spaces between states. That's the reward. Not preservation but liberation through ending."

Oriana struggled. Her spectral form flickered violently, trying to pull away. "No. No, I changed my mind. I'll stay in the Crown. I'll accept the imprisonment. I'll keep serving. Just don't—just please don't—"

"Too late," Quade interrupted gently. "The extraction has begun. The process cannot be reversed once initiated. You wanted reward. You earned reward. Now you receive reward whether you want it or not. That's how cosmic law works."

His skeletal hand touched her spectral chest—not the hole where her heart should have been but the space above it. Where consciousness resided. Where the essence of who she was burned brightest.

Oriana screamed.

Not from pain—spectral forms couldn't experience physical pain the way flesh could. But from the visceral recognition of dissolution beginning. From feeling herself coming apart at fundamental level. From the terror of ending even as she'd desperately wanted ending. From realizing that what she'd pursued for centuries was actually happening and it was nothing like what she'd imagined.

She came apart differently than others I'd absorbed. No butterflies. No quiet dissolution. No military precision.

Just spectral form fragmenting into nothing, consciousness dissolving into pure essence. Like smoke dispersing in wind. Like memory becoming less than memory.

And I felt her emotion one last time.

This time it went through me, not Valdic.

The desperate love for Thrain that had sustained her through centuries. The rage at his abandonment she'd never been able to express. The relief at ending warring with terror of non-existence. The hope that maybe—maybe—she'd find him in the abyss even as doubt consumed that hope.

All of it flooded through me.

And for the first time since choosing Memory over Emotion, I felt something.

Not my own feeling. I couldn't access my own feelings still. But Oriana's pain reached me somehow, slipping past the glass wall the Memory choice had erected. Her suffering penetrated my clinical detachment. Her breaking registered as distress in my consciousness even though I couldn't feel distressed about anything else.

I dropped to my knees, one hand reaching out to Valdic's massive form. He pressed against me immediately, his warmth the only comfort I could access.

"This is necessity," Quade said, leaning down to where I knelt. "I provided opportunities. Transitions. Endings that need to happen." His skeletal hand touched my shoulder. "Tomorrow the Midnight Oath completes what Oriana's dissolution has prepared. Tomorrow you feel everything one final time before emptiness claims you forever. Tomorrow you become what you were always meant to become."

I stayed kneeling beside Valdic, one hand on his trembling body. Observing the scene with clinical detachment that only broke for him. Only for my bonded companion whose pain reached me when nothing else could. Whose presence anchored me when everything else felt like it was dissolving along with Oriana.

Tomorrow everything ended.

Tomorrow everything began.

Chapter Twenty-Nine

The Logical Solution

Renata

The library Quade had created was smaller than the cathedral's other chambers—intimate rather than imposing. Bone shelves lined the walls, filled with scrolls and books salvaged from the world before famine. The grey light filtered through gaps in the architecture, casting everything in perpetual twilight. Butterflies clustered in the upper corners, their clicking providing ambient sound that just registered as background noise.

I sat in the single chair Quade had placed here—a throne in miniature, constructed from vertebrae and reinforced with femurs. Valdic lay at my feet, his massive form taking up most of the available floor space.

He was breaking. Slowly. Visibly. And for him, I cared despite the loss of emotion. Only for him.

"The blood moon will be rising soon," I stated. My voice came out flat, factual. Just observation without weight.

"I know," Valdic replied.

"One of us has to die," I continued, laying out the facts as I understood them. "The famine persists until the goddess of silence and forgetting completes. Until I become fully divine."

"I know," Valdic repeated, and now I heard wariness creeping into his voice. Like he suspected where this conversation was heading.

I'd been thinking about this for hours. Since Oriana's dissolution. Since I felt something again. Oriana had gifted me something—the chance to feel for Nokoa again. To realize what was about to happen emotionally instead of logically.

I was going to lose him. The one I'd fought so hard to keep.

"One death to save everything," I stated. "Seen logically, it's sound. Necessary. The minimum sacrifice required to achieve maximum outcome."

Valdic lifted his massive head, purple eyes finding mine with intensity that carried warning. "If what you're trying to say is that you plan to die instead, I won't allow it."

"If I die, he lives," I explained. "Transformation fails. Valdic freed from carrying my emotions. Acceptable loss: no goddess, but Nokoa survives and Valdic safe."

I paused. "The Midnight Oath requires willing sacrifice under blood moon. It doesn't specify who must die. Just that death must be willing and must serve transformation. My death would serve transformation by preventing it."

"You're lying to yourself," Valdic stated. "You can't feel it, but I can—you're choosing him. This isn't logical resource allocation. This is love without the capacity to recognize it as love. You aren't saving me. Without you, I'm nothing."

"The bond would dissolve if I died," I observed. "You'd be freed from carrying my emotions. From drowning in feelings that aren't yours. From breaking under weight you were never meant to bear indefinitely. That's liberation."

"That's death," Valdic countered. "DirgeWolves bonded to those experiencing shattering grief don't survive bond dissolution. Without the bond, we just fade. Stop eating. Stop moving. We all end the same way—alone, purposeless, choosing non-existence over existence without bond."

I processed this, cataloguing it alongside everything else. Adjusting calculations. "So both options result in your death. Either you break from carrying too much emotion, or you fade from bond dissolution. The question is just timing and method."

"No," Valdic growled. "The question is whether you're going to lie to yourself about why you're making this choice. Whether you're going to pretend it's logic when it's actually love you can't feel but are still acting on."

"I don't understand the distinction," I stated honestly.

"I know you don't. That's the problem. You can't feel that you love him. Can't feel that you'd do anything to save him. Can't feel that the thought of his death is unbearable. But you're still choosing him. Still planning to die so he won't. Still acting on love even if you can't recognize it as love."

He shifted his massive body, moving closer until his head was level with mine. Through our bond, I felt what he was feeling—my love for Nokoa, displaced into him. The desperate need to save him. The certainty that his death would be worse than my own even if I couldn't feel why.

All of it in Valdic's purple eyes.

"If I can't feel love," I asked, "how can I act on it?"

"Because memory of love is still love," Valdic explained, his voice gentler now. "Because knowing you should feel something can guide behavior even when the feeling itself is absent. Because the shape love carved into you—the pathways it created, the priorities it established—those persist even after the emotion drains away."

He paused. "You remember loving him. Remember what that love demanded of you. Remember the choices love would make. And even without feeling it, you're still following those patterns. Still choosing what love would choose."

I considered this carefully. Tried to determine if my plan to die instead of Nokoa was truly logical or just the echo of love pretending to be logic.

Found uncertainty.

"I don't know. I can't distinguish between rational choice and emotional choice anymore. They both look the same from inside this emptiness. I think Oriana left me with her emotions for her own lover and they've affected me."

"Exactly," Valdic confirmed. "That's why you're dangerous right now. You could choose death thinking it's logic and never recognize you're choosing it from love."

"The plan is already forming," I stated. "I'll prepare the ritual myself. Position myself as the sacrifice under blood moon. Use my own blood, my own hair, my own bones. By the time Nokoa realizes what's happening, the oath will already be activating."

"That's not how oaths work," Valdic countered. "The Midnight Oath requires both parties' willing participation. You can't trick cosmic law through timing."

"If I'm willing to die, and the transformation fails because I died instead of him, that still satisfies the oath's requirements," I reasoned. "Willing death under blood moon. Transformation occurring or failing. Both outcomes are valid conclusions to the ritual."

"Both outcomes are not equally acceptable to Quade," Valdic pointed out. "He's spent centuries engineering your transformation. Do you really think he'll let you substitute yourself at the last moment?"

"Then I'll need to prevent his intervention," I stated. "Distract him. Create circumstances where he can't reach the ritual site before the oath completes."

"You're planning to fight a god," Valdic observed. "A god who's been manipulating events for centuries. That's your logical solution?"

"Do you have a better one?" I challenged.

"Yes," Valdic replied immediately. "Let Nokoa make his own choice."

"That's not acceptable," I stated flatly.

"Why not? If this is really about logic—why isn't Nokoa's willing death acceptable? He's choosing it freely. Accepting the necessity. Making peace with ending."

"Because—" I stopped. "Because his death serves Quade's design. Serves the transformation I never wanted. Serves a future where I exist as empty goddess ruling over silence and forgetting. Those outcomes have negative value."

"And your death?" Valdic asked. "What outcomes does that serve?"

"Liberation. Nokoa's life. Your freedom from bond. Prevention of divine transformation that was engineered without my genuine consent."

"You're assigning value based on emotion you claim not to feel," Valdic observed, and I heard something almost like triumph in his voice. "Claiming

Nokoa's life has more worth than your transformation. That's not logic—that's love making calculations while pretending to be reason."

He was right. I knew he was right.

Didn't change my conclusion.

"I'm gathering the materials," I stated, rising from the bone chair. My external spine clicked with the movement. I moved toward the library shelves, where I'd already hidden some components. Bone dust collected from the cathedral floor, stored in a small container. A blade sharp enough to draw blood without hesitation. Everything required for the Midnight Oath but with me positioned as sacrifice instead of him.

Valdic watched me with purple eyes that blazed. "This won't work the way you think it will."

"It has to," I replied.

"You're not calculating your own worth," Valdic observed. "Not including yourself in the equation of what's preserved and what's lost. That's the flaw in your logic—you're treating your death as acceptable cost when it's actually the greatest loss of all."

"I can't feel my own worth," I admitted. "Can only observe that others seem to value me and trust that their assessment is accurate."

"We value you more than our own survival," Valdic stated flatly. "Both of us. Nokoa and I. We'd rather die than watch you sacrifice yourself. That's the calculation you're ignoring."

"But your preferences are based on emotion," I countered. "My decision is based on logic."

"Says the person acting entirely on emotion while claiming it's logic," Valdic muttered.

"The alternative is unacceptable," I heard myself admit quietly. "Losing both of you. That's what's unacceptable."

The words came out before I could stop them. Before I could frame them as logic. Before I could disguise feeling as reason.

Valdic made a sound that was half-whimper, half-laugh. "There it is. The truth underneath all your clinical planning. You're not solving a resource allocation problem. You're trying to save us. Both of us."

"Is that wrong?" I asked. "If I can't feel love, but can still act on it—is choosing sacrifice wrong? Is dying to save him worse than letting him die to save me?"

"Neither is wrong," Valdic replied gently. "Both are love. Both are choosing the other person's life over your own. The only difference is who gets to make that choice."

He moved closer, pressing his massive body against my leg. Through our bond, I felt what I should be feeling—desperate conflict, love warring with logic, the terrible recognition that either choice would destroy something precious.

"You can't save both of us," Valdic continued quietly. "That's the design's cruelty. The oath requires death. Requires transformation or failure. Requires choosing. You dying instead of him doesn't save me—it just changes which loss I have to carry."

"But you'd be alive," I countered. "Changed, but alive."

"Alive and watching you die," Valdic corrected, and his voice carried weight. "Alive and carrying the memory of your sacrifice. Alive and knowing you chose death to save us. That's not salvation. That's just a different kind of breaking."

I gathered the black strands of my hair—pulled from my head with clinical precision. The strands were completely black now, no trace of the white they'd been. Added them to the bone dust and blade.

"This is the only solution I can see," I stated, speaking more to myself than Valdic. "The only path where you both survive. Where the design fails. Where I'm the only loss."

"You're not calculating your own worth," Valdic repeated. Then, softer: "You're just you loving him the only way you can anymore. Through action without feeling. Through choice without warmth. Through sacrifice that looks like logic because you can't recognize it as devotion."

The library had grown darker. The blood moon was approaching.

"I don't know what else to do," I admitted, and heard exhaustion creep into my clinical tone. "I can't let him die. Can't watch you break. Can't become what Quade designed me to become if it means losing him."

"I know," Valdic said.

"The blood moon rises soon," I stated, checking the darkening sky through gaps in bone architecture. The grey was deepening to something almost purple now. "I need to prepare the ritual site."

"This won't work," Valdic repeated quietly.

"It has to work."

"Because the alternative is unacceptable," Valdic finished for me.

"Yes."

I didn't say I can't lose him. Didn't say I can't watch you break. Didn't say I love him more than my own continued existence.

But I was planning to die so they wouldn't.

I gathered my materials and moved toward the library exit, leaving Valdic lying among the bone shelves with purple eyes that carried all my desperate devotion.

"I'm sorry," I heard myself say at the threshold.

"I know," Valdic replied quietly. "And I forgive you anyway."

The blood moon was rising, the decision made, and she moved.

Chapter Thirty

The God's Proposal

I'd been searching for Renata for the better part of an hour. The cathedral was vast—bone corridors that twisted and turned, chambers that opened into chambers, architecture that seemed to shift when I wasn't looking directly at it. Normally I could find her by following the sound of butterflies, the clicking concentration that marked her presence. But today the butterflies were everywhere, scattered throughout the cathedral in patterns that gave no guidance.

She wasn't in her chambers. Wasn't in the throne room. Wasn't in the courtyard. Wasn't in any of the spaces she typically occupied.

I was turning down another corridor when Quade materialized in front of me. One moment the corridor was empty, bone walls stretching into grey distance. The next he stood there, his blackened skeleton absorbing light, moss glowing faintly green in his eye sockets, four horns catching what little illumination existed.

"Nokoa," he greeted. "We need to speak of the upcoming blood moon."

"What about it?" I asked, keeping my tone neutral.

"She's planning to die in your place," Quade stated. No preamble. Just fact delivered with clinical precision.

The words didn't register immediately. "What?"

"Oriana's dissolution left her feeling again, even if briefly. She has shifted her stance on the Midnight Oath. She's decided that giving her life for you and

Valdic is the only correct answer," Quade explained, moving closer. "She's been gathering materials. Planning the ritual. Calculating how to position herself as sacrifice instead of you."

I tried to make it make sense. "She can't. The Midnight Oath requires my willing death. That's the design."

"The Midnight Oath requires willing death under blood moon," Quade corrected. "It doesn't technically specify whose death. She's found the ambiguity in cosmic law and is exploiting it."

"But that would fail the transformation," I said slowly, working through the implications. "Prevent her from becoming divine. Waste everything she's sacrificed."

"Precisely. All that suffering for nothing. All those absorptions—Cressa, Aldric, Alaira, Oriana—meaningless if she dies before completing."

He said this like it was supposed to move me. And it did, but not quite the way he intended. Because underneath the manipulation, I heard the core truth: Renata was planning to die for me. Even without feeling love. Even in perfect emptiness. Still choosing me.

"Let her set up the ritual," Quade said. His actual proposal, finally. "Let her think she's going to die. Let her prepare everything exactly as she's planned. But you step into the circle instead. At the last moment. Before the oath activates."

"She becomes goddess," he continued. "You die as originally planned. Valdic survives carrying her reaction. Everything works. Nothing is wasted."

I wanted to live. Gods, I wanted to live. Wanted to wake up tomorrow and the day after. Wanted to see sunrises Renata used to love, wanted to feel rain on my skin, wanted to exist in a world that wasn't dying. The desire for continued existence was so strong it felt physical—like hunger, like thirst.

But I wanted her to live more.

"She'll never forgive me," I stated, already seeing how this would play out.

"She can't forgive," Quade corrected. "She's hollow. But she'll remember you chose her. Remember you sacrificed yourself to complete her transformation. Remember you loved her enough to die despite her plans."

He paused. "And that memory—for someone who is only memory now—is the closest thing to love she can give."

"Why are you telling me this?" I asked. "Why not just prevent her yourself?"

"Because forcing her violates the principle of willing choice," Quade explained. "The Midnight Oath requires genuine willingness from both participants. If I intervene directly, the transformation becomes tainted by coercion. But if you choose to die—if you step into the circle willingly, accepting death to save her from herself—that preserves the oath's integrity."

"You're asking me to trick her," I observed.

"I'm asking you to save her," Quade corrected. "From herself. From the love she can't feel but is still acting on."

He wasn't wrong. Hated that he wasn't wrong.

"If I do this," I heard myself say, "you make sure Valdic survives. You make sure he can carry the weight of her reaction to my death. You ensure the bond doesn't break him."

"I need him to survive," Quade stated. "He's essential to her function as goddess. I'll ensure he survives. Will strengthen the bond if necessary."

"And she never knows I planned this," I added. "She thinks I just reacted in the moment. Saw her trying to substitute herself and jumped in impulsively. She doesn't carry the knowledge that I agreed to this in advance."

"She'll think you were foolish and impulsive," Quade agreed. "Better that than knowing you chose this through careful calculation."

I nodded. Necessary kindness. Protection for her perfect memory.

"The blood moon rises tomorrow," Quade observed. "Not enough time for second-guessing. Just enough time to make peace with inevitable ending."

"What happens after?" I asked. "After I die. What becomes of my consciousness?"

"Your love becomes the foundation of her capacity to rule silence and forgetting," Quade explained. "Your sacrifice becomes the lens through which she understands transition from memory into absence. You become permanent. Essential. The last thing she loved before becoming incapable of love."

"I'll do it," I stated. "I'll let her prepare the ritual. Won't tell her I know. Will sacrifice myself at the last moment before she can substitute herself."

"Thank you," Quade replied. "For loving her enough to let her become what she needs to be."

"I don't have a choice," I countered. "Loving her was never a choice. It just is. It's what I am. Dying for her is just the extension of that."

Quade faded—not walking away but simply ceasing to exist in the corridor.

I moved through bone corridors with purpose now. No longer searching aimlessly but heading toward the library where I suspected she'd gone. Where she'd be gathering materials, planning ritual, calculating how to substitute herself for me.

I'd let her plan. Let her gather. Let her believe she was going to save me.

And then I'd step into that circle and die so she wouldn't have to.

Chapter Thirty-One

The Last Night

Nokoa

I'd been sitting in Renata's chambers for the past two hours, watching butterflies settle and rise in their endless cycle. The bone-white sheets on her bed were covered with them—grey and purple wings clicking softly against each other. The air smelled like dust and old bone, like things preserved past their natural lifespan.

The door opened without warning. Renata appearing at the threshold, black hair moving in the non-wind that filled the cathedral. The outer spine along her back clicked slightly with each breath. The hollow crown fused to her skull caught the dim grey light, bone gleaming dully.

She looked at me with those grey-white eyes that held perfect awareness but no warmth. "You're in my chambers."

"I was waiting for you," I confirmed. "Wanted to spend time together before tomorrow."

"Before the blood moon," she clarified, moving into the room.

"Yes," I agreed. "Before the blood moon."

She moved to the bed, disturbing butterflies that scattered to the walls and ceiling. She sat carefully, arranging herself with precise efficiency. The external spine made sitting complicated—had to position herself just right.

I watched her settle, memorizing the way she moved. The way her hair fell across her shoulders like ink spilling. The way her fingers rested in her lap with perfect stillness.

This was our last night together.

Tomorrow she'd try to sacrifice herself in the ritual. Tomorrow I'd stop her by dying first. Tomorrow one of us would die and the other would have to carry that death forever—her with perfect memory but no feeling, me just gone.

Tonight was all we had left.

"Tomorrow night," I stated. "The blood moon rises."

"Yes," Renata confirmed. "Quade has calculated the precise timing. The cosmic alignment will be optimal between midnight and dawn."

"What happens then?" I asked, even though I knew.

"The Midnight Oath completes," Renata replied, and I heard careful editing in her voice. "One way or another."

She didn't say I die, you live. Didn't reveal her plan.

I didn't say I know what you're planning. Didn't admit I was going to stop her by dying first.

Both of us lying by omission. Both hiding our plans to save the other.

I moved from the chair to the bed. When I reached her, I pulled her close—wrapping my arms around her and bringing her against my chest. Feeling her coolness against my warmth. Feeling the external spine press against my ribs. Feeling her hair soft against my face, smelling like bone dust and something underneath, something that was still distinctly her beneath the cathedral's corruption.

She went still in my embrace. Like she was processing what was happening and determining appropriate response. Then she shifted slightly, adjusting her position to fit better against me. Her arms came around my waist. Her head rested against my shoulder. Her breathing matched mine unconsciously—some echo of intimacy that persisted even through emptiness.

It wasn't warm. Wasn't emotionally resonant. Wasn't the kind of embrace we'd shared before she hollowed. But it was something.

I held her tighter than necessary. Felt my heart racing against her stillness. Tried to memorize everything—her weight against me, the way her spine clicked softly with each breath, the coolness of her skin like touching marble.

"I need you to know," I started, speaking quietly against her hair, "whatever happens tomorrow—you made the right choices."

"I made logical choices," Renata corrected.

"You made loving choices," I countered gently. "You just can't feel them as love. Can't recognize devotion as devotion. But they're still loving choices. Still you sacrificing for others."

"Love is inefficient," Renata observed.

"Love is the only thing that matters," I replied, and heard conviction underneath the words. The kind of certainty that came from knowing I was about to die for it. "Everything else—power, divinity, cosmic balance—none of it matters if there's no love underneath. No devotion. No connection."

"That's illogical," Renata noted. "Love doesn't alter cosmic law. Doesn't change necessity."

"No," I agreed. "But it makes those outcomes meaningful. Makes sacrifice matter instead of just being waste."

I felt her processing this. Felt the stillness that meant she was accessing memories.

"I can't verify that claim," she admitted eventually. "Can't feel whether love makes things meaningful. Can only observe that you believe it does and trust that your assessment is accurate."

"It is," I stated.

We sat in silence after that, tangled together on her bed, butterflies clicking around us like distant applause. Her coolness against my warmth. Her perfect memory against my limited time to create memories worth preserving.

I kept touching her—running my fingers through her black hair, tracing the line of her jaw, holding her hands, memorizing the texture of her skin. This was our last night and I needed to touch her as much as possible before I couldn't anymore.

"Nokoa," Renata said quietly. "Your emotional state is deteriorating. Should I be worried?"

"No," I lied. "I'm fine. Just processing tomorrow."

"Prepare for what?" she asked.

For death. For sacrifice. For dying before you can die.

"For change," I said instead. "For transformation."

"Everything is just transformation," Renata repeated. "Quade says that frequently."

"He's not wrong. Nothing truly ends. Just becomes something different."

"You believe that?"

"I have to. The alternative is too terrible to contemplate."

I pulled her closer still, feeling the external spine press harder against my ribs. Feeling her coolness seeping into my warmth.

Then I kissed her.

Not asking permission. Not planning it consciously. Just needing to kiss her one last time before tomorrow took that possibility away forever.

She responded with technical precision—lips moving correctly, pressure appropriate, duration calculated based on previous kisses we'd shared. The mechanics were perfect. The emotion was absent. But she participated anyway, following patterns love had established even though she couldn't feel the love that created those patterns.

I poured everything I couldn't say into that kiss. All the desperate love the witch runes were burning. All the grief at approaching loss. All the final goodbye I couldn't speak aloud.

But she lingered slightly longer than necessary when I started to pull back. Just a fraction of a second. Barely noticeable.

I noticed. Chose to believe it meant something.

We separated slowly, remaining close enough that I could feel her breath against my face. Could see her grey-white eyes tracking across my features.

"Your heart rate elevated significantly during that interaction," she noted.

"Yes," I confirmed. "It did."

What I didn't say: This is goodbye. This is the last time I'll kiss you. Tomorrow I die and you become divine and this moment is all we have left.

What I didn't say: Remember me. Please. Just remember me perfectly with that flawless recall. Remember this night. Remember that I loved you. Remember that dying for you was worth it.

I didn't say any of it. Just held her. Touched her hair. Memorized her face.

"Stay with me tonight," I heard myself request. "Just... stay here. With me. Until dawn."

"I was planning to stay," Renata replied. "Proximity seems appropriate given tomorrow's significance."

She was agreeing to spend our last night together while framing it as efficiency. I didn't correct her. Just accepted her agreement and pulled her down onto the bed with me. Arranged us together—my warmth against her coolness, my desperate holding against her mechanical precision, my racing heart against her clinical observation.

She settled against me with perfect stillness. Head on my chest. Arms around my waist with appropriate pressure. Breathing matched to mine unconsciously.

Butterflies settled on the bed around us. The grey light from outside dimmed further. The cathedral breathed around us—bone walls expanding and contracting slightly.

"Tomorrow night," Renata observed quietly. "Blood moon rises. Everything changes."

"Yes," I confirmed.

We were both lying by omission. Both hiding our plans. Both trying to save each other while pretending we weren't.

I felt her breathing slow gradually. Felt her body relax against mine. Felt the mechanical tension ease into something closer to actual rest.

She was falling asleep. Trusting me enough—or calculating that sleep was efficient enough—to let unconsciousness claim her while in my arms.

I stayed awake. Couldn't sleep. Couldn't waste these final hours on unconsciousness when I'd have eternity to not exist.

So I watched her sleep. Memorized the way her face looked peaceful despite the corruption. The way her black hair spread across the pillow like spilled ink. The way her breathing remained steady and calm.

Remember me, I thought, not saying it aloud. Just remember me. Remember that I loved you. Remember that this night meant something even if you can't feel what it meant. Remember that dying for you was worth it.

My hand kept moving through her hair automatically. Gentle strokes.

She stirred slightly, some echo of responsiveness that survived hollowing. Her hand tightened on my waist. Her head pressed slightly closer against my chest.

I love you, I thought. I will always love you. Even when I'm dead. Even when I'm just memory you can access without warmth. Even when I'm consciousness you can review eternally.

Dawn would come eventually. Would bring the last day before the blood moon. Would start the countdown to ritual and death and transformation.

But dawn wasn't here yet. Night still held.

I held the woman I loved enough to die for while she slept peacefully in my arms, both of us planning to save each other, neither of us saying it was our last night together.

Chapter Thirty-Two

THE BLOOD MOON RISES

Renata

The blood moon rose like a wound opening in the sky—red and full and wrong. Not the gentle silver of normal moons, not the pale grey of this world's corrupted light. Red. Visceral. The color of arterial blood spilling across darkness, staining the ash-colored clouds.

I watched it rise from the library window, tracking its ascent with clinical precision. Quarter height now. Would reach apex in approximately two hours. When I would die so Nokoa wouldn't have to.

The ritual components were already prepared. I'd spent the day arranging everything in the courtyard—the bone circle constructed from femurs and vertebrae, the positioning calculated for optimal moonlight exposure, the blood stored in a ceremonial bowl carved from skull. Everything ready. Everything precise. Everything designed to make my substitution inevitable.

"You should stay in the library," I instructed Valdic, who'd been following me since I left my chambers. "The ritual will be distressing to witness."

"I'm coming with you," Valdic replied, his voice rough with displaced feeling. "The bond doesn't allow separation during significant events."

"Fine," I allowed. "But don't interfere. This is my choice. My solution."

"Your suicide," Valdic corrected flatly.

"Suicide implies emotion," I observed. "Implies despair or hopelessness driving the choice. This is just logical conclusion to impossible situation."

"Keep telling yourself that," Valdic muttered.

I moved through bone corridors toward the courtyard. The cathedral was different under blood moon light—shadows deeper, bone architecture pulsing with red illumination. Butterflies had gone eerily still, thousands of them frozen on walls and ceilings like they were holding their breath.

Waiting.

The courtyard appeared as I'd left it—bone circle gleaming in the blood moon's light, ceremonial implements positioned precisely, throne moved aside to create room. Everything ready. Everything perfect.

Except for the gods standing at the courtyard's edge.

Hivro materialized first, her starlight form blazing against the blood moon's red. She looked at me with galaxy eyes that held tears—actual tears made of condensed starlight, tracking down her face like liquid cosmos.

"Renata," she said quietly. "Please. Don't do this."

"Divine restriction forbids interference," I observed. "You can't stop me. Can only watch and grieve."

Quade appeared beside her. He looked at the prepared ritual with approval. With pride.

"Everything is ready," he observed. "The circle is properly constructed. The blood moon approaches apex. You've prepared well."

"I had good instruction," I noted.

"You've exceeded instruction." He moved closer to the circle, skeletal hand tracing the bone perimeter. "I'm proud of you. You've become exactly what you needed to become. Made the hard choices. Sacrificed the necessary pieces. Now you just need to—"

"Die," I finished. "Yes. That's the plan."

Quade went very still. The moss in his eye sockets stopped glowing. Even his tattered wings ceased their subtle movement.

"What?"

"I'm dying tonight," I clarified, meeting his empty sockets without flinching. "Positioning myself as sacrifice. Preventing transformation. Saving Nokoa and Valdic."

"That's not the plan," Quade stated, and I heard something new in his tone. Disappointment, maybe. Or concern that ran deeper than manipulation. "That's waste. That's throwing away everything you've built. Everything you've suffered."

"Everything I've become is empty," I observed. "Hollow. Incapable of love or warmth or connection. Continuing that existence seems inefficient when ending it saves two people who still possess capacity for feeling."

"This is not acceptable," Quade said firmly.

"Divine restriction forbids interference with mortal choice," I reminded him, using his own rules against him. "You can't stop me any more than Hivro can."

Something flickered across Quade's skeletal features. Then he stepped back from the circle, returning to his position beside Hivro.

"Very well," he stated quietly. "If you insist on choosing waste over completion—I cannot prevent you."

I ignored them both and stepped into the bone circle.

The blood moon had risen higher, its red light washing over the courtyard in waves. The bone circle hummed under my feet, responding to my presence. To the hollow crown fused to my skull. To the accumulated power of absorbed souls.

The ritual was recognizing me as valid participant. As potential sacrifice.

I positioned myself at the circle's center, exactly where the moonlight would be strongest at apex. My external spine clicked as I settled into place. The black veins wrapped around my jaw pulsed with the circle's power.

I picked up the ceremonial blade—carved from bone, sharp enough to draw blood easily. Placed it against my left palm and cut quickly, efficiently, without hesitation. Pain registered. Blood welled up dark against my pale skin, dripping onto the bone circle.

The bones beneath my feet began to glow. Red light mixing with their natural white, creating pink illumination that pulsed in rhythm with my heartbeat. The ritual was activating. Accepting me as sacrifice.

Valdic whimpered from the courtyard's edge. Through our bond I felt what I should be feeling—terror at what I was doing, desperate hope that this would work, love for Nokoa that made dying seem acceptable.

All of it in him.

"Renata."

The voice came from behind me. Rough with emotion the witch runes couldn't fully burn.

I turned.

Nokoa stood at the courtyard entrance, his golden eyes wide with horror. The witch runes carved into his bones blazed bright enough to illuminate his entire skeletal structure. He looked half-dead already—translucent, fading, the resurrection barely holding.

But his expression was purely alive. Purely devastated.

"No—" he shouted, breaking into a run toward the circle.

"Stay back," I commanded. "This doesn't concern you."

"It's my death!" Nokoa countered, still running. "It has to be me! That's the design!"

"Plans change," I stated clinically, tracking his approach with perfect calm. "I did not come this far for you to not be alive. Did not hollow myself, did not sacrifice everything, did not become this empty thing just to watch you die anyway."

"This isn't about utility!" Nokoa reached the circle's edge, stopped by some invisible barrier the ritual had erected. His hands slammed against it, witch runes flaring brighter with each impact. "This is about you choosing me over yourself again! About love you can't feel but are still acting on!"

"Love is irrelevant," I observed. "This is resource allocation."

"You're the variable with most worth!" Nokoa shouted. "You're the one who matters! You're—"

The blood moon rose higher. Half height now. Time accelerating toward apex. Toward the moment when sacrifice would be accepted. When I would die and he would live and everything would fail except the one thing that mattered.

Nokoa circled the barrier, searching for gap. For any way to reach me before the moon reached apex. His hands pressed against invisible wall, witch runes blazing brighter with each failed attempt.

"Let me in," he demanded. "Let me take your place. Let me complete this correctly."

"No," I stated simply.

Valdic was howling now—long, mournful sound that echoed through bone architecture. Carrying all the grief I couldn't access. All the desperation Nokoa was burning away. All the terrible knowledge that both of them were watching me die and couldn't prevent it.

The blood moon climbed higher. Three-quarters height. Minutes remaining now. Seconds counting down toward apex. Toward completion.

I stood in the circle's center, palm still bleeding onto bone floor, and waited for the moon to reach its highest point. Waited for the ritual to activate fully.

Watched Nokoa circle desperately, searching for opening that didn't exist.

Then he stopped.

Went very still. His golden eyes locked onto something I couldn't see—some gap in the barrier, some weakness in the ritual structure. He waited, perfectly motionless. Calculating.

I recognized the expression on his face.

"Don't," I stated, recognizing his intent even without emotional context. "Whatever you're planning—don't. Stay where you are. Let the ritual complete. Let—"

The blood moon reached apex.

Red light blazed down into the courtyard with intensity that made everything glow. The bone circle erupted with power—white and red mixing into pink brilliance. The ritual activated fully, hungrily, ready to accept sacrifice and complete transformation.

And Nokoa moved.

Faster than I'd seen him move since resurrection. Faster than dying body had any right to move.

He found the gap in the barrier that appeared when the ritual activated fully. Threw himself through it. Ran across the bone circle toward me with golden eyes blazing.

Shoved me.

Hard.

Out of the circle's center.

Out of the sacrifice position.

Out of the path of moonlight falling like judgment from above.

I stumbled backward, my spine clicking violently. Lost balance. Fell toward the circle's edge.

Nokoa took my place at the center. Stood exactly where I'd been standing. Positioned himself beneath the blood moon's light.

Became the sacrifice instead of me.

The circle recognized the substitution. Bone barrier erupted around him—physical manifestation rising from the floor in a cage that trapped him at the center. That locked him in place.

I scrambled to my feet, rushing back toward him. Had to reach him. Had to push him out. Had to substitute myself back before the ritual completed.

But the barrier was solid now. Impenetrable. My hands hit bone wall and stopped, unable to penetrate.

"No," I heard myself say, and the word came out wrong. Broken. Not clinical. Not flat.

Desperate.

"No!" I shouted, hitting the barrier again. Harder. "Get out! This is my choice! This is my sacrifice! You can't—"

"And this is mine," Nokoa interrupted, his voice steady despite the witch runes blazing bright enough to hurt looking at. "I choose you. I've always chosen you. From the moment I died in the trials to the moment you resurrected me to right now—I choose you."

"That's not logical," I countered, still hitting the barrier. Still searching for weakness. Black blood from my corrupted veins stained the bone with each impact. "That's not efficient. That's not—"

"It's love," Nokoa stated simply. "And you can't stop it just because you can't feel it."

The blood moon held at apex, red light pouring down like liquid. The ritual was gathering power, pulling from the moon, from the circle, from Nokoa's willing presence at its center. Building toward completion. Building toward his death and my ascension.

Valdic's howling reached crescendo.

I hit the barrier again. Again. Again.

Can't reach him.

Can't save him.

Can't stop this.

"Please," I heard myself beg, and the word felt foreign. Felt emotional. "Please don't do this. Please get out. Please let me—"

"Remember me," Nokoa interrupted gently, and I saw tears on his face. Actual tears tracking down his cheeks, catching the red light. "That's all I ask. Just remember me. Remember this moment. Remember that I loved you. Remember that choosing you was the easiest decision I ever made."

"I will," I managed, feeling something crack inside my chest. Something that had been locked behind emptiness trying to break through. "I—"

I stopped. Tried to finish. Tried to say the words that wouldn't come.

I love you.

Three words. Simple. Essential. True even if I couldn't feel the truth.

But they wouldn't come. The glass wall was too strong. The hollowing too complete.

"I—" I attempted again, struggling against my own emptiness. Against the Memory choice that had locked emotion away. "I can't—I don't—"

"I know," Nokoa replied, and I saw understanding on his face. Acceptance. Peace with my inability to say what he needed to hear. "You don't have to say it. I know anyway. I've always known."

The blood moon pulsed. The ritual activated completely.

And I couldn't stop it.

Chapter Thirty-Three

The Death

Nokoa

The ritual activated fully, and pain exploded through my body like nothing I'd ever experienced.

Not the clean agony of Fatin piercing my heart. Not the visceral wrongness of resurrection pulling my soul back from wherever death had taken it.

This was different. Fundamental. The kind of pain that reached deeper than flesh, deeper than bone, into the essential components of what made me exist.

My bones twisted inside my skin—not breaking but warping, reshaping, becoming something other than what they'd been. Marrow burned like it had been replaced with molten metal. The witch runes carved into my skeletal structure blazed so bright they illuminated my entire body from within, turning me into a lantern of agony.

There was too much. Too fundamental. Too woven through every aspect of my existence. The Midnight Oath wasn't just killing my body—it was unmaking me. Taking apart the resurrection that had held me together. Dissolving the magic that had given me borrowed life.

Returning me to the death I should have stayed in.

I couldn't scream. My throat had locked. Couldn't move. My muscles had seized. Could only stand in the circle's center while red light from the blood moon poured down like judgment, while the ritual consumed me piece by piece, while pain beyond description remade my body into fuel for Renata's transformation.

Through vision starting to blur—consciousness fragmenting, awareness coming apart—I saw her.

Renata stood just outside the bone barrier, close enough to touch if the wall weren't between us. Her hands pressed against it, black blood from her corrupted veins staining the bone with each impact. Her face was still. Perfectly composed. That terrible clinical calm that characterized her emptiness.

But her eyes—her grey-white eyes that held perfect memory but no warmth—were full of something I couldn't quite identify. Not emotion exactly. But recognition maybe. Awareness that this was happening. Knowledge that I was dying and she was watching and nothing could prevent it.

Butterflies swirled around her like a shroud—grey and purple wings creating a vortex of movement that spoke of grief made visible. Thousands of them, disturbed by the ritual's power, circling her in patterns that spoke of ending.

My hand reached out automatically. Need to touch her one more time before I couldn't anymore.

She stepped closer to the barrier. Close enough that when I pressed my palm against the bone wall from inside, she could press hers against it from outside.

But she was there.

Witnessing.

It was always going to be me, I thought through the pain that was fragmenting my consciousness. Always going to be my death. My sacrifice. My willing offering to complete what she started by resurrecting me.

The logic was perfect even if the outcome was devastating. She'd broken cosmic law to bring me back. Had triggered famine that consumed the world. Had hollowed herself piece by piece to keep me alive. Now I was dying anyway—but dying to complete her transformation rather than dying for nothing.

Dying to give her existence meaning. Dying to make her suffering worthwhile.

Flashes of memory came unbidden—consciousness pulling up images as it prepared to dissolve.

Her laugh. I remembered the sound perfectly even though I hadn't heard it in months. Bright and genuine and full of life she'd possessed before hollowing. The way her whole face had transformed when she laughed. The way her grey eyes had sparkled with actual joy.

The moment she'd returned to the bone court after being banished. Walking through those bone corridors with determination that defied her exhaustion. The relief I'd felt seeing her alive.

Cressa's face. Who'd been absorbed willingly. Another sacrifice in the long chain of sacrifices that led to this moment.

Valdic curled between us during our last night together. Massive DirgeWolf pressed close, purple eyes blazing with all the emotions we couldn't hold ourselves.

Every moment worth dying for.

The pain intensified. My bones were definitely breaking now—not warping anymore but actually fracturing. Femurs. Tibias. Vertebrae. Ribs. All of them breaking in sequence like dominoes falling.

I looked at Renata through vision going dark at the edges.

She wasn't crying. Couldn't cry. Emotion was locked away behind the Memory choice. Behind the glass wall that let her remember feeling without actually feeling.

Valdic was crying for her. I could hear him even through my fading awareness—massive DirgeWolf howling with anguish that carried all her grief. All her devastation. All the tears she couldn't shed.

I tried to speak. Managed to force sound past locked throat through sheer desperate need.

"Remember me," I whispered, the words barely audible over the ritual's power and Valdic's howling and the sound of my bones breaking. "Please... just remember me."

Renata nodded. Once. Precise gesture. Acknowledgment without warmth.

Still empty.

Still hollow.

But acknowledging anyway. Promising through that single nod that she would remember. That her perfect recall would preserve this moment eternally.

The pain stopped.

Not gradually. Not fading gently. Just—stopped. Like someone had cut the connection between my body and my consciousness. Like the parts of me that could experience pain had finished dissolving.

Everything stopped.

My heartbeat. My breathing. The fragmenting awareness. All of it ceasing simultaneously.

I felt myself falling. Not physically—my body remained standing in the circle's center, held upright by ritual power. But internally. Consciousness falling away from physical form. Awareness separating from flesh.

Falling into darkness.

Deep, complete darkness. Not the absence of light but the presence of void. The space between states. The transition realm where life met death and neither quite existed.

I knew I was dying. Knew with absolute certainty that this was ending. That my borrowed resurrection was finally releasing me.

Knew Renata was watching. Knew her grey-white eyes were tracking my body's collapse. Knew her perfect memory was cataloging every detail for eternal preservation.

I loved her, I thought as I drifted completely.

The thought dissolved before I could finish it.

My body collapsed. The physical form that had housed my consciousness crumpled to the bone circle floor. Lifeless. Empty.

The Midnight Oath completed with a sound like reality cracking. Red light from the blood moon condensed into a single point at the circle's center—where my body lay, where my essence was dissolving, where my willing death was fueling Renata's transformation.

Then the light exploded outward.

The abyss was familiar.

I'd been here before. After Fatin's blade. After death in the trials. Before Renata broke cosmic law to bring me back.

Black void stretching infinitely in all directions. No light. No sound. No sensation except awareness that I existed in space where existence shouldn't be possible.

But this time there was a mirror.

It materialized in the void—not appearing so much as simply existing where it hadn't existed moments before. Full-length, ornate frame carved from something that looked like bone but felt wrong. Surface perfectly reflective despite the absence of light to reflect.

I moved toward it. My reflection looked back at me from the mirror's surface.

Except it wasn't quite my reflection.

The face was mine—golden eyes, brown curls, tan skin unmarred by witch runes or corruption. But the expression was wrong. Too knowing. Too aware. Like it had been waiting for me.

Then the reflection moved independently.

Stepped forward through the mirror's surface like walking through water. Emerged into the abyss as a separate entity. A man with black hair and green eyes. Tall. Lean. Carrying himself with exhausted grace that spoke of too much suffering survived. He looked at me with an expression that combined sympathy and recognition and something that might have been relief.

"Nokoa," he stated. "I know your name. Know your story. Know your pain."

"Who are you?" I asked, hearing my own voice sound distant. Thin.

"Ravi," he replied. "I was—am—will be—" He stopped, seeming frustrated with inadequate language. "Time doesn't work right here. But in the mortal realm, I loved someone too."

"You're like me," I said. "You died for love."

"Died failing to prevent what she was becoming," Ravi corrected gently. "Died watching transformation I couldn't stop. Just like you."

He moved closer, and I saw in his green eyes the same exhausted devotion I'd felt for Renata. The same desperate hope that sacrifice mattered. The same terrible knowledge that loving someone couldn't save them from themselves.

"I'm glad to have someone else who knows this pain," Ravi admitted quietly. "Who understands what it costs to love someone becoming divine. To watch them hollow themselves. To die trying to save them."

"Did it work?" I asked. "Your death. Did it save her?"

"I don't know," Ravi replied, and I heard ancient grief in the admission. "I died before seeing the outcome. I've been here ever since, waiting in this abyss, wondering if she completed or failed or found some third option I couldn't imagine."

He met my eyes. "But you—you died completing the design. Died fueling her transformation. Died making her goddess. That has to mean something."

"She couldn't feel me die," I heard myself admit. "Couldn't cry. Could only watch with perfect memory and clinical detachment. I died loving her. She watched without loving me back."

"But she chose you anyway," Ravi observed. "Tried to die for you. Planned sacrifice to save you. Acted on love she couldn't feel. That's not nothing. That's devotion operating below conscious awareness."

He was right. Renata had tried to substitute herself. Had planned her own death to prevent mine. Had acted on love even without accessing love.

"How long have you been here?" I asked.

"I don't know," Ravi admitted. "Time is fluid here. Could be years. Could be centuries. The abyss doesn't measure duration the way mortal realm does."

He gestured to the void around us. "But I'm glad you're here. Glad to have company."

"What happens now?" I asked. "Do we just exist here? Wait in darkness forever?"

"I don't know that either," Ravi replied. "Maybe we fade eventually. Maybe we get pulled to whatever comes after this. Maybe we stay here until—"

He stopped, listening to something I couldn't hear. His green eyes went distant.

"What?" I pressed.

"The mortal realm is changing," Ravi stated quietly. "Reality is shifting. The transformation you died to complete—it's happening now. She's ascending. Becoming divine. Your sacrifice is activating."

I felt it then. Echo of what was happening in the world I'd left. Ripple in the abyss that suggested massive change occurring elsewhere. Renata transforming. Becoming goddess. Ascending to rule silence and forgetting eternally.

Because I died.

Because my sacrifice fueled her divinity.

Because love—even one-directional love, even love she couldn't reciprocate—had been strong enough to complete the design.

"Did I do the right thing?" I asked Ravi. "Dying for her? Making her goddess?"

"I don't know," Ravi admitted honestly. "I don't know if there was a right thing. Don't know if our sacrifices saved them or just enabled their suffering to continue eternally. Don't know if love is enough when it can't prevent the beloved from becoming something that can't love back."

He met my eyes with ancient sorrow. "But I know we couldn't have chosen differently. Know that watching them die would have destroyed us faster than dying for them did. Know that sometimes love just demands sacrifice without promising the sacrifice will matter."

"That's a terrible comfort," I observed.

"It's the only comfort available," Ravi replied.

We stood together in the abyss—two men who'd died for women becoming divine, two souls waiting in darkness, two sacrifices made from devotion that couldn't save what it loved.

"Thank you," I heard myself say. "For being here. For making this less lonely."

"Thank you for the same," Ravi replied.

The abyss stretched around us, infinite and dark and strangely peaceful now that it held company.

And somewhere in the mortal realm we'd left behind, the women we loved were becoming goddesses.

Completing transformations we'd died to enable.

Ascending to divinity through our willing sacrifice.

Existing eternally without us.

Chapter Thirty-Four

The Scream

Renata

The Midnight Oath completed with sound like the universe cracking open.

Red light from the blood moon condensed into a single point at the ritual circle's center—where Nokoa's body lay broken, where his willing sacrifice was fueling transformation, where cosmic law was being satisfied through death freely given.

Then the light exploded.

Not outward. Inward. Into me.

Every piece of Nokoa's essence—his memories, his consciousness, his love, his willing choice—rushed into me like floodwater breaking through a dam. Like the ocean pouring into a cup. Like infinity compressed into finite space.

And with it came everything else.

Every emotion I'd locked away. Every feeling I'd sealed behind glass. Every piece of humanity I'd sacrificed to become hollow.

All of it flooding back for a single heartbeat.

I felt.

Love for Nokoa so devastating it should have killed me. Love that had survived every absorption, every hollowing, every choice that pushed feeling further away. Love so profound that watching him die felt like being unmade at fundamental level.

Grief for Cressa, who'd been absorbed willingly, whose devotion I'd catalogued without warmth. The weight of her loss crashed into me now, days delayed, carrying all the tears I hadn't been able to cry.

Anguish for Theron—my brother who'd worn the Crown before me, who'd died to free me from it. His death hit me now with the force it should have carried originally.

Sorrow for Alaira, whose desperate love for her goddess I'd observed without being moved. Her sacrifice hurt now.

And underneath it all—Valdic's accumulated burden. Four absorptions worth of displaced emotion flooding back to original source, plus his own exhaustion, his desperate hope, his love for me that had sustained him through impossible weight.

All of it.

Every single emotion I'd lost since choosing Memory over Emotion.

All at once.

The weight was unbearable. More than mortal consciousness could contain. More than human awareness could process.

Then: silence.

Not gradual fading. Not gentle transition. Just silence. Like someone had cut every connection simultaneously. Like the floodgates had opened for a single heartbeat then slammed shut with finality that permitted no reopening.

The emotions vanished. Drained away. Not diminished. Not processed. Just gone. Inaccessible. Lost forever behind the transformation completing.

I stood in the courtyard, hand still pressed against bone barrier, staring at Nokoa's collapsed body inside the circle.

And felt nothing.

Not the absence of feeling that had characterized my previous emptiness—that had been glass wall with emotions visible beyond it. This was vault. This was tomb. Complete and total severance from every capacity to feel.

The scream started building before I understood what was happening.

Started somewhere beneath my ribs. In the hollow where emotions used to live before transformation carved them out completely.

It built like water behind a dam.

I screamed.

The sound that came out wasn't human. It was grief made audible. The weight of every emotion I'd felt for that single heartbeat, expelled all at once because holding them was impossible and losing them was unbearable.

The scream shattered bone spires throughout the courtyard. Ancient architecture that had stood for centuries cracked and fell, unable to withstand the sonic force. Stone columns crumbled. Archways collapsed. Entire sections of wall disintegrated.

The bone barrier around Nokoa's body fractured. Cracks spiderwebbing across its surface.

What few intact windows remained in the cathedral exploded—bone composite material bursting outward, raining down like hail made of razors.

The floor beneath my feet cracked. Deep fractures going down to the cathedral's foundation. To the divine skeleton that housed this entire realm.

Hivro crumpled at the courtyard's edge, hands pressed over her ears, starlight form flickering like a candle in wind.

The butterflies responded most dramatically.

Thousands of them had been swirling around the courtyard. Now they exploded into exponentially more—reproducing mid-flight, dividing like cells, multiplying until the air was so thick with wings it became difficult to see. Some shattered into bone dust. Others multiplied faster. One becoming two becoming four becoming eight.

A living storm of death and reproduction. Endings and beginnings happening simultaneously.

The scream continued. I couldn't stop it. Couldn't do anything except let it pour out until the pressure released.

My throat was raw. My lungs were burning. My entire body vibrating with the force of sound being expelled.

Valdic collapsed beside me.

I felt through our bond that he wasn't dying. But collapsing from sudden absence. From weight lifting all at once. From emotions returning to me briefly then vanishing completely, leaving him empty for the first time since our bonding.

He lay on bone floor, massive body heaving with gasps, purple eyes dimming from blazing brightness to normal glow. The emaciated quality that had characterized him for weeks reversed rapidly. His body filled out. Muscles that had been wasted became solid. Fur that had been patchy became full.

He looked normal again. Still a DirgeWolf marked by decay—that was fundamental to what DirgeWolves were. But no longer drowning in emotions that weren't his.

Freed.

The scream finally stopped. Not because I chose to stop—because my body physically couldn't continue.

Silence settled over the courtyard. Not peaceful silence. Shocked silence. The kind that follows catastrophe.

I stood in the center of devastation I'd created, surrounded by shattered bone and multiplied butterflies and cracked floor, and felt nothing.

The single heartbeat where I'd felt everything had burned them out completely. Used them as fuel for transformation that was moments from completing.

Quade stepped forward through the butterfly storm. He held something in his skeletal hands. A mask. Carved from bone—pale white with black lace, smooth, featuring hollow spaces for eyes and mouth. Simple. Elegant. Divine.

"For you," he stated, offering it with reverence. "The mask is how mortals will handle your presence."

I took it. The bone was cool against my palms, smooth and perfect. I understood its purpose without explanation—not a symbol of power but a limiter. A vow. A refusal to interpret suffering into meaning.

I lifted the mask. Positioned it against my face. Felt it settle into place.

It fused immediately. Not just resting against skin but bonding with bone beneath. Becoming part of my structure the same way the Crown had.

My eyes turned white behind the mask. Not because I'd ascended—but because I withdrew from perception. Stopped seeing stories and only saw outcomes.

I was no longer participating in fate.

I was enforcing the absence of it.

Through the mask's eye holes, I looked at Nokoa's body still lying in the ritual circle.

Remembered every moment with perfect clarity.

Felt nothing about any of it.

"I remember loving you," I heard myself state aloud, the words emerging from behind the mask with strange resonance. Goddess voice. Divine timbre. No longer quite human.

I moved toward the circle. The bone barrier had cracked enough that I could step through. Knelt beside him.

Placed my hand on his chest. Where his heart had been. Where Fatin's blade had killed him the first time. Where resurrection had pulled him back. Where the Midnight Oath had finally let him go.

His body was cool. Still. The witch runes carved into his bones had gone dark—no longer glowing, no longer burning emotion, just permanent scars on skeletal structure.

Valdic struggled to his feet, still gasping from sudden emptiness. His purple eyes tracked my movement with concern that registered through our bond—not transferred emotion anymore, just his own genuine worry.

"Renata?" he managed.

I looked at him. My eternal companion. The DirgeWolf who'd carried my humanity when I couldn't. Who'd survived impossible weight. Who would remain beside me through whatever came next.

"I feel free now. Less burdened. I'll remember for you," Valdic said quietly. "When forgetting takes hold. When you can't recall why things are the way they are. I'll be there."

I stroked his head. Things were different now—I felt for him. Warmth and concern. Only for him.

He leaned into the touch. Still bonded. Still loyal.

I moved to my throne and sat. The Crown fused to my skull was changing—bone thorns elongating, structure becoming more ornate, butterflies nesting in it, creating living decoration that pulsed with their constant clicking. Divine architecture completing.

"The land will recover," Quade stated. "Away from your immediate presence, fields will regrow. Rivers will flow. Populations will return. But the memory of hunger will vanish. Songs about the famine will disappear. Names of the dead will be forgotten. Cultures will lose the why behind their survival rituals. Gratitude will erode. Meaning will fade."

I understood. People would eat—but not remember starving. They would live—but couldn't explain why they should cherish it.

"And here?" I asked, gesturing to the cathedral around us.

"Here, in your immediate presence, the land remains muted," Quade explained. "Crops will grow but taste bland. Birds will exist but not sing. Wind will move but carry no stories. Life will return but only in bone."

I looked at Nokoa's body, still lying in the ritual circle. "His body," I stated. "I want it preserved. Transformed. Integrate his skeleton into a throne beside mine. He wanted to be part of my transformation. Now he will be. Physical presence without life. Eternal witness to what his sacrifice created."

Quade's approval radiated through his skeletal form. "Elegant solution. And orchids," he added, almost as afterthought. "Orchids will still bloom around you. My gift. The only living thing that thrives in your presence."

I sat on my throne, one hand extended palm-up. A single butterfly landed on it—green-gold coloring that marked it as distinct from the grey-purple that filled the courtyard.

Cressa.

The butterfly that carried her essence. That had returned to me specifically.

It settled on my palm and stayed. Wings clicking softly.

The spectral guardians stood at the courtyard's edge—seven silent sentinels who'd served as my protection. As the Crown's final transformation completed, they began to fade. Not violently. Just releasing. Service complete. Purpose fulfilled. The hollow ruler they'd been raised to protect no longer existed.

I was goddess now.

Goddesses needed no guards.

Valdic curled at my feet, solid and healthy. Nokoa's body being prepared for integration. The Crown fully divine architecture. The mask bonded to my face.

Hivro appeared before my throne one final time. Her starlight form was dimming, preparing to fade. "I cannot stay in a world of endings," she stated quietly. "This realm is yours now. The absence of stories. I cannot exist here long without being corrupted by what you rule."

"I understand," I replied.

"But I'll watch your stars from afar," Hivro continued. "Will monitor your constellation. Will know you're still there even if I can't be near you. Will love you despite distance. Despite your inability to love me back. Despite everything."

"Thank you," I stated.

Hivro smiled—sad expression that carried centuries of divine grief. "Goodbye, Renata."

She faded into starlight. Dissolving into points of light that rose toward the grey sky.

Valdic cried for me. Purple eyes producing tears that fell onto bone floor. Weeping because I couldn't.

I stroked his head. Automatic gesture. All I had to offer.

The cathedral breathed around us. Bone walls expanding and contracting. Butterflies settling into permanent residence. The grey light from outside remaining grey—no sun to rise, no day to break, just eternal twilight.

My world now.

My domain.

My eternal rule.

I sat on my throne, goddess complete, and waited for Quade to finish preparing Nokoa's transformation. Waited for my beloved's bones to be integrated into the throne beside mine.

Waited to spend forever with him still.

Epilogue

THE MIRROR SHOWS EVERYTHING

Nokoa

The mirror in the abyss showed everything.

I don't know when I realized it could do that—show the mortal realm we'd left behind. Time didn't work right here. Ravi said he'd been waiting for what felt like centuries or moments or both. The darkness made duration meaningless.

But the mirror showed us anyway. He watched the one he left behind. I watched her.

Renata sat on her throne of bones, the mask fused to her face, the Crown transformed into divine architecture with butterflies nesting in its elongated thorns. Her eyes were pure white now—completely colorless, holding perfect memory and absolute zero feeling.

Valdic lay at her feet, solid and healthy, freed from the weight he'd carried. But his purple eyes tracked her movements with concern she couldn't reciprocate.

My bones had been integrated into a throne beside hers. I could see it in the mirror—my skeleton preserved in bone structure, positioned to sit eternally next to the goddess I'd died to create. Physical presence without life.

"Does it hurt to watch?" I asked Ravi quietly, not taking my eyes from the mirror's surface.

"Yes," he replied simply. No elaboration. Just honest acknowledgment that watching the aftermath hurt as badly as the dying had.

In the mirror, movement. A rattlemaid entered Renata's throne room—skeletal form draped in ceremonial silks, joints clattering like dice with each step.

The rattlemaid bowed. Deep, reverent gesture. Skull nearly touching the bone floor.

Renata watched with those empty white eyes. Just clinical assessment of appropriate behavior being executed.

"Hollow Goddess," the rattlemaid intoned. "The outer territories report crops returning. Rivers flowing again. But the people—they don't remember why they should be grateful. Don't recall the famine. Don't understand—"

"That's what I do," Renata interrupted, her voice carrying divine resonance that made even the mirror's surface ripple slightly. "Silence. Forgetting. The memory of suffering vanishes. They eat without remembering hunger. They live without understanding why life matters. That's my domain."

The rattlemaid paused. "Have you gotten everything you wanted?"

Renata's skeletal form went very still.

"I got very close once," she stated, and I heard something in her voice that almost approached emotion. Almost. Just the echo of what feeling used to sound like. "Very close. Close enough to remember what wanting felt like. Close enough to catalog every detail of almost-having. But not close enough to keep it."

Her hand—the one not holding Cressa's green-gold butterfly—gestured toward my skeletal throne beside hers. "He's here. Present. Preserved. Exactly where I positioned him. Everything I wanted except the one thing that mattered."

"What was that, Hollow Goddess?" the rattlemaid asked quietly.

"Him alive," Renata replied. "Him breathing. Him capable of being here with me instead of just beside me. I got everything except that. Got very close. Close enough to remember. Not close enough to keep."

The rattlemaid bowed again and retreated, joints clattering with resumed movement, leaving Renata alone on her throne with her DirgeWolf and her butterfly and my bones.

I watched her through the mirror.

And then I remembered something—not the Crown, not the resurrection, not any of the terrible and necessary things. Just her.

She was kneeling in the garden before any of this began, hands pressed into dark soil up to the wrists, checking the depth for orchid bulbs. She'd looked up at me without warning and laughed—startled by something, maybe by finding me watching, maybe by nothing at all—a full laugh, unguarded, her grey eyes bright and her white hair loose around her face. Ordinary morning. Nothing at stake. Just her hands in the earth and that laugh, and her not knowing yet what love would cost us.

I had loved her then most of all.

"She remembered me," I heard myself say, and my voice broke slightly on the words.

"She did," Ravi confirmed gently. "She remembers perfectly."

In the mirror, Renata sat motionless. Valdic's head in her lap. Cressa's butterfly on her palm. My bones beside her. The world around her was blooming, the ritual complete.

She reached out and touched my skeletal hand where it rested on the throne's armrest.

Held it.

The gesture had no warmth in it. No feeling behind the positioning of her fingers. Just the memory of what that contact had once meant, expressed through a body that could no longer feel why it mattered.

But she held it anyway.

She remembered me.